Arctic Restitution

Lynn Kelling

I0687507

ForbiddenFiction
www.forbiddenfiction.com

an imprint of

Fantastic Fiction Publishing
www.fantasticfictionpublishing.com

ARCTIC RESTITUTION

A ForbiddenFiction book

Fantastic Fiction Publishing Hayward, California

© Lynn Kelling, 2017

CREDITS
Editor: Rylan Hunter, D.M. Atkins
Cover Design: Siolnatine
Cover photo: Original art by Natalya Nesterova
Production Editor: Kaye O'Malley
Proofreading: Jae Knight
Font: Wellrock Slab, by Manfred Klein

SKU: LK1-1.000298-01 FFP
ISBN: 978-1-62234-326-3

Published in the United States of America

As he approaches his twenty-second birthday, the three-year anniversary of the brutal attack in an alley that nearly cost him his life in a few different ways, Jaye Larson thinks he's left behind the ghosts from his years spent incarcerated, but when he's delivered a mysterious letter with terrifying implications, old monsters rear their ugly heads. His normal new life in remote Zus, Alaska, with his lover, Dixon Rowe, the heart of a found-family that supports Jaye in ways he's never before dreamed possible, is threatened by old deals and ties he begins to fear may never be broken. While old alliances strive to draw Jaye backward, Dixon and the rest of their family are called to step up to keep him steady. When the letter turns out to be just the first clue in a chain leading both Jaye and Dixon back inside the walls of the Federal Corrections Institute of Sheridan, Oregon, all of them are left facing carefully-held secrets and terrible new truths that refuse to be ignored.

Also recommended…

You may also enjoy these other ForbiddenFiction works:

My Brother's Lover , by Lynn Kelling

Growing up gay in a small town with no mother, Evan Savage learned the hard way to cherish his secrets above all else. Now he's 18, not even his father can hurt him anymore. When his long-lost twin brother Brennan shows up out of nowhere looking for a new home, Evan's world, and his very identity, comes crashing down around him all over again. (M/M+)

Broken Ink , by Jack L. Pyke

Carrying a tattoo on your skin no longer just comes with a risk of infection. Get the composition right, you have the latest mind-control drug on the market. It's the sex-traders' dream, or worst nightmare, depending on the concentrated dose of the ink—and just who's wearing it. Together or apart, Kiyen's on the run and Fal's in for a fight for his sanity. (M/M)

DISCLAIMER

This book is a work of fiction which contains explicit erotic content; it is intended for mature readers. Do not read this if it's not legal for you.

All the characters, locations and events herein are fictional. While elements of existing locations or historical characters or events may be used fictitiously, any resemblance to actual people, places or events is coincidental.

This story depicts fictional BDSM; it is not intended to be used as an instruction manual. It contains descriptions of erotic acts that may be immoral, illegal, or unsafe. The characters are not models for the Safe, Sane and Consensual forms embraced by most current practitioners of BDSM. The author takes license with the use of BDSM for dramatic effect. Do not take the events in this story as proof of the plausibility or safety of any particular practice.

Such content should not be read as a depiction of the desires, opinions, or fetishes of the author or the staff of ForbiddenFiction.com.

Dedication

For Talulla and Caelan,
My hope, my love, my everything

Contents

Chapter 1:
Beginning in the Ending

Time had been draining away at an alarming speed, with only a week left before Jaye Larson completed his sentence and would be officially released from the Federal Corrections Institute of Sheridan, Oregon. The closer the end came, the less Jaye felt prepared to handle it. He had nothing waiting for him on the outside — or rather, no people. Just an empty cabin in the middle of nowhere. But there was no money, and no one who gave a fuck about him existed on the face of the whole planet, other than the people who'd become his family inside FCI Sheridan. Now, his gang — the Disciples — were his family, and he was losing them. Most of all, he was losing Cash.

The deal with Cash, boss man of the Disciples and a bad-ass, tattooed, scarred and scary motherfucker, had started out as a straightforward barter. In exchange for sexual favors and the ability to have full ownership of Jaye's body, Cash had agreed to protect Jaye to the best of his ability. Cash had most of the prison deathly afraid of him — so much so that when his enemies came after him, they targeted his crew rather than the man himself. That meant Jaye had often found himself in the crosshairs of one evil piece of shit or other. Yet, he'd survived through sheer force of will alone.

Even after two years together, night and day, every day, Jaye knew little about the full extent of what Cash had done both to land himself behind bars, and otherwise. He never bragged, or let old stories slip, even to boost his own reputation. There were some little clues, like the three blue-ink tears on his face, to hint at the lethal quality of his actions. Cash bore the gnarled remnants of those old fights and crimes on his body, had tattooed mysterious, countless symbols into his skin, was muscle-bound, bald and angry as hell. He didn't have a soft side, and it wasn't an act.

But...

Jaye now had over seven hundred days of memories filled with all of the ways Cash had looked out for him. Sure, Cash had scared off the rival gangs and thugs hard up for someone pretty to fuck over in any way possible. He had done his best to keep the guards off Jaye's back, too. He also made sure Jaye ate when he was having a rough time, or if his mental health went on the fritz. If someone did hurt Jaye — and they had, plenty of times — Cash meted out payback in spades. Eyeless and blinded Tio was proof enough of that. However, even all of that didn't do enough to cover everything Cash had been to Jaye.

He'd been family.

A lover.

A friend.

A solitary, unbreakable lifeline when Jaye had been ready and willing to die.

He'd kept Jaye together when he'd fallen completely apart and somehow caused him look forward to waking up in the morning when everything else kept on tearing him down.

He'd been kind when there was no reason. He'd kissed Jaye, laughing. He'd made love to him daily, tenderly, giving Jaye as much pleasure as he took for himself, without being asked or expected to do so.

And Jaye knew what his leaving meant for Cash.

It meant all of that was gone. Maybe Jaye would be alone out there, in the world, but Cash would be alone too. Only, he'd have nowhere to run, no escape in sight. He was here for the duration, with years tacked on years and no end promised, except in a body bag. He'd have no promise of someone who appreciated him sharing his lonely nights in the cell, or even that he'd hear from Jaye again. Jaye hadn't been able to promise it. He didn't want to give Cash hope of something he wasn't sure he could deliver. Jaye wasn't making any plans past walking out of Sheridan and into the rest of his life. There were no guarantees, and Cash wasn't stupid. He knew how it was.

Maybe Cash had cared about someone before, like he'd cared about Jaye. But as the months whittled down to weeks and then days, Jaye saw something in his boss that had never been there before.

Cash was scared.

He didn't show the crew, and he tried not to show Jaye, but when Cash was inside him in the dark, Jaye could feel how tight Cash held on, how hard he breathed, and heard the desperation in his moans.

Neither of them knew what to say. They weren't good with words, or talking about emotions.

So they kept putting it off. There was a goodbye coming, which they had no way to know how to face.

It made Jaye jittery. The voices came back, louder than they'd been in a long time. His nerves were fried.

The corrupt guard who'd given him hell his whole sentence — Ecker — was in prime form. He took Jaye whenever he could, fairly regularly, to get bent over and reamed out with both his baton and his pathetically tiny dick. Since Jaye knew Cash had no way to make the rapes stop, and that Cash was already upset about Jaye going, Jaye kept it to himself as much as he could. Still, he was worn right out — emotionally, physically, mentally.

It made him slow. Unobservant.

That's why he hadn't seen it coming.

It was seven days before his release when they raided Cash's bunk. Jaye had been coming back from a work assignment. He hadn't been in Unit Four to see it go down, but had heard the commotion and quickened his approach.

Five guards kept Cash out of the cell while they tore up his shit, including the sketch Jaye had made for him of a blue jay over an open field, with mountains in the distance, done painstakingly as a gesture of deep gratitude. Remembering his promise to his mother, Cora, when she'd still been alive, that he would always try to fly free, no matter what it took, Jaye had wanted to give that to Cash too. Even if it was just a drawing, it still meant something.

They ripped it to shreds.

They found drugs, probably planted by Ecker.

When Cash realized what was going on, he started to scream.

The whole Unit got quiet in a bad, piss-your-pants kind of way.

3

The sound of Cash's screaming carried far.

Jaye stopped breathing. Then, he ran.

A pair of guards held him back, wouldn't even let him go inside the Unit. But he could see Cash through a narrow, shatterproof window.

Cash was fighting, punching one guard in the eye, another in the jaw. They wrestled him down to the ground and all piled on him to keep him there.

"JOHNNY!"

Jaye opened his mouth, trying to speak, to yell, to do something.

"Get him the fuck out of here," Ecker snarled. "Throw him in ad-seg for the week."

"NO! JOHNNY! I'm never... I'm never gonna see him again... I'm..."

There was no air. Jaye clawed at it. Pushing his lungs hard enough to burst. He couldn't see, his last sight of Cash smeared and watery.

Pathetically, too broken to be heard, especially with how loud Cash was growling and crying out in pure, rage-fueled panic, Jaye tried to call out to him, "Cash! Please! Please just let me... Let me say..."

"JOHNNY!"

They carried Cash out a different door a couple of hundred feet from where Jaye stood. It took all five guards, because he fought the whole way, even in leg irons and handcuffs. It was the last time Jaye saw him.

They never got to say goodbye.

The world had turned sideways and inside-out. Drop four hundred and fifty or so days' worth of sand through the hourglass. Feeling like he had hardly anything in common with the kid who'd come out of Sheridan, there Jaye stood, with an envelope addressed to Johnny in his hands. It bore no return address.

It had been delivered to his post office box address, which no one but his ghosts and the government had any use for anymore.

Jaye drove back to his cabin, parked in front of it, then sat in the car staring blankly forward for nearly an hour. It was the ass-end of winter and a surprisingly nice day, with the temperatures solidly above freezing. The wind was almost non-existent, making it feel like the whole world had taken an indrawn breath and held it. What would come out when they let it go? A scream? A cry? A whimper?

He couldn't move from the driver's seat.

Whatever he did next would be a choice made in light of the fact of the envelope in his possession.

It lay in his lap. He kept running his fingers over the crinkled white envelope and the jagged, handwritten letters spelling out *Johnny Larson*. It wasn't Cash's handwriting, or sent on prison stationary, but Jaye wasn't stupid either. He knew who it was from.

As Jaye sorted facts and fears in his head, he counted the things that were true. One was that Dixon would be coming home in a few hours. Another certainty was that the confines of the snug little cabin that had been his and Dixon Rowe's painstakingly crafted home for over a year held no comfort for him in that moment. Sometimes, being in a confined space made him feel better. It reminded him of the pleasures of living out of a cinderblock cell, where no one could sneak up on you and everything was in its place.

This was not one of those times.

Instinct told him one thing:

Run.

It wasn't a letter he held. It was a bomb. A kind even the most paranoid couldn't understand the fear behind. The only person in the whole world with the ability to comprehend how fucked he was, just because that letter existed, was Jaye himself.

That letter would blow everything up. Jaye's progress. His mental health. His emotional stability. His ability to form words or do anything.

And it wasn't even about him anymore. Dixon came first in a lot of ways. He was Jaye's life, his love, his reason. Nothing that might lie in wait in that envelope would be good for Dixon.

Yet... in Jaye's mind, from another life, traveling through time, there was screaming. All over again, his heart was breaking. That bald-headed, mean-ass, stubborn and brutal man was bigger in Jaye's head than anyone. Even Dixon. Though Dixon had saved him too, Jaye had been doing pretty well at the time. He had been relatively sane. He hadn't had hundreds of convicted felons salivating at the thought of carving him up or raping him to death for any number of reasons. Cash had saved him from all of that, over and over again, for years.

Then there was the kick-in-the-balls certainty that Cash deserved a hell of a lot better than what he'd gotten.

If ever a person had owed another person…

Jaye got out of the car. It was a shitty one, and almost ten years old, with stained upholstery and a faulty stereo, but it had a good engine and a great heater. The gray exterior was beat to hell and rusted at the edges, but he liked it that way. Every dent, scratch, and scuff told a story. Some he knew, most he didn't. But, there was no way to erase the past. Not completely. An ugly truth was always going to be better than a pristine lie. He was a firm believer that the outside should sometimes match the inside, and cars were the type of possession that should speak to the personality of the owner.

To his right loomed the cabin, set up on its thick foundation, holding back the wild forest beyond through plain old ballsiness. It was a crappy, hand-built monstrosity, but he loved every quirk it held. It symbolized a lot — everything Jaye had lost, everything he'd fought with teeth, blood, and multicolored pain to keep, and everything he'd been tearing himself apart to build. It was hope. It was the future, present, and past. He sensed its warmth, the food stocking the fridge, the soft coziness of the bed, the invigorating sight of his artwork decorating the walls. It was their place. His sanctuary.

He didn't deserve it. Couldn't stand it.

To his left a field opened up to the wider world. It was covered in melting snow. The sun beat down on it as hard as it could, withering the ice, forcing white to give over to brown. Straight ahead, the road reached all the way out to the horizon.

Turning, Jaye made his way into the field. When his shoes began to crunch over the frozen mounds and brittle, muddy grass, he enjoyed the sound and feeling of ruining something pure and untouched. He knew he left footsteps, so he didn't worry much about not taking his phone or leaving Dixon a message.

Some things were never explainable with words anyway.

Chapter 2:
Warning Signs

Dixon's big, black Expedition rolled up to home, right behind Jaye's gray sedan. Shifting into park, he tumbled the details of Sesi's missing person's case over in his head again. Twenty-four-year-old female. No relatives unaccounted for. Gone for a week. No sign of stolen cash to fund a bus ticket. Not much, if anything, missing from the residence. Maybe she had a go bag? They should check the interviews again to look for signs of long-term planning for an escape. She was Iñupiaq, or Alaskan Inuit, like his co-worker and best friend, Sesi Ahnah. There was a history and tradition of youth running away without a word to friends or relatives, but something didn't sit well with him this time. The bloody rag in the bottom of the closet and the missing keys to an old shed pointed in other directions.

He had to shake it off. Snap out of it. He never liked to bring work home if he could help it. It wasn't Jaye's job to solve Dixon's cases for him, and Dixon didn't think he should have to suffer a distant, inattentive boyfriend when their new schedules had them passing in the night so often lately.

He took the key out of the ignition and grabbed his bag with the clean change of clothes he hadn't had time to change into. In the rearview mirror, he caught sight of his golden-red hair and teal-blue eyes — a dash or two of pure color in a desaturated world.

Hand on the handle, he glanced up at the cabin.

Dark.

Weird.

No smoke trailed from the chimney. No lights burned inside.

But the car was there.

"Fuck."

A chill raced up his spine, which for once had nothing to do with the weather.

Something was wrong.

He left his things, jumped down from the vehicle and walked to the sedan.

A hand placed on the front hood told him the engine was cold. The car had been there a while.

He scanned the area, looking for signs of a scuffle or trouble. Possibilities swirled through his head. Some made sense — like maybe his sister, Brekken, or her husband, Grant, had picked Jaye up in their truck for some reason. Others weren't even logically possible — his ex, Marcus, rising from the dead to enact more revenge or complete the murder he'd once attempted, bringing Jaye to his knees for some rape and a sliced throat.

"Get it together, you dumb shit," Dixon muttered to himself. It was always so hard to be reasonable when it came to Jaye, who had been in trouble since the moment they first met, and continued to terrify Dixon just because he loved Jaye so much.

No debris by the car. Nothing under the car either, when he bent to check. He started to pivot and run to the cabin when he saw it.

The trail led off into the field across from the cabin.

One set of footprints.

Taking a deep breath of pure relief, Dixon tried to calm down. His racing heart slowed to a more normal pace.

"You owe me one, kid," he groaned, running a hand over his face and feeling the cold sweat that had already started to form on his brow.

Glancing all around, seeing nothing but the twinkling stars up in the inky dome stretched in all directions above him, Dixon headed to Jaye's trail and began to follow.

The walk invigorated him, and might have even been pleasant if not for the length it took to find any additional sign of Jaye's whereabouts.

When he saw a small, dark form seated on the ice, Dixon yelled, "You scared the shit out of me!"

"Just keeping you on your toes, Trooper Rowe," Jaye's gravelly purr of a voice replied.

Quickening his pace, it still took a few more minutes for Dixon to make it to Jaye's side. When he got close enough to see Jaye's shivering, Dixon's confusion got a dash of anger and fear to give it more depth and flavor.

"What the hell are you doing out here? Let me see your fingers. Have you lost any feeling in your toes? We need to get you into the cabin and — "

"Hey," Jaye interrupted, his light-green eyes staring up at Dixon from where he sat cross-legged. "I'm fine. I needed some air. You know how that goes."

"Why do you need air?" Dixon worried.

"To breathe," Jaye replied.

With a tense chuckle, he rolled his neck to work out some stiffness and squeezed his eyes shut.

"Did something happen at work?"

Jaye got to his feet, stretched his legs. Chocolate-brown tendrils fell in a tumble over his pale forehead. His hands shoved down deep into his pockets. There was a look on his face that Dixon didn't like, didn't know how to interpret.

"Come on." Jaye grabbed Dixon's hand, tugging him back towards the way he'd come. Somewhere nearby, a wolf howled. A gust of icy wind tossed Dixon's hair and nipped at his ears.

Jaye's fingers were icy, too. Dixon stared at him as they walked, wanting to figure it out but unable to ignore the persistent voice of pessimism that warned him to be afraid. Marcus had honed that instinct in Dixon for a long time. It was a hard one to un-learn.

"Please talk to me," Dixon asked more softly, dropping his walls a little, with effort.

"Let's get warm. Time just got away from me."

Backtracking Jaye's initial snaky trail, now marred with Dixon's following footsteps, they trampled the way even more, crushing crisp snow and drawing up mud. Slowly, the cabin drew closer. Jaye stayed quiet, avoiding eye contact and seeming far, far away. Dixon tried to rub some life back into Jaye's fingers.

Jaye finally looked over at Dixon, wearing an unreadable expression. Whatever he saw in Dixon's face pulled him closer. He looped his arm through Dixon's, their sides brushing as they walked. The dark ink of his tear seemed stark in the glow of the moon on snow, Jaye's fair skin too blue in the dim light for Dixon's liking.

"I know you know this, but don't take chances with the weather out here, okay? I want you warm. Safe. Not in the middle of an empty field getting frostbite."

He could still feel shivering radiating from deep down in Jaye's slim body.

"I know. I promise I'm okay."

Jaye dug his keys out first, with Dixon too worried to beat him to it. They finally arrived at the cabin's door, and Jaye got it open. While he closed and locked it behind them as well, Dixon rushed for a blanket, drawing it around Jaye's shoulders, ignoring the slight eye-roll Jaye gave him for it.

"Sit down. I'll start the fire," Dixon instructed.

Jaye went to the couch. Dixon crouched by the fireplace and stacked some kindling.

Once he'd gotten the fire going, and heat began to fill the small space, Dixon let himself begin to unload his gear and duty belt.

"You know," Jaye said, pushing the blanket off and pulling out of his coat, too. "Sharing body heat is the best way to warm up. I don't know if you've ever heard that or not."

He pulled his sweater over his head, then his undershirt too. His hands went to his fly, parting it.

"That sounds like a distraction tactic," Dixon said, prepared to put a halt to any advances meant to stall conversation. "I really think we should…"

Jaye stared at him, dead in the eyes. He came right up to Dixon, letting him get a good look, then bowed his head to rest on Dixon's shoulder, pushing Dixon's shirt open, sliding a chilly hand up under the fabric of his undershirt to touch him, skin on skin.

"…talk about this," Dixon finished lamely. He sighed and kissed Jaye's dark curling hair, embracing him. The shivers were awful. Hugging Jaye didn't make them stop.

He let Jaye help him get the other shirt off too. Right away, Jaye pressed himself up against Dixon's chest. He kept his wind-chilled face turned away, his body posture speaking clearly that he was looking to get lost in other ways.

"Let's get you closer to the fire," Dixon suggested.

"Just lay with me? Please?" Jaye asked, his voice sounding like it came from far away.

Dixon cupped the side of Jaye's face, tilting it up so he could see it. "What is this?" he questioned as Jaye frowned, nuzzling Dixon's palm.

Jaye pressed him back, walking him to the edge of the bed. Dixon spared a second to unbuckle his pants and shed them. Jaye was naked by the time he was done.

They crawled under the covers.

It was too dark to see Jaye's face well, but he felt upset. It came off of him like steam.

Jaye pulled the covers up over them, breathing against Dixon's neck, pressing down on top of him as if to absorb all of his heat and energy. Dixon tried to rub the cold away from Jaye's form, but the trembling continued. Even his breaths were softly chattering.

Dixon whispered, "If this is about your birthday, remember I promised you don't need to worry about it, okay? I have it all taken care of and I'm not going to forget, I — "

"It's not," Jaye protested, but he sounded distraught. His lips dragged over Dixon's jaw. His arms wound around behind Dixon's back. Dixon wrapped his legs around behind Jaye's body and just held on, caressing through the silky curls of his hair.

"I love you. I love you so much," Dixon told him. "Whatever this is, we'll fix it, okay? We'll do it together."

A harder shiver had Jaye quaking in Dixon's arms. Dixon tried to absorb it. To drain away the pain and whatever had disturbed the fearless man he cherished so deeply.

"I'm scared," Jaye confessed, barely loud enough to hear.

"Whatever this is, I'll protect you. You're safe. I swear you are. No one hurts you."

Jaye sighed. Dixon hooked a hand around Jaye's jaw, brought it up within kissing range. He felt the quiver of his lips, the chill on his breath. Jaye reached out for something on the nightstand. Dixon realized what it was when he felt two fingers enter him as they kissed.

"Please, can I?"

"Yeah." Dixon moaned when Jaye pulled out and lined up. With gentle pushes that had goosebumps racing out over his skin from head to toe, Jaye claimed him a little at a time. He rocked against him until fully sheathed, then let out a deeper exhale, dragging soft kisses over Dixon's temple.

"Better," Jaye sighed, starting to move and build a rhythm.

"Mmm. Good." Dixon groaned, moving counter to Jaye's gentle thrusts into him. When Jaye's hand found Dixon's cock, toying with it as he rode him, Dixon used his legs to draw Jaye in tighter and panted with the rush of stimulation. As Jaye found his gland, dragging against it on each thrust, Dixon didn't try to bite back the desperate sounds coming from him. The more he gave over to it, the steadier Jaye felt against him, moving more deliberately, with need, vigor, and control.

"So much better," Jaye moaned, then gave it to him harder.

"Fuck," Dixon whined, shooting over Jaye's fingers.

Hooking his arms under Dixon's legs to pull him open wider, Jaye shifted their position slightly and began giving it to him deeper, with even more force. Dixon palmed the back of Jaye's head and drew him in for a rough, dirty kiss that lasted until Jaye moaned, quaking with orgasm.

"Love you, Dix," Jaye vowed in a breathless whisper by his left ear.

"I know you do."

Dixon had told Jaye to stay in bed where it was warm as he washed up before going to make dinner. Lying there, under the covers, the fire crackling away, Jaye stared at his coat draped over the arm of the couch. The letter was inside it.

His hand crept down the edge of the mattress, to the seam where he used to tuck away a hunting knife.

Piggy.

His fingers dug into the seam, his eyes squeezed shut. A chill raced down his back and the stark fear of ghostly touching felt strong enough to conjure it. He tried to think of something else. Anything else. A bear tracking prey in the woods. The flow of electrons through a closed circuit like water through a pipe. Service entry cables connecting remote homes to an ordered grid, returning the isolated back to the community. The carefree way Brekken laughed. The sight of Grant sitting on the porch, shotgun in hand, ready and determined to safeguard their family.

The night was soundless, making it feel like their cabin existed alone in the universe — a satellite orbiting through inky space. The only thing Jaye heard was the tapping of water in the shower, a few feet away.

Instinct told him to shred the letter and burn it. He could pretend it never came. Dixon would never have to know. It wouldn't get a chance to destroy the good they'd built. Future could stay far away from past.

But one particular ghost spoke up, and it was screaming. He heard the fight as it was wrestled to the ground, bound with chains. It called for him with the most primal desperation. Jaye knew if he burned the letter, that ghost would never let him go. It would be screaming at the back of his mind forever. There would be no peace.

It felt like a choice between them — past and future. Maybe he wasn't meant to have both. Maybe he didn't deserve that much happiness.

He wanted to choose Dixon, but... the screaming.

He jammed his palms against his ears and breathed more deeply, burrowing into the soft, warm covers in a sparsely populated corner of remote Alaska. No matter how far he ran, the ghosts always found him.

The water stopped. A minute later, creaking footsteps crossed to the bed, which shifted under the weight of someone sitting beside where he lay. A gentle hand moved over his side through the blankets, the touch filled with so much terrifying love.

"I'm always here for you. You know that," Dixon reminded him.

"I know. I fucking know."

"Whoever put you back in this place, J-bird, is in one hell of a lot of trouble with me. Is it someone in town giving you a hard time? Was it a trigger? Was it — "

"It's a letter. It's a-a fucking piece of paper, okay. Fuck. I shouldn't have..." He sat up, pushed the blankets back. Dixon took his hand and Jaye said, "Look, just forget it, all right? Please forget it?"

Dixon's blue eyes were the sweetest thing Jaye had ever known. The most decadent indulgence he'd experienced. They looked on with so much patience and understanding, it pulled at all of the frayed ends of Jaye's psyche. "Why?"

"Dixon, I need you to hear me, all right?"

"I am. I'm listening. I always listen to you."

Jaye felt tears of pure helplessness gathering and hated it. He blinked and shook his head, staring into the fire instead.

"Jaye, please," Dixon begged.

"It's a… a fucking hook, okay? A snare. Don't touch it."

"I don't understand you, babe. Can you explain it from the beginning?"

Jaye blew out a breath, pushed a hand through his short hair, expecting to feel long, twisting curls.

"The beginning. What the hell would the beginning be?" He laughed, but it sounded crazy, so he stopped. He cleared his throat, sniffled, then looked up at Dixon through the dark hair fallen into his eyes. Tripping a little over his words, he said, "Okay. There was once a very scared, very sick boy named Johnny, who was all alone in a cage with many monsters, and the worst monster of all was named Ecker. He liked to capture the boy and had fingers like tentacles which he used to violate and torture the boy over and over again, until the boy's mind broke, and he resolved to stop eating in a pathetic attempt at slow suicide. Some of the other monsters tried to bite and scratch at Ecker, but he was too big, too powerful. Nothing hurt him. When the other monsters tried to fight Ecker, it only made him madder at the boy. So when Ecker captured the boy again and took him to secret places to be hurt and raped, the boy didn't tell anyone about it. Anyone. He just let it keep happening because he knew that soon, he would be let out of the cage, and that's all that mattered."

Dixon's mouth was a tight, straight line, his eyes wide and glassy, his posture tensed. His hand gripped Jaye's with brutal strength.

"Where's this fucking letter?"

"In my coat pocket."

"The hook in the letter. It's Ecker's?"

Jaye drew the blankets back over himself.

"I'll fucking kill him," Dixon promised in a soft, deadly whisper.

"Too late," Jaye sighed.

Chapter 3:
The Letter

Dixon found the envelope addressed to Johnny Larson in the inside pocket of Jaye's coat. It was crumpled and folded in half twice. It bore no return address and the street address wasn't just incorrect, it was for a street that didn't even exist — Memory Lane. Jaye's P.O. Box number was correctly listed, though. Just looking at the outside with its hand-carved writing gave Dixon the creeps.

No wonder Jaye had wandered off into the field.

Time and experience had given Dixon tools, though. He understood Jaye better than he had, and a lot better than anyone else did.

Before daring to open the envelope's flap, Dixon returned to the bed upon which Jaye was curled in a fetal position under several layers of sheets and blankets. Only some of the short, dark curls at the top of his head were visible. Laying a hand on what seemed to be Jaye's lower leg, Dixon promised, "There's no one else here. We're partners, aren't we? You and me? We handle things together. We're a team. And this is just a letter."

"It's not just a letter," Jaye said ominously.

That morning, Jaye had woken much earlier than needed in order to cook chocolate chip pancakes with plenty of syrup. He'd served them with a smile and flirty laugh, wearing nothing but a pair of too-loose and soft pajama pants slung low on his slim hips, while straddling Dixon's lap to face him at the table and hand-feeding him small bites, letting Dixon lick the syrup and melted chocolate from his fingers.

The change in Jaye compared to how he had been just that morning was jarring. Witnessing Jaye's hopelessness, turmoil, and pain made Dixon frantic, desperate to help but unsure how to do it. Knowing Jaye well only assisted Dixon so much in his understanding of how to tackle the problem. The period of Jaye's life lived in FCI Sheridan was still murky and clouded for Dixon. Jaye gave him glimpses, but hid most. Dixon didn't pry in order to spare Jaye more pain, wanting to allow time for him to feel comfortable opening up on his own. Now, Dixon missed not having that insight. He could tell Jaye was just trying to protect him from something, but what? It wasn't only a sense of loyalty to Dixon causing this mood shift. Jaye was being torn up inside. It left Dixon scrambling to stop a process well beyond his reach.

Not for the first time, Dixon thought of Cash, an inmate Jaye had paired up with in order to stay alive while incarcerated. In Dixon's mind, Cash was nothing but a meathead thug using a vulnerable young kid, breaking him down, and taking advantage in ways that might not ever completely heal for Jaye.

Dixon had trouble picturing the man Jaye had been while with Cash and in prison. He'd gotten glimpses of that version of his personality when they'd first met — the cockiness, seduction, bravado, and miserable certainty that no one could help him in any way that mattered. Every time he began to sense what that implied for Jaye's mental state while with Cash, Dixon's anxiety spiked. It was a feeling built of fear and helplessness which he'd become an expert in while with Marcus. The sense of having no way out, that no one in the entire world understood or cared enough to make a difference, was a prison of its own. Dixon hated imagining Jaye feeling that way, especially because the solution wasn't as apparent as it had been with Marcus. Then, Dixon had needed to figure out a way to escape and get Marcus out of his life for good. Jaye had helped that happen, and now Marcus was really gone.

But Jaye wasn't trying to escape in the same way Dixon had been. Jaye was no longer locked up. Cash and Ecker and all of the rest of them were out of his life.

Weren't they?

Before Dixon found the nerve to open the envelope, he saw the blankets push back a little. Chewing at his lip, worry painted all over his beautiful face, Jaye watched the paper in Dixon's hand like he expected it to catch fire at any moment.

Dixon looked at the writing on the envelope spelling out Johnny Larson. He blew out an uneasy, sickly breath. He knew what it meant as well as Jaye did. Some of the pieces started to come together for Dixon, just a little — why Jaye was so upset, why something so seemingly insignificant had so much power over him.

The piece of mail had been sent from Portland, Oregon. Setting the envelope aside, Dixon cleared his throat and turned his attention to the letter.

He unfolded the paper with one hand, pressing it flat against his right thigh.

It wasn't a letter. Jaye was right about that. Inside the folded paper were two things — a newspaper clipping and a printed transcript. The newspaper clipping's headline caught Dixon's attention first, due to the size and boldness of the type.

Prison Guard Found Dead Outside of Sheridan

Local prison guard at the Federal Corrections Institute of Sheridan, Ned Ecker, was found inside his apartment Tuesday after failing to appear at work for several days. Sheridan officials say there were signs of a struggle following a break-in that likely occurred late Sunday evening. Details about Ecker's death are being withheld as the investigation continues.

The rest was torn away.

"Jesus," Dixon muttered, scanning the accompanying transcript before slowing down to read it. He felt nauseous, his skin clammy with a creeping dread he couldn't shake off.

There was a time stamp at the top: *2:34 am 3-22-16*

Yeah, we've got one hell of a mess over here. You need to come down and take a look at this shit.

Pre-meditated, definitely. Clean work. Deliberate. Nothing about this is accidental. Whoever did this knew what they were doing, that's for sure. So far, no fingerprints or physical evidence found at the scene, but we're still looking.

We figure the struggle happened when they were trying to get the cuffs on and prior to the sexual assault. The damn batons were still in him when he died. They likely stabbed him in the side during the assault, maybe to subdue him. He's not a small guy, but we don't know how big or how many were here to take him down. At some point, they cut his throat, ear to ear.

You're gonna think I'm nuts, but I think they were wearing those shoe covers service people wear when they're checking out your A/C, because there are smears in the blood, but no clear footprints. Damnedest thing.

Whoever did this had some real beef with this guy. This is some sick shit.

Yeah, we'll be here a while longer. Okay. Bye.

Shit. Okay, keep looking, people. There's gotta be something we're missing here.

Dixon folded the paper and set it aside with the envelope, near the foot of the bed. He took a deep breath and caressed Jaye's leg, wondering at how small and fragile he looked, curled up like that. Not at all like a thug, or someone capable of handling an entire crew of thugs, though Dixon knew his experience limited his appreciation of just how deep Jaye's iron will ran.

Dixon just wanted to know what the letter meant, and why they'd mailed that shit to Jaye. Were they trying to frame him for the murder? That was impossible, wasn't it? Ecker had been back in the lower forty-eight. There was documented proof Jaye hadn't been in Oregon for almost a year.

But then… what? Why would they send such a cryptic, unsettling communication?

Dixon watched the dark piece of the world he could see through the window, trying to make sense of it all, trying to figure out the best way to protect Jaye from something Dixon didn't even begin to understand.

Jaye promised to get out of bed and washed up if Dixon agreed to make dinner and give him a little time alone to get his head together about it all before they talked.

A half-hour later, they sat at the small table with plates of reheated stew Brekken had given them the previous weekend to tide them through the days when their schedules didn't mesh. Jaye thought it was a wonder to have someone like that in his life, without any motive in mind besides wanting to see him and Dixon happy.

The closest Jaye ever had to someone willing to cook pots full of homemade food for him was an elderly neighbor back in Anchorage named Angela Traylor who had known enough of his and Cora's situation to be concerned Jaye wasn't getting his proper nutritional allowance of all the food groups every day. Usually when Cora was out at work, Mrs. Traylor would knock at their apartment's door with a Tupperware container full to the top with warm food inside. She would tell him to eat as much as he wanted, then save the rest for another day. She gave him things like chicken parmesan, fettuccine alfredo, sausage and mashed potatoes, and stir fry. He wasn't sure why she waited to give Jaye the food directly rather than give it to Cora. Maybe she had tried once, and Cora's pride had sent the needed food away when Jaye's growling stomach would have appreciated it. It wasn't that Cora hadn't fed him or didn't make sure there was something in the fridge to eat, but her priorities weren't entirely organized in those days. Managing life as a working mom while dealing with a gig as a stripper during the nights meant sleeping most of the day, and fighting various drug habits used to keep reality tolerable. Keeping a roof over their heads was as much as Cora could handle. Planning balanced menus for Jaye's breakfast, lunch, and dinner was mostly beyond her capabilities. It wasn't her fault, but he'd been glad for people like Mrs. Traylor.

Now, he had Dixon, and Brekken, and Grant. He was getting better at cooking, too, but having loved ones willing to cook for him was a private pleasure that always warmed his heart as well as his stomach.

The stew was full of beef, vegetables, and potatoes with a richly seasoned brown sauce. Dressed in a warm, long-sleeved shirt, jeans, and thick, woolen socks, Jaye sat slightly hunched over in his chair across from Dixon, pushing food around in his bowl with his fork. His sense memory was full of two years' worth of days in the FCI Sheridan cafeteria, seated at the long table on a hard bench and protecting his tray of bland carbs while surrounded by the Disciples. Meal time meant keeping his guard up, doing as he was told, and acting like everything was fine when it usually wasn't.

The stew smelled incredibly appealing, but Jaye's fork wasn't making it to his mouth. Dealing with Ecker had always zapped Jaye's appetite. It seemed time hadn't changed that either.

The ghosts didn't have him like they used to. He didn't feel them touching, sliding down his throat or up his ass, but he remembered all of the countless times they did. It had been going on so long, Jaye was left exhausted by it all. The ghosts were part of Ecker's legacy.

It would have been better to walk while they talked rather than try to eat, but Jaye needed to watch out for Dixon as well as himself, and Dixon had worked a full shift. He needed fuel even if Jaye didn't want any.

He wasn't sure what Dixon had made of the contents of the envelope, but Jaye had taken more than enough time to think it all over. There was no question what the real message was. It was only a matter of deciding to follow through or not.

"They must have bugged the room," Jaye said. "Fuckin' Cash, man. He's got some real sons of bitches on his crew. Real fuckin' professional. He always promised me, but then nothing ever happened. I just... can't figure out one thing, though. Why now? Why the hell did he do it now? He always said it was impossible. Was it always a lie? And if so, what changed?"

"Cash did this?" Dixon said, watching Jaye, looking lost.

"Remember all of those stories," Jaye started. He pulled all of the comfort brought of being in their cabin together closely around him like thick armor for strength. "About the guard who'd come to my cell to scare me, as payback against Cash? Then later, when he'd come snatch me up and..." Jaye's voice broke. He shook his head, shaking it off, or trying to.

"The baton," Dixon guessed. "The guy who called you piggy."

He sounded so angry, and it made Jaye want to curl up into a ball again, so all of Dixon's anger would just wash over him without being able to get through and get at his weak spots to draw out the ghosts again.

"That's Ecker? Are you shitting me?" Dixon dropped his fork and sat back, the anger pumping him up. He blew out a breath, seemed to try to calm down. "Okay. Okay. You think Cash did this? But he's still inside. So... it was his crew? The Disciples?"

"Yeah, far as I can tell. Or else he had some people who owed him a favor. A big favor."

For a minute or so, they just sat there looking at each other across both the table and a gap built of wildly different experiences. On one side was law and order, the other chaos and crime. And all around them was open miles of Alaskan wild, filled with hardly any people or civilization, but only raw nature in all its glory. They were so far away from everything, but then why did the fear make it all seem so close?

Maybe it was because despite how far Jaye had run, way out into nowhere, Cash had still found him. So had Ecker, from beyond the grave and now perhaps even better able to haunt Jaye's every attempt at recovery.

"They wanted me to know how he died," Jaye explained. "They killed him like that to let me know they'd done it for me. The rape. The stabbing. The way they'd cut his throat."

Dixon just sat there, hands on the tabletop, eyes wide, looking ready for anything, but scared as hell.

In a place where there was no sound at all but the wood crackling in the fire, Dixon said quietly to Jaye, "You don't owe him shit, J-bird. You don't."

But that wasn't true. Cash had followed through. He'd made Ecker pay. Plus, he'd gone out of his way to let Jaye know he'd made Ecker pay.

Jaye owed Cash now.

Jaye was in Cash's debt.

When Jaye said nothing, Dixon repeated himself, sounding a little frantic. "You don't!"

"Dix — " Jaye sighed.

21

"No," Dixon said abruptly, cutting him off. "No. He doesn't get to tug at the leash like that anymore. He doesn't own you. It was done. He's fucking... he's in prison, hundreds of miles away. You're not his anymore. He doesn't get to pull this shit and expect you to follow along."

Jaye closed his eyes. The inviting scent of the stew, the warmth of the flames in the hearth, the softness of his clothes against his skin all held him in a safe place, helping to fortify his spirit. Because no matter how secure he was, physically and mentally, he couldn't escape the creeping certainty of what needed to happen next.

"You didn't ask for this!"

"I did, though. I did ask."

"That was a long time ago," Dixon argued.

"Doesn't matter."

"So... what? Now you go down there and fuck him? Conjugal visit?"

Breathe, Jaye told himself. In. Out. In. Out.

His eyes stung, but he refused to let tears gather. There was a squeezing in his chest, and a feeling of being crushed, of being made smaller and smaller and smaller.

It only got away from him for a second. He started to feel the touching start between his legs, prying them apart and a horrified moan slipped through his defenses.

"Fuck. I'm sorry. I'm sorry." Dixon said heavily, in a rush. He got out of the chair, came around. Jaye felt touching. It was real — Dixon crouching down to grasp Jaye's arm and the side of his jaw. Jaye flinched.

"Don't."

"I'm scared, okay? That wasn't fair to you, and — "

"No. It was. You're right. I'm a whore. That's how I've always paid him back, isn't it?"

"No. You survived by making impossible choices and I know that," Dixon said, filled with sorrow that Jaye couldn't let him touch him, or get inside his head. "That world you lived in? That role you played? That's gone. It can't affect you if you don't want it to. Shut it out. We'll... I don't know. Burn the fucking letter in the fireplace. Forget it ever came. You're a different person now. You're not his. You're not Johnny."

From far away, in places only Jaye knew existed, Cash was screaming. So was Tio. So was he. Heavy prison doors slammed and locks engaged. Voices echoed down long corridors. Footsteps squeaked on tile. No one answered the screaming. No one could or even cared.

Slowly, painfully, Jaye opened up just enough to sling his arms behind Dixon's neck. For months, he'd been nothing but Dixon's. But as Jaye heard Dixon whisper against his neck, "He can't have you back," Jaye knew that, deep down, he'd always be Johnny. Just a little. Just enough. And, after all, a deal was a deal.

Chapter 4:
The Breakdown

The whole thing was totally Cash's style. Jaye could easily fill in the missing pieces of information just by using his imagination. Cash outsourced the job, made sure nothing tied back to him in any concrete way, but included enough particulars for Jaye to know, without a doubt, why Ecker had been killed, and by whom.

It was another deal, still in play. Jaye had made the request, back when he was in Sheridan. Cash had come through in a big way. Now, Cash expected compensation.

Only, Jaye had no idea what it could be that Cash wanted from him.

Maybe he really was lonely, and would ask for Jaye to visit. The idea of walking back into that hellhole of his own accord was stomach churning, but Jaye knew if it came down to it, he'd go. For Cash, he would.

The creeping dread like icy fingers tickling up his spine told him it wouldn't be as easy as that.

Maybe they'd want to make another video.

Maybe it would be even worse.

I'm straight now, Jaye told himself. *No more breaking the law. No more fucking up. I won't ruin what I have with Dixon. I can't take the chance. Not even for Cash.*

Standing in the kitchen, scraping his uneaten stew back into the container to save for later, Jaye felt closed in and too exposed at the same time. The conflicting types of paranoia made him a little crazy. That damned letter had him pinned down, unable to stop thinking about it. But it also made him feel like all of the wilderness in Alaska wasn't enough to hide him. Cash, and his crew, knew right where he was.

Jaye set the container back in the fridge, then wandered across the cabin.

Dixon tended the fire, staring into the licking, amorphous tongues of orange and red. As he set some more wood on the charred pile, he glanced over a shoulder at Jaye, lingering nearby. "Where'd he get your P.O. address?"

"Mm," Jaye grunted, chewing at his lip. "My fault, obviously. Another cock-up. I wrote him once, right after I got up here. It was stupid. I was just lonely, looking for someone to talk to. As nice as the solitude was... there was a fuck-ton of it and it was kind of hard to deal with. I gave him the P.O. Box so he could write back, but he never did."

Dixon paused with the poker in his hand. After a moment's thought, he stuck it into the flames, using it to arrange the fresh wood. "I didn't even think of that," he admitted. "You coming way out here, with no one to talk to, trying to get your life together."

"I was closer to him than anyone. After the attack, I lost everyone — my mom, my boyfriend, my regular friends. That was harder than being locked up, and when I got out I couldn't escape the isolation."

"Yeah, I've noticed you don't talk about that stuff a lot." The fire was growing again, the wood popping, the flames feeding on the wood. Dixon stood and turned his attention back to Jaye. The size difference between them hit Jaye, turning him on and setting him on edge a little. Dixon's cotton shirt pulled tight over his muscular chest and shoulders. He loved the way Dixon made him feel helpless and safeguarded. Only wanting more of that, Jaye was tempted to submit to everything he knew Dixon could give.

"Yeah." Jaye dropped his gaze. Dixon walked closer, touched Jaye's arm and guided him over to the bed. Jaye sat on the edge next to Dixon and rubbed at his thighs as his nerves jangled and surged. "There was no way to deal with it all. I just had to put it behind me. It felt like proof of what a worthless person I was. No one wanted me. I was nothing. No one. But Cash made me feel like I was worth something. He taught me how to keep fighting for myself, even when it seemed like I had nothing left to give. You can always dig deeper."

Matching Jaye's hushed tone, Dixon said, "I can't imagine what that must have felt like to have all of the people you thought you could count on fail you in such a huge way, right when you needed them the most. I'm so sorry you felt so alone. I swear you're never going to feel like that again. You have family and friends, and we love you. We're here for you. It makes me so angry knowing what you went through, and I feel so goddamned powerless, knowing that there's nothing I can do about it."

Jaye shook his head. "No, we've been through this. It was some hard times, sure. But you had your own to deal with. No looking back. Only forward. And there's plenty you do for me every day, every fucking minute, just by being here."

He took a good long look at Dixon, seeing all of his frustration and protectiveness. It made Jaye grin. Dixon was his living, breathing reminder of how something amazing could enter life at any moment. Jaye was determined to hold on to him as tightly as he could, now that he had him. He'd lost too much not to realize how good he had it.

But that letter meant something. Cash was waiting, but for what?

Jaye paused, just to see if the ghosts would speak up, now that they had new fodder for torment, but they'd remained silent. All he could detect was faint, far away laughter. It sounded dead, and cold. All of his enemies were dead now.

The thought should have been more comforting than it was.

With goosebumps lingering on his skin, Jaye turned to Dixon and shifted, moving to straddle Dixon's lap.

"Hey," Dixon protested, holding Jaye's hips and trying to keep him from advancing. "You don't need to."

"Maybe I do," Jaye countered. He was able to settle on top of Dixon, facing him, breathing in his scent. It felt nice, soothing, real. The goosebumps went away. Dixon caressed Jaye's back.

"I can't believe he's anything but a bad guy," Dixon confessed, so quietly Jaye barely heard him. "Even if he was there for you sometimes."

Chuckling despite himself, wearing a crooked grin, Jaye rolled his hips against Dixon's crotch. "Mm, so this is your jealous side, huh?"

"No," Dixon scoffed, gritting his teeth against the distracting movements of Jaye's body. After another firm thrust, Jaye could feel Dixon getting hard, and it only made Jaye's smile grow.

26

"I was a bad guy, too. We were all bad guys in there."

Dixon groaned, then kissed Jaye like he needed to but was trying hard not to. It was quick, dirty, and Dixon's hand grabbed at Jaye's ass, squeezing. Using the grip there, he pulled Jaye's crotch in even harder against him.

They fell back onto the bed, lying on it as they rutted against each other.

"No fucking way. You were innocent."

"Of what?" Jaye grinned darkly. Dixon's eyes flashed in warning, like he wasn't going to let Jaye speak badly about himself, which only egged Jaye on even more. "It's okay to be bad sometimes, Dix."

He had Dixon's belt open, then his fly, and pulled out his cock. With a hungry, hard grunt, Jaye pushed off against Dixon's chest, sliding quickly down to kneel at the foot of the bed. He yanked Dixon toward him a few inches, then swallowed his cock like he was starving for it. The taste, the heat, the wet, easy slide over his tongue made Jaye moan wantonly.

Dixon hissed, "Fuck," and palmed Jaye's head.

Drawing it out as long as he could, Jaye sucked Dixon until he was close to coming. Knowing what he needed to come next, Jaye pulled off with a wet pop, stood, then hurriedly pushed his pants down. He climbed onto the bed next to Dixon, and got into position on his knees, ass up and waiting.

The funniest part was how clearly Dixon was fighting against the moment, trying to tell himself it was inappropriate or something, but instincts were getting in the way.

He shifted behind Jaye. After just a second, two licked-wet fingers pressed inside.

"Just fuck me," Jaye begged.

"No. It'll hurt without prep."

"So fucking what? You would never hurt me in any way that matters."

Dixon's pair of fingers pumped harder, making Jaye gasp and spread even more, wanting it intensely. A third finger slipped in on the next push, nice and slow, and Jaye gasped around a moan, shivering. Dixon's name became a mantra when the fingers pulled out, leaving him empty. As soon as he felt pressure, Jaye bit his lip and pushed back onto the thick cock burrowing into him, claiming him.

Lowering his head so it was resting against the bed, Jaye gasped. Sure, it still hurt a little, but he drank the ache down, needing Dixon inside him where he belonged. Once he was fully seated, he let Jaye catch his breath and just caressed the sides of his ass and along his thighs.

"Love you," Dixon whispered.

Needing those words so desperately, it was terrifying, Jaye frowned against the bed. It used to be so easy to be hard, to not care. Dixon had changed all that — changed him.

"I'll take care of you. I promise," Dixon told him, starting to move. The intimate tug and press, stuffing him full, kept him in a vulnerable mindset.

Jaye could only moan. When Dixon began stroking Jaye's dick counter to each thrust, it was only seconds before Jaye came, shuddering, his breath choking off completely with the force of it.

Dixon slowly pulled out, then pushed right back in on a steady, never-ending thrust that took Jaye apart. "Fucking love you so much, Dix."

Three hard rutting pushes, hips slapped against Jaye's cheeks, and Dixon came too, growling through the climax. Jaye laughed breathlessly. He reached for Dixon's hand, pulling him closer, not letting go.

—▭—▭—▭—

Jaye's body wound around Dixon, his arms and legs holding on tightly. The fire crackled in the fireplace but the world beyond the cabin's wooden confines was peaceful and still. The blankets covering the entangled pair were warm and cozy. A stubborn, subtle frown lingered on Jaye's expression. Dixon tried to soothe it away with kisses, to no avail.

He knew it was easier for Jaye to face things physically. Talking out problems still brought out his defensive side, his walls closing him in intentionally. That's why he wasn't surprised Jaye's instinct had been to seek comfort and connection through sex before either of them had really faced what they were dealing with. But talking needed to happen. Dixon knew he had to try to assure Jaye it was going to be all right.

"What are you going to do?" Dixon asked, knowing Jaye had thought it through just from the pure unease in the quirk of his mouth.

"I can't call him. He doesn't have my number and he can't call cell phones anyway. Has to be a landline. I could write him, but what would I say? I mean, really? Hey, got your message, thanks for bumping off that piece of shit Ecker? Prison staff reads everything that goes in or out."

Dixon propped himself up on one arm. The more he pulled away, the more Jaye tried to prevent it by clinging even tighter to him.

"You're not going down there."

He'd intended it to be a question, but when it came out as a command, Jaye smirked a little.

"Yes sir, Trooper Rowe, though I'm pretty sure I went down already," Jaye teased.

"I mean it," Dixon pressed after a pause for a little inward reflection. "I'm not delivering you to that dangerous nutcase. You don't owe him anything."

"Don't I? I would probably be long dead if it wasn't for Cash. That's worth something to you, isn't it? Because it is to me. I've got my whole life ahead of me now, because of him. I have you. I have hope. That's pretty fucking huge. He's doing his time. It doesn't hurt anything just to touch base with him."

"Yes. It does. He ordered a hit on that guard. He fucking had a man murdered in cold blood."

"Hey, I murdered a guy too. Someone just as monstrous as Ecker."

"That's not the same. You were being actively killed and violated. It was pure self-defense. Cash wasn't anywhere near Ecker when he died. It was pre-meditated."

"I don't know, Dix. Some days I think a killer is a killer, no matter what kind he might happen to be."

"What if he expects you to do something illegal for him? That seems pretty likely to me. Tell me it isn't."

Jaye's expression shifted. Dixon couldn't get a read on it, it was too shadowy, hiding things that barely reached the surface. "It isn't," Jaye said after a long while.

"You had to think about it a long time," Dixon frowned.

"He wouldn't put me in danger like that."

Dixon had to laugh. Flashes of memory came back, of the things Jaye had hinted to in private confession. He hated to think of what Jaye had been made to suffer in prison. Imagination conjured unspeakable horrors, especially when he had Jaye naked, spread and vulnerable beneath him. There had been other, crueler men in his place, taking advantage in the most awful ways of the person Dixon loved more than any other. Letting Cash have any contact with Jaye felt like stepping aside to let the unhinged thug climb back on top of Jaye's nude body to have at him in whatever ways he wanted. Dixon had no concept of how to be okay with that on any level.

He stroked through Jaye's dark curls, afraid for him all over again.

"Tell me he never put you in danger in there," Dixon dared.

Jaye's gaze slipped to the side. He sighed. It was answer enough.

"Cash wasn't responsible for anything I hadn't agreed to ahead of time," Jaye replied. It was a cautious, telling response and it made Dixon angry as hell.

"He offered you up to people," Dixon growled. "How would you feel if Marcus had offered me up like that?"

"Dix," Jaye hushed, "I would never agree to anything that would make you uncomfortable. You know that, right? You're the only thing that matters to me. It was about surviving in there. It's not about that anymore. Cash knows it. He knows he doesn't have that kind of leverage. He's not stupid."

"Fuck leverage and fuck the past. You don't owe him anything," Dixon snapped.

He could see it now. Jaye felt like he needed to contact Cash. He was going to do it.

"I'm asking you not to contact him," Dixon said, trying to get it together and to stop imagining Jaye being raped, being held down by criminals and hurt, over and over again, with no end in sight. "Please? Please don't?"

Jaye avoided eye contact and stayed silent. Dixon caressed Jaye's arms. Their fingers wove together. He held Jaye down and kissed him gently. "You're mine now," he whispered against Jaye's warm, kiss-bitten lips.

Exhaling heavily, undulating up against Dixon, Jaye gave every sign of being turned on by the position and Dixon's words. His legs were hooked behind Dixon's lower back. Grinding in little movements against Dixon's body while they kissed, Jaye slowly got hard, his breathing uneven and rough.

Dixon let go of Jaye's hands, hooked his arms under Jaye's legs instead, pulling him wide open as he folded Jaye's legs back. He entered Jaye in one push, going deep fast. Jaye's mouth fell open around a cry, drinking down air. His lower lip quivered. As Dixon started to move, rocking right against Jaye's gland, Jaye let out a rough yell of pure pleasure. Clawing at the back of Dixon's neck, Jaye met every hard thrust. He glanced down where their bodies met, watching Dixon's swollen dick fucking him wide open.

"God yes," Jaye moaned, back arching.

He reached for his cock, but Dixon commanded, "No. Just lay there. That's an order."

"Fucking love when you give me orders," Jaye chuckled deliriously. The sound twisted, broke apart on a gasp.

"Then I order you not to contact him."

"Yes, sir, Trooper Rowe," Jaye replied with a submissive purr.

"Obey me," Dixon growled, giving him a hard, complete thrust, feeling Jaye's lithe, toned body yield and spread easily to receive.

"Oh Jesus," Jaye moaned, his eyes rolling up, his dick an angry, stiff red, dripping pre-come. Dixon kept rocking against his gland, making Jaye whimper and tremble. His ass pushed down into every thrust. His chin tipped up, his head thrown back in ecstasy. "Don't fucking stop," he begged.

"Obey me," Dixon repeated, his lips brushing against Jaye's. The heat came off him in waves, sweat slicking his brow and chest.

"Always," Jaye promised.

Dixon came with a rough groan, pumping seed deeply into Jaye's ass.

He guided Jaye's arms above his head, curling there. Crossing his wrists, Dixon pinned them with one hand. When he reached, slowly, for Jaye's straining dick with the other, Jaye made a fragile, pleading sound. Dixon rubbed gently with the pad of his thumb under the head of Jaye's dick, barely brushing the silky, hot skin. Jaye shuddered hard, frowning. His hips chased into the touch, but he was impaled on Dixon's cock, his arms trapped. He wasn't going anywhere. Dixon kept the light, tickling touch from providing much relief, making Jaye ride the edge of his orgasm. His inner muscles clenched up around Dixon as he fought it, trying to thrust, to come.

He drew it out as long as he could. Brushing with his fingertips around Jaye's cockhead, Dixon watched Jaye's mouth as he made broken, breathless little cries. He kept shuddering, his cock dripping. Reading his cues, Dixon kept relief just out of reach. Jaye's frown melted away. A sort of peace transformed his expression and body language. The stimulation was too intense for any worries to slip through.

Dixon pulled slowly out and fed Jaye's ass three fingers instead. Going right for his gland, Dixon massaged it carefully.

Jaye yelled, his naturally rough voice even more ragged. Fingering him over and over again, Dixon gradually let go of Jaye's wrists and crept down his body.

"Fuck... Dix... please..."

He licked with long strokes of his tongue up the underside of Jaye's cock. Swallowing down the pre-come, he cleaned it all away. Then he licked over the head, up the sides. When he closed his lips around Jaye's cockhead and let the shaft slide back to fill his mouth and throat, Jaye came with a strangled sound, convulsing. He rode Dixon's mouth, fucking it, twisting on the fingers taking him apart. Jaye's come tasted sweet and Dixon sucked him hard through the aftershocks.

Once he was fully spent and lay boneless on the bed, Dixon crawled back up and settled down beside him. Without a moment's hesitation, though he was clearly exhausted, Jaye curled up like a kitten at Dixon's side, under his arm, his head pillowed on Dixon's chest as he caught his breath.

Cruel men like Cash might have been good at building up Jaye's walls, but Dixon took great pride at his ability to get Jaye to let all of those walls come tumbling down.

Chapter 5:
No Going Back

The Expedition pulled into the gravel lot outside of the Zus utilities building which was the base of operations for Jaye's work. It was located downtown, a short walk from the station. The pre-fab structure was divided into several offices for electric, plumbing, water, and sewer services. Having their workplaces near to each other helped on days when their schedules didn't mesh. That morning, Dixon had left before dawn — hours before Jaye was due to work. He would also get home well before Jaye. A similar schedule the next day meant he'd need to catch some sleep instead of wake up to spend time together.

But they still had the chance to steal moments together if they needed to.

Sitting behind the wheel in the cozy confines of the SUV, Dixon sipped a mug of lukewarm coffee and watched Jaye. He stood a few steps around the corner from the building's entrance, chatting and laughing with one of his co-workers — a guy in his thirties named Oki. While Oki leaned back against the building's wall, smoking a cigarette, Jaye stood nearby, hands pushed way down in his pockets. Just watching body language said a lot. Jaye turned toward Oki. His shoulders were back. When he tossed his head, Dixon glimpsed Jaye's wide smile and crinkled eyes, squinted shut to block some of the bright, mid-day sunlight.

That was how Dixon loved seeing him — carefree, interacting with people in a way that served not to gain him anything, but just to make him happy and more fulfilled.

Oki was a nice guy with a wife and three kids. He was born and raised in the towns around Zus. A tried and true local who treated Jaye, the ultimate outsider, with only friendliness and understanding. Jaye deserved as many of those types of friendships as he could get, so Dixon sat back and waited. As much as he'd been looking forward to his desperately needed talk with Jaye, it could wait.

A few sips later, Oki nodded toward the Expedition, idling well beyond Jaye's turned back. Jaye spun, finally seeing the vehicle. Giving Oki a wave, his lips sounding out words Dixon couldn't hear, Jaye took his leave of his friend and jogged over to Dixon.

The passenger door swung open.

"Hey, you should have honked or something."

"Nah. No rush. Didn't want to interrupt," Dixon told him. He gave Oki a wave, which was returned with a smile. Stubbing out his butt, Oki tossed it in a small receptacle left for the employees and began to walk back into the building. "How's he doing?"

"Good," Jaye said, climbing into the seat, shutting the door and huddling around the heater's vent. He rubbed his hands in the jet of hot air. "His wife's been trying to get him to quit, since they have the baby. They try to keep the smoking outside only, to keep it away from the kids, but that means he's outside a lot of time, in the cold, while she's in with all three kids and no help. It's tough, though. I've never been there, but I saw how desperate some guys get if their supply runs low or out. Anyway. How are you? How's your day been, Trooper?"

"Here." Dixon passed him the other coffee in the holder. "It's probably not hot anymore, but Sesi brought in some imported coffee beans from somewhere or other. Tastes different, but good."

"Thanks." Jaye cupped his hands around the paper container, his eyes watchful, locked on Dixon, as he took a sip. Then he set the cup down between them in the center console and leaned over to give Dixon a kiss. Their lips grazed and Jaye's keen gaze searched deeply into Dixon. "What's wrong?"

"Nothing's wrong," he said, but knew his behavior was all the alert Jaye needed to spark his acute intuition. It was a talent that helped keep him alive in FCI Sheridan, but translated in strange ways out in the real world. Such as making him about five times as observant as everyone else Dixon encountered in his private life or in the course of his job.

"Bullshit." His hand wrapped Dixon's thigh, sparking distracting want. It was tempting to give in and indulge, wasting away precious minutes with some physical release. As always, Jaye was easy to turn on and ready to get dirty with the slightest hint it was welcomed or wanted.

Dixon felt the inviting heat coming off of Jaye's lean body. The natural scent of his skin and hair got in Dixon's head in all of the right ways. Jaye wasn't one for cologne or fancy toiletries. The fragrance was all soap, water, and Jaye. Dixon loved it.

The feel of Jaye's fingers moving over Dixon's thigh, caressing, gently kneading, was intended, he knew, to turn him on and draw him out. The caresses drew higher, close to dangerous territory. Then the pad of Jaye's thumb dragged over the swell of Dixon's crotch. Dixon loved that too — how Jaye could cross lines instinctively, with all of the bravery, confidence, and love in the world. When they were together, there was nothing standoffish in him. All of Jaye only worked to draw Dixon in closer, taking him deeper. He was the greatest intoxicant Dixon had ever encountered.

There was more, too — the softness of his silky lips, the flirtatiousness of his dark eyelashes working to give Dixon only glimpses of the sharp intellect and wit found in his gorgeous eyes, the dark tumble of his hair over his forehead, the peek of his tattoos always hinting at his inherent wickedness, the pure sex of his body...

It was a lot to say no to.

"I've been thinking. I've made a decision."

Jaye's ministrations paused, only for a moment. Everything in him that actively worked to loosen Dixon's ties hesitated. Dixon had spoken with authority and conviction, so he knew that it was his tone more than his words that had the effect they did.

"And what have you decided, Trooper Rowe?" Jaye murmured.

"I've decided," Dixon explained slowly and deliberately, "how this is going to go."

"Yes, sir," Jaye said with a crooked, sinful grin. "How do you want me?"

"In ways you could never even imagine, gorgeous," Dixon smiled, giving Jaye's jaw a gentle brush of his fingertips.

There was a silence, then, and he saw the shift in Jaye happen, right before his eyes. Somehow, without any explanation, Jaye knew. Maybe he actually just flat-out read Dixon's mind. Maybe he simply knew Dixon that well, after having so much time to study him in detail — physically, psychologically, and emotionally.

Did Jaye know Cash as well, too? After two years incarcerated together, he must. Dixon hated the thought of it, and it only strengthened his resolve further.

The nature of Jaye's continued little caresses changed. The sex and lure of them became more soothing and placating instead. His gaze lowered submissively. His lips softened and his breathing became more rapid in exceedingly subtle ways.

So, Dixon took firmer hold of Jaye's jaw, their bodies slightly turned toward each other in the front seat of the SUV. He didn't care if anyone could see them, or was watching. They were the only people in existence in that moment.

Better than anyone, Dixon knew never to underestimate Jaye Larson, who was stronger and more capable than anyone else Dixon had met. But he also knew — better even than Cash, he would bet — the exact, fine webbing of the cracks in Jaye's heart and soul. Cash had caused those, along with Ecker and so many others. Now, it was Dixon's job to make sure the splintering not only didn't worsen, but that nothing got close enough to break the most precious person in his life.

The more Jaye fell into his submissive role, the more Dixon rose to dominate. It felt right.

"I'll be sending Cash a letter, requesting he call my work number. I'll also request that he add me as an approved visitor."

Jaye's jaw clenched, but his gaze remained lowered. He didn't say a word.

"You are not to contact him further, in any way. I will be the one to contact him."

He watched Jaye breathe through his nose, his nostrils flaring momentarily. His head bowed slightly further.

"Yes, sir."

"Swear to me that you'll obey my command."

"I swear."

"Look at me, J-bird."

He did it instantly, confidently. Cool and hot at the same time, his gaze locked onto Dixon's eyes, dancing back and forth between them.

"Do you understand why it has to be this way?"

"Yes, sir."

"Explain."

"You're protecting me."

"We don't know his intentions, and I don't trust him not to hurt you. I know you feel indebted to him, so I am going to be the buffer between you two. You're not his anymore. You're mine. I intend to make that clear, as well."

Jaye took a deeper breath and let it out.

"What?"

"He won't talk to you like he talks to me. You're law. And he won't like you for being close to me."

"If he has a message to convey to you, he'll find a way to give it to me instead."

There was another too-long pause. A glance to the clock on the dashboard told Dixon that Jaye's break was almost over.

"What?"

"You're not really going to see him face-to-face are you?"

"Why?"

"Seeing him will upset you."

"You sound pretty sure of that."

"I am sure. You know who he was to me. You know what he did to me. I was his whore for two years, and it wasn't a private deal. He showed me off. He force-fucked me in front of the whole gang more times than I can count."

Dixon refused to think about it. He instantly shut down the mental images, because the words alone were making him want to vomit or smash his fist through the windshield.

He closed his eyes. He started to let go of Jaye, and that must have been the opening he was looking for, because he took it.

His hand clasped over Dixon's, keeping it in place, against the side of his jaw.

Just like that, Dixon had lost all power. Jaye had taken it.

"It would happen a lot in the showers. I'd be naked. Helpless. Without Cash, they would have all come in and raped me to death right there on the greasy tile with cockroaches hiding in the corners. And they would have done it laughing. The dirty guards would have let it happen. But I was a possession to Cash. I added to his value, but he had a reputation to uphold, so he wasn't gentle. He'd pull my hair nearly hard enough to rip my scalp off, jam his cock up my ass, choke me a little. He wanted me to cry and fight with real fear, so he let it hurt enough to make the act sell. And that was all the time, Dix. That was daily. It wasn't just Cash fucking me, either. He used me as payment. Gave me to others to fuck or touch as much as they wanted to, to pay off debts, and they were even less gentle. The things they called me? The things they did to my body? The ways I hurt, all the time? That's why I have ghosts. That's why I lost my fucking mind."

"Stop," Dixon demanded, his voice breaking.

"I owe Cash this call, this visit. I do. Because there is no way in hell I'd still be in one piece or above ground without him. But this is not someone I want you in contact with."

"This is the way it has to be," Dixon countered, standing his ground. "It's this or nothing. I'm not bending on this. I won't. He doesn't get to have you anymore. He only goes through me."

Jaye's beautiful eyes searched his, but this time Dixon had to look away. It was too much. It was far too easy to believe not only every single word Jaye had said, but that he was still hiding the really bad stuff from him. Dixon couldn't take it away, or help more than Jaye would let him do so, and it hurt. A lot. And when Dixon hurt, it showed. Always. He couldn't help it. It's what kept Marcus around, feeding off of Dixon's anguish and shame like a vampire.

He started to cry, soundlessly, avoiding eye contact, jaw clenched. The tears rolled down his cheeks. Jaye brushed them away and kissed him over and over again, on his closed eyelids, on the tip of his nose, his cheek, his lips.

Dixon gathered him up in an awkward hug over the center console, holding him so tightly. He buried his face against Jaye's skin, the soft curl of his hair, with one hand clasped behind his head and one on his back. Jaye brushed the skin at the back of Dixon's neck.

"No one hurts me anymore. No one touches me but you," Jaye told him.

Dixon's breath hitched. In his mind, Jaye was screaming for help that wouldn't come, sobbing to deaf ears, bleeding and breaking, and there was nothing he could do.

"It's just a conversation," Jaye said.

"We could just let it go," Dixon begged.

"I can't."

"I know."

Dixon relaxed his hold, sniffled and tried to get it together. Jaye kissed his forehead, his cheek, his knuckles.

"I love you so much," Dixon breathed, his voice breaking and vision blurred.

"What I would have given," Jaye replied, "to have had you sooner, Dixon."

Dixon just gathered him up again, kissing his hair and caressing his back. "There's no going back, for either of us."

Jaye took his hand, weaving their fingers together. They stayed like that for several minutes, letting the clock wind down. When Jaye had to go, he closed his eyes while kissing Dixon, then turned, almost running back to the building as if by looking at Dixon at all, he would never leave.

Much later that evening, hours after Dixon had come home from his shift and gone to bed for some sleep after eating an early dinner of more re-heated stew, Jaye drove home from work. The sound of the car pulling up to the house and the gentle bang of the driver's side door closing didn't wake him — it didn't usually — but he did roll over in bed with a sleepy grunt as Jaye closed the door as quickly as he could to shut out the chill. He saw Dixon draw the blankets up to cover himself more completely. Shedding his coat and shoes and going to stoke the waning flames in the hearth, Jaye crept around as silently as he could.

He set a few pieces of split logs into the dancing tongues of gold and orange, liking the heat on his hand and arm. Staring into the shapes made as the wood was consumed, Jaye thought back again on the looping process his thoughts had made that day after Dixon's orders had been delivered.

He understood Dixon's logic, and was prepared to honor it, but Dixon not only didn't have the full story — he never would have the full story. There were aspects in the power dynamics long since established between Jaye "Johnny" Larson and Cassius "Cash" Jones that were so alien to a lawman like Dixon, Jaye knew he had to speak up. But what to say?

He'd spent so long keeping Cash and Dixon's worlds apart, not only practically, but in Jaye's mental space as well; he resisted with all his might the thought of them colliding. No good could come of it. But Cash was so determined, he'd had a man tortured and murdered just to send a message. And Dixon was equally determined to safeguard Jaye, with every bit of a lover's whole-hearted devotion. How could something as immaterial as discomfort stand in the way of those types of motivations?

Jaye's whole life had been a series of weird and wild balancing acts.

As a child, he had to strive for his own success and health while dealing with his only family in the form of a troubled, drug-addicted mother on a less-than-ideal career path. Love for Cora got him through until he met Kris, his first boyfriend, and a third dynamic was added to the mix. Then it became a dance of keeping both Kris and Cora happy or safe enough while also taking care of his own basic needs as a teenager with limited resources, trying to build a life for himself.

Once the attack happened, Cora and Kris quickly became non-factors. Then it was all about staying alive.

After the initial adjustment period, merely striving for survival wasn't the only thing on Jaye's plate. He also had to keep Cash, his owner and protector, happy. No matter what that meant. He also had to bob and weave around the guards. Some were in the pocket of Cash's gang. Others were in the pocket of rivals. In that isolated world of FCI Sheridan, there were many players on the board and none of them were to be underestimated.

Now, having left Sheridan behind, Jaye was tasked with honoring Dixon as his partner, protector and true love, while simultaneously honoring Cash's unfailing follow-through in keeping Jaye breathing air.

Just because Cash wasn't physically nearby didn't mean he wasn't still in the game. He was, and might always be, a major player in Jaye's life. Just because Dixon wanted Jaye to pretend Cash had been knocked off the board didn't make it true. It had nothing to do with Jaye's commitment to Dixon as his primary relationship and priority. It was about balance, and honor in the most basic sense.

Jaye never wanted to have to play Dixon and Cash off of each other. He wanted them each far, far away from the other. Now, he had no choice. He had to allow Dixon to call the shots in this. He had to let Dixon have his say. He'd earned at least that much.

"Hey," he heard from a few feet behind him.

"Hey," Jaye replied without turning around. The warmth of the fire heating his face, chest, and hands helped anchor him in the tangible rather than the psychological puzzle shifting around in his head.

"You want me to heat you up some food?"

"I can get it, Dix. But thank you. It never fails to stun me that I actually have someone willing to provide hot food for me on a regular basis."

"C'mere. Sit with me a second."

Jaye sighed and stood. With the cabin's only light behind him, Dixon was in deep shadow as Jaye approached the bed. For a second, he imagined Cash there instead, taking up the left side of the bed, his many tattoos and scars only visible in the orange firelight when Jaye moved slightly to one side.

Strangely, the idea didn't horrify Jaye. It just made him sad.

Cash would never get out. He would never have a home, or a lover kept only out of mutual devotion, and with no ulterior motives.

Way back in his mind, Jaye heard Cash screaming again. He heard the fight and the futility of their last moments together, and it hurt. There was a lot that wasn't fair in the world, but something about Cash's situation spoke deeply to Jaye of the massive failings of many levels of reality.

When Jaye turned to sit, the firelight caught Dixon's golden-red hair, his bright blue eyes and creamy skin.

Dixon took Jaye's hand, folding it up in a different kind of living, consuming warmth.

"We going to Brekken's for dinner on Friday?"

"Yep. That's the plan," Dixon agreed. "The big day."

Jaye felt instantly uncomfortable at the mention of his birthday. There was too much riding on it. He wished he could just skip the day entirely, sleep through it and call it a win. It would mark the third anniversary of the night of his attack.

"Maybe we shouldn't go."

Dixon gave him a disbelieving look. "No way. We've been over this. We need to give you some happy memories to associate with it. You deserve that. As someone who loves you very much, I want to see you happy on that day more than anything. It means a lot to me too."

"All right," Jaye surrendered. "We don't need to get into it."

"Okay. What's up?" He rubbed the back of Jaye's hand and gave him a patient but knowing glance. "I know that look. Makes you seem fifty-two instead of twenty-two. Whatever you're carrying, gimme some."

"You didn't send the letter yet, right?"

Dixon's expression softened into a humble little smile. "No, I'm not that good."

"Okay. I know you can be compulsive with this stuff once it's on your To Do list, so I just wanted to make sure."

"Why?"

Jaye let out a heavy breath and tried to figure out how to say it. It used to be so much easier to get what he wanted from Dixon. He could seduce the decisions out of him. But they were way beyond that now. Their relationship had matured along with them. Now, talking things out had become key — not that he was any good at it.

"He won't trust you. Cash. As hard as he's tried to get me his message, he might just rip up your letter without even reading it at the first sign it's from a lawman. And he'd just try to come at me some other way."

"So what do you suggest?"

He gazed down at his hand, cocooned now in both of Dixon's. He wished Dixon could do that with all of him — just hold him so gently and keep him far out of harm's way.

"You need to let me tell you what to say. Cash sent his message in code. Our message back has to be the same. They'll read it. Screen it. So it has to be carefully considered to let Cash know I had you send it for me, and that you know enough of what's gone on to cement your status as a reliable link to me."

"You need me to tell him things only the two of you would know," Dixon paraphrased.

"Yes. You have to understand how smart this guy is. He's excellent at reading people. He will know you hate his guts. That alone will only contribute to his mistrust of you."

"J-bird, I don't give a flying fuck what this guy thinks of me. The goal here is to find out what the hell he wants with you, then to be abso-fucking-lutely done with all of it. For good. I know you think

42

you owe him, but my job here is to mediate, resolve whatever this is, and make it go away. I see it in your face, how you do care about him, and that fucking kills me, kid. But I get it. I'm not dumb either. But if you're looking for anything more than closure here, tell me now. Please."

Just like it was yesterday instead of three years ago, Jaye heard...

You feel that, right? How I'm still fucking that hole? How that's gonna be throbbing for days? And you ain't gonna sit or shit right for a long damn time? That's our deal. That's my hole, now. It's mine, not yours. No one else touches it. You do what I say, no matter what it is.

God, but it made him tired. He let it sag his posture and drain a little more of his fading energy. It had been a long day.

"No, you're right," Jaye said. "I used to argue with the ghosts all the time. Nightly. About whether it was rape or not. He made me bleed. He made it hurt. As long as he was out of solitary, he hardly ever gave me a night off. It was only when I was on death's doorstep and high as a kite that he laid off a little. He gave me to other men as payment, to fuck. He'd watch and monitor it usually, but for the most part just let them have at it and say whatever shit they wanted to me. He wasn't a good guy. But you don't understand the life he's living in there. You just don't. You don't know what it was really like, for him or me. The promises we made to each other? Those are just as binding as any other type of vows. They mean something. Cash is locked up in there for the rest of his life, and what we had together was the closest thing to something good and real and meaningful that he will likely ever have, and they didn't..." His voice choked off. He angrily wiped his eyes dry and tried to pull the awful truth of it all out of him somehow. "They didn't let us say goodbye. They planted drugs in his cell to prevent it, so he'd be out of the way the whole week before I left and it was such a fucking low blow, Dix. I hear him screaming. He was screaming my name and..." He shook his head. He couldn't give anymore.

Dixon pulled him down into a soft hug. Jaye swung his legs up onto the bed, buried his face against Dixon's skin and tried to breathe.

"I can't love him, but I have to respect him," Jaye managed.

"I know. I know you do." Dixon kissed the top of Jaye's head and held him in the embrace. "We'll work it out, all right? The best way we can."

"Thanks."

"I just don't want you to have to carry this alone. You've already got way too much on your shoulders, and I'm here for you in whatever ways you need."

The words were so perfect, they physically hurt Jaye to hear. With a soft moan, he curled further into the hug and let it soothe some of the old aches, wondering what he'd ever done to deserve such kindness.

Chapter 6:
Some Big Hero

"Hi," Brekken said in a cheerful sing-song voice, wearing a beaming smile. She opened her arms and came forward. "I'm gonna kiss you. Fair warning."

"Noted," Jaye grinned. She pecked his cheek with her pursed lips, then gave him a tight hug.

"Happy early birthday," she said, pulling back and shifting her purse strap on her shoulder.

"You've still got more than a day to go, but thanks. I know Dix told you it was a big deal, but it's really not something you need to worry about. I mean, I appreciate everything, but I don't want to be a hassle to anyone."

"Oh, come on, Jaye." He stepped aside to let her in, then shut the door behind her to block out the cold. "I do know you well enough by now to know you're not just saying that to be polite. I can tell you mean it, but that's even more reason why I do need to make a fuss. You have so much to celebrate! And so do the rest of us, to be honest."

"Make yourself comfortable. You need a drink or anything?" he asked, trying to remember how to be hospitable. Everyday manners still weren't things that came to him easily. He had to work at normality more than others seemed to need to.

"No thanks. I'm good. He'll be home soon, by the way. I texted him a few minutes ago."

"Oh. Good."

"But what was I saying?" She dropped her bag and sat on the couch like she'd been on her feet all day. Settling back into the cushions in a way that spoke of her ease with both the place and Jaye, she let out a heavy breath and let go of some tension in her frame. Jaye noticed it mainly because it was odd for others to feel so comfortable around him. He tended to set people on edge rather than the opposite.

The realization of Brekken's acceptance caused a painful spark of gratitude, deep in his chest, that he wasn't sure how to process or accept.

"Oh, right. Celebrating!" She gave him a knowing smirk, as if calling him on his curmudgeonly attitude. She pulled a hairband off of her wrist and tied her long blonde hair up in a knot behind her head. Not for the first time, he marveled at how sisterly she felt to him, when he'd never been blessed with siblings, or had been close enough to someone to feel like they fit the role. He knew Brekken and Grant watched out for him, and not just because he was with Dixon. It underscored for him that he needed to watch out for them too, and repay the favor, but lately it felt like they were doing all of the giving. It made him uncomfortable.

"Maybe you do need to hear this," she told him. "I know how clever you are, Jaye, but it's different to have things said to you than to just assume them in your own head. I need you to understand that Dixon has been so different since he's been with you. I credit you with the whole Marcus thing, and only in good ways. I hated him more than anyone, Dixon included, but you probably know that, right? I mean, come on. He's my only brother, and that piece of shit was beating on him and doing God knows what else behind closed doors for too damned long. And I knew it. And I couldn't do anything! But you did. You came in there, and in no time, you'd figured that shit out and made a huge difference. You saved his life. Hell, you probably saved our lives too. I'm sorry you had to deal with all of that, but you've made a massive difference in my family. You're my hero."

"Brek…"

"No. Nope. Sorry. You don't get to contradict me on that. It's my opinion. So, yes. I know only a smidgeon of the shit you've been through in life, but I know enough to be aware that you deserve the best fucking birthday of your life. Pardon my French."

"Pardoned," Jaye smirked. He bit at the end of his thumb, trying to think of a comeback and failing. In fact, the more he stood there and thought about what she said, the more temptation there was to get upset, and she seemed to sense that too.

"Don't you dare cry on me, Jaye Larson. Let's change the subject. Dessert. What's your favorite flavor?"

"Of what?" he laughed.

"Anything. Tell me favorites. Favorite cake? Cupcakes? Um, cheesecakes… ice cream… candy…"

"Candy?" he smiled.

"Whatever," she said, flapping a hand. "Give me something. Just keep in mind the limitations of my grocery shopping access. Weird stuff takes time to ship in, and we don't have it for this one. Maybe next time."

Before answering, he just smiled at her a moment, watching her sitting there in his cabin, cross-legged on the couch, caring about things that wouldn't benefit her in the slightest, knowing most of his biggest secrets and still invested anyway. She wore an eager smile of the sort he figured came easier to her brother before he met Marcus. In fact, he bet their smiles would have matched identically. Maybe there were photos somewhere of them, arm-in-arm, like two peas in a pod. Both with that red-gold hair — since that would have been before she started to dye it blonde — and bright blue eyes. Brekken still had the innocence that had been stolen from Dixon forever.

She was part of his responsibility now. This woman who wouldn't have looked at him twice a year ago.

And now here he was, trying to get back in touch with Cash, who could only bring bad things to his new, hopeful life, and to people like sweet-hearted Brekken Rowe.

It wasn't just Jaye's hide on the line anymore. Now he had to come through for a bunch of people.

"Chocolate cake would be amazing," he told her, rubbing warmth into his arms as a chill ran down his back. "My mom wasn't," he cleared his throat, "always great at getting me a cake, so I'd go look for something chocolate at the store. Kind of became a tradition."

Brekken's cheer faded a little at that. "She was a single mom, right?"

"Yeah."

"I'm sorry, Jaye," she said, with more sincerity than he was comfortable hearing. "Birthdays are a big deal to kids. That must have broken your heart. But I'm sure she did her very best."

"Always," he agreed. "But it was good practice for dealing with the record-breaking Worst Birthday Ever a few years back, so it all worked out."

"You must think about her a lot," she guessed, gently.

"Good days and bad days. You know how it goes."

He'd visited with Dixon and Brekken's parents via Skype a few months ago. It had been as awkward as expected. Their mother's shock at his appearance had been evident, but she'd been polite enough. Mrs. Rowe had been a blonde, just as naturally as her daughter, Jaye guessed. She also had oodles of Southern charm and an accent. Gray-haired, blue-eyed Mr. Rowe had Dixon's strong jaw and rugged masculinity. Seeing the echo of similarity between the generations had caused Jaye to wonder about his own relatives, and what they might have looked like at an advanced age. He hadn't had much chance to find out. Neither did they.

He glanced at the front door at the sound of a vehicle pulling up out front. A peek at the window told him Dixon was home.

"Jaye," Brekken asked almost hastily, sitting forward. "Is it just the whole birthday thing, or is something else wrong? Are you okay?"

He thought of how impatient he was to send the letter to Cash, just to have it done with, and also to hurry along whatever fate was trying to throw his way. He hadn't felt incredibly patient at the thought of having to wait a while to find out what was going on. At least with the attack that had sent him to prison, and the final, deadly confrontation with Marcus, he hadn't seen them coming at all. There'd been no time to be scared of the possibilities.

Now, not so much.

He never knew why he said it. Then again, his verbal filters had been mostly broken off long, long ago.

"An old friend has been in touch," he said without managing to conjure any levity at all.

"An old friend," she echoed, staring at him like it might help her figure out his meaning. "You don't mean... Oh, you do. Does Dixon know?"

"Yeah."

Heavy booted footsteps ascended to the door, which then opened. Dixon stepped inside, decked out in full Alaska State Trooper regalia. Seeing him like that still did weird things to Jaye's insides. It was equally alluring and terrifying.

He saw Brekken glance between them both.

"Hey, Dixie," Brekken said offhandedly.

"Hey," he smiled, setting down some of his gear. He came over and gave Jaye a kiss hello.

"So what are you gonna do?"

Dixon glanced back to see who the question was directed toward.

She was looking right at Jaye.

"Do about what?" Dixon asked.

"Hold onto my ass and hope for the best, pretty much," Jaye replied.

"What are you talking about?" Dixon persisted.

"The letter."

"You told her about the letter?" Dixon said with shock.

"Why, what was in the letter?" Brekken asked with wider eyes.

They both looked at Jaye.

"Should I tell her the monster story?" Jaye asked Dixon.

"Please don't." He sighed. "This isn't something you need to be concerned about, Brek."

"Maybe it is," she insisted. "Look at him. He's freaking out and even Marcus didn't make him freak out. He was cool as a cucumber around that psycho. I'm in this family too, you know."

"Christ," Dixon groaned. "Now Grant is gonna hear about this too, because she tells him everything, and it's gonna turn into a big thing again and — "

"Stop keeping secrets, Dixon," she snapped.

Jaye just smiled.

"There was a guy," Jaye told her. "A guard. He had a beef with my boss, so he went for the easiest target. Me. Tortured me on the regular for the majority of my sentence, factoring in one long break when my friends arranged to have him sent to a different post for a while."

"Okay, so when you say torture, you mean…"

"Brekken," Dixon complained.

"Invasive body searches for stashed drugs I didn't have. Forced vomiting. Anal rape. Over and over and fucking over. Towards the end, it was just straightforward rape, beatings, and brutality."

"No. Jaye, no," she breathed.

"Yep."

She got up off the couch. She started to walk towards him, and he was surprised enough to back up a step. Then she was hugging him, and he was hugging her back. Her hair smelled like flowers and his chest was burning. He pushed down on the pain and hugged her tighter.

"I'm so sorry," she whispered. Pulling back, she held him by the shoulders and persisted, "What was in the letter?"

"They killed him."

"They killed the guard?" She glanced between them again. "Who killed the guard?"

"We don't know," Dixon told her. "But we know what the real message was."

He looked to Jaye to finish the thought.

"My old crew needs a favor."

After some more explanation and a private little conversation outside between brother and sister, Dixon and Jaye were once again alone. Jaye was busy cooking chili for dinner. Dixon came back inside, stripped down to work pants and a white t-shirt, his feet bare on the wood, and came to lean against the wall beside where Jaye worked away at the stove.

"We're never gonna hear the end of this, you know. Grant might fucking drive over here once he hears. Wouldn't put it past him."

With a glance over his shoulder, Jaye said, "It's good to have people who care that much about you. Who have your back. These aren't your secrets to keep."

"I'm not saying they are, I just..." he blew out an angry breath.

"Not talking about that shit doesn't make it less true. Do you realize how crazy it is that I can talk about it? To people who care? Who'll feel that sorry for me once they hear the truth?"

Dixon came up behind him, took the spoon out of his hand, set it on the stove and drew Jaye into a hug. His hand slid down Jaye's back. His warm lips touched Jaye's cheek.

"I don't want to see you hurt," Dixon admitted.

"Too late. Years too late."

"I know."

"I want to write it up tonight. We need to get it done."

"Okay."

They ate the chili before starting. Jaye could tell Dixon's appetite would vanish quickly once they got down to business, so he stopped pushing until Dixon was fed and restless.

Dixon got out a few pieces of stationery from the department, with the logo and contact information for their division of the Alaska State Trooper Zus outpost. Jaye wasn't sure how Cash would respond to the official stationery, but Dixon insisted on it as verification of his position. Jaye knew it was just a way to compare dick lengths. Cash was definitely packing in that regard, but what Dixon carried was impressive in other ways.

Dixon began to write, speaking what his pen scrawled. "I'm aware you're interested in hearing from Jaye Larson — I'm not calling you Johnny and this fucker can kiss my ass." He shot Jaye a glare, then kept writing, "I'm the person in charge of his wellbeing. If you want to talk to him, you'll talk to me."

"You're gonna piss him off," Jaye told him.

"I don't care. He's asking for a lot here."

"He has guys who kill for him."

"I understand that. Either he can show me some fucking respect, or he can go to Hell."

"Dix…"

"Come on. We doing this or what?"

Fire blazed behind his cool blue irises. Jaye smiled to see it.

"Maybe instead, I climb up here," he leaned forward, hand resting on the table, "Strip down, spread myself wide open, and let you fuck me through the wood?"

Dixon bit down on his back teeth. His nostrils flared. Jaye chuckled.

"That's not helping."

"Yes, Master. Sorry, Master."

"I swear to god."

"I'm trying to get you to calm down. You're gonna give yourself an aneurysm this way."

Dixon sat back, closed his eyes and took a deep breath.

"Tell me what to say," he invited.

Jaye thought about it. "Say... You did a good job on his ink. He hasn't gotten any new pieces but says he's saving room for a portrait of the original J.C., whatever that means. I say some things last forever when they shouldn't. He says sometimes it's just a matter of paying respect."

Dixon coped it all down, then kept going. "Jaye's moved on. He's not the person he used to be. But if you have something to say, you can write me at this address, or we can speak on the phone."

Jaye sat there a while, staring at that sheet of white on the dark wood, and the words scrawled in blue upon it. He thought of the past, and the present, and tried to glimpse visions of the future, somehow. Not just for himself, but for his old prison family, too. They were all stuck in Hell. Filled with fire and brimstone, pain and screaming. They were never alone and simultaneously always alone.

"It's good. Send it," he said, in his soft growl of a voice.

"I want you to be able to let this stuff go. To move beyond it, not be dragged back in."

"I want that too. But he helped with that by taking Ecker off the board. He did that for me. Just me. I need to pay my respects. Doesn't mean I'm getting dragged in. You made your peace with Marcus. Let me try to make mine. We've all got our demons."

He sipped his wine and swirled the dark crimson in the glass.

Dixon's cell phone began to ring. He glanced at the caller ID and rolled his eyes.

"Fuck me."

Jaye saw who it was and laughed.

"I love that guy. He's as reliable as the sunrise," Jaye grinned.

With a groan, Dixon answered, "Okay, Grant, before you start in — "

Jaye heard yelling from the other end and kept laughing. How could he not?

Chapter 7:
Devil's Doorway

Dixon carried around the letter to Cash in the glove compartment of his Expedition for almost two days before he found the resolve to set it in the mail and on its way. On Friday, the day of Jaye's birthday, Dixon had arranged for a shorter shift on duty. It started early and ended even earlier. That meant he hadn't been there for Jaye when he woke up, which he regretted, but hoped to make up for in the second half of the day.

In lieu of his physical presence, Dixon had cooked breakfast at four in the morning, as silently as was humanly possible given the one-room nature of their small home. The chocolate pancakes were then wrapped up and stowed in the fridge, along with a can of whipped cream and a small container of sprinkles. On the table, he'd left directions to reheat the food, along with a good morning, happy birthday, love you always note meant to hopefully bring Jaye a smile as he woke.

Once Dixon had gotten on his way, the presence of the letter to Cash weighed even more heavily on him than it had before. He kept glancing to the glove compartment where he'd stowed it, like Cash's spirit was in that folded paper instead of a few carefully chosen sentences directed towards him.

If it had been only up to Dixon, he never would have mailed it. The secretive, fearful part of him, which Marcus had nurtured, whispered the temptation to not mail it but tell Jaye he had. Then the lack of a response would be all of the message they needed. But Dixon knew all of the reasons that was a terrible idea. He had no plans to lie to Jaye, first off. But he also had no plans to witness any fret on Jaye's part as he contemplated the why's and how's forever with no good explanation for them. To cheat his way out of the situation would have been a coward's way out.

He had no plans to act a coward either.

So he drove to the post office, and sat there for longer than he should, staring at the horizon. Not so long ago, that horizon was a symbol of danger and fear that Marcus might arrive on it at any moment, bringing nothing good in his wake. Day and night, Dixon would watch it in front and behind him, trying to be ready for anything.

With Marcus dead, killed by the gun in Dixon's holster, for a blessed while that horizon was a peaceful symbol. It held the future and possibilities. Once that letter left his possession, the horizon would once more become a threat. He would have opened a devil's doorway leading right for him. And if they could find him, they could find Jaye.

He hated it.

But it wasn't only his call to make. He had obligations to Jaye. They had to win out over immaterial and possibly negative turns of fate.

He walked into the office, located in a small side office inside the home of an elderly couple with the last name of Peterson, and said hello to the clerk. Mrs. Peterson gave him a patient stare as he stood there, holding the damned letter. A few rooms away, he heard the Maury Povich Show playing.

"Mail that for you?" she offered when he did and said nothing.

"Yeah," he surrendered, passing it over to her.

He hated Cash. He hated every part of the man, even more than he'd hated Marcus. Part of Dixon had understood Marcus and the measly benefits his existence brought to Dixon's life in the forms of sexual pleasure and monetary reward.

Cash held no such benefits. This was a man who had assaulted Jaye daily. For years.

No matter what Jaye said or felt on the matter, Dixon knew there was no real consent there. Cash wasn't an ex. He was the man who had enslaved, repeatedly violated, and terrorized a sweet, injured, abandoned teenage boy. There was no forgiving that. He wasn't able to set it aside, even for the sake of Jaye's conscience. The only allowance Dixon knew he was able to make, was to interrupt Cash's attempts to hook Jaye directly. That needed to stop.

He suspected that if no response came to the transcript and newspaper clipping, they would try something else. Something even more drastic. They wouldn't stop and they wouldn't let Jaye go.

Walking back to the Expedition, knowing he was already late for work, Dixon felt the lag on his muscles and mind.

Against his will, he kept imagining it. The things Cash had done to Jaye. Heavy breathing mixed with Jaye's small cries. A cluster of cruel criminals laughing and goading the burly crime boss with his dick stuffed inside a terrified, slender, long-haired boy's ass. Jaye pulling his pants down when he only wanted to run. Jaye screaming in fright of approaching attackers as he was shackled and held down for more pain. The scenarios were endless.

He saw Jaye, barely out of childhood and scared out of his mind, with not a soul in the world to worry for him, locked in a cramped, rotting cell with a monster who climbed into his bed at night to strip him naked and force-fuck him as long as was desired. Every night.

And it froze Dixon up each time the images started to play. If he was walking, he stopped dead. If he was driving, he forced himself to pull over, unless he was in the open roads where he could see for miles. Then he just stopped where he was and idled in the middle of the highway. If he was out on a call, he let the civilian try to snap him out of it.

Back toward the beginning of their relationship, there had been plenty of times when Jaye had waking or sleeping nightmares. He would scream and fight like ghosts were trying to rip him to shreds or turn him inside out. And they were. Sure they were.

The nightmares and daymares had lessened in frequency and strength since then, but Dixon knew he'd never forget the sound of that screaming, or the look that sometimes entered Jaye's eyes. It was cold, empty, vacant and dead inside. That was Johnny. That was Cash's legacy.

All of Jaye's submitting had left him with empty spots. Things he should have had in his mind and heart were carved away, the hollow cavities healed over with scar tissue. Dixon was actively trying to give that monster access to his lover. That was on him.

Once upon a time, Jaye had burned down a house with men inside, just from wanting to protect Dixon from further harm.

Now, Dixon handed Jaye back to his demons and ghosts. He couldn't say no, couldn't stop, and would never, ever forgive himself.

In contrast to his last birthday out in the wide world, when he had been over-the-moon excited for the day's events before being skewered on a filleting knife, Jaye mostly wanted to get the damned thing over with as quickly as possible.

Little faggot's gonna squeal. Gonna squeeeeeal...

Jaye hummed to cover the words, bubbling up from three years back, and rubbed his forehead. Dixon glanced at him from the driver's seat.

"You okay?"

Just need to grab hold of one of these ropes, start pulling 'em out, like a magic trick.

"Yeah. Fantastic."

Gonna take a while to pull 'em all out, too. That's what we do to monsters like you.

Jaye pulled his legs up to his chest, closed his eyes, tried to breathe.

When Dixon had gotten home from work, he'd quickly read Jaye's signals and guessed he wasn't in the mood to fool around, possibly for the first time since they'd met. Jaye had been sitting out on the front stoop, pad of paper in his lap, pencil in his hand as he'd worked on capturing the view from the front of the cabin. It was something he'd drawn numerous times already, but something in the repetition and focus on his surroundings helped ground him and clear his mind.

Dixon had left him to it, knowing to let Jaye have his say in how he wanted the day to go. Inside the cabin, Dixon had put on some classic rock. Jaye could just barely hear it through the closed door. It was nice, having that as a background to his drawing, and nothing much flying through his head other than decisions on where to shade darker and where to add in details like the delicate tips of grass or bits of rocky gravel.

When Jaye had finally gone inside, Dixon lay on the couch, reading a book. Shortly thereafter, they were on their way to Brekken and Grant's home across town.

Gonna slice open your belly. Pull your insides out. Make you watch.

Rolling along the mostly deserted streets, with expansive nature in all its mostly untouched glory stretched out around them in all directions, and only modest little structures to hint at civilization, Jaye knew where he was, and where he'd been. Of course he did.

He hated that it was real. That it had happened. That he could see the scar every time he got undressed. That part of him couldn't let go of certain phrases. Some of the original inflection had worn away with the passage of time. He was sure he remembered the pieces with more cartoony maliciousness than they once had. Burt and Earl had been idiots. Dangerous idiots, but still. They had been real guys with a whole lot of hate carried around inside them, and a reason to let it all come flooding out.

Jaye tried to focus on his last glimpse of Earl, blade buried in his back, the handle jutting up stupidly, wiggling back and forth as Earl twisted and tried to reach to pull it out. The dark stain around the wound seeped outward. There had been a startling, human quality to the way being stabbed had stopped Earl short. His confusion was almost tragic as he'd collapsed.

Jaye wished he'd seen them take Burt's body away, or heard the surely preposterous explanation from Earl of what had happened in that alleyway.

"Hey," Dixon said in a verbal nudge. "Where you at?"

"An alley in Anchorage, watching bad men begin to die."

"You're not including yourself in there, are you?"

Jaye shrugged. "I'm no good guy. Maybe I was then, but I don't know anymore."

"Why? Because of Sheridan?"

"No. Because of the things I would do, if I could. Oh, the things I would do."

"But you don't. You have a conscience. You know the law, and why to follow it."

"Damn right, I do," Jaye murmured. He felt so tired. It wasn't just Burt and Earl. It was fucking Dorrance in a storage closet while being called the prettiest come rag he ever did see. It was knowing Cash was out there, right now, thinking of Johnny and planning something Jaye couldn't pretend to know. Each piece, each person, pulled at him, spreading him out thin.

"Should I take you home? If you're not up for this — "

"No. No, I want to do this. What you said, earlier? You were right. I need to look forward, not back. It's just hard when I hear things behind me and try not to look."

Dixon reached over and took Jaye's hand.

They pulled up to the house, and Jaye breathed out a small laugh. He shot Dixon a look, chewing on his lower lip. "You sly fucker."

Dixon grinned and shut off the engine.

There were several cars at the house. Some of them Jaye recognized. Some, he didn't.

"If there was ever a man who needed a good party," Dixon said in a dreamy way, reaching for the door handle. He added under his breath, "I did tell those assholes to carpool, though."

"Did you invite the whole damn town?"

"J-bird, you're not the only one out here in desperate need of a solid good time."

They got out of the Expedition and Dixon walked around to where Jaye stood, stunned and smiling despite himself.

Chapter 8:
Happy Birthday

As Dixon opened the door, revealing the guest of honor to the packed house, a roar of excitement erupted within.

"Woo!"

"Jaye!"

"The birthday man!" yelled a guy named Bill Simmons who was the official town plumber and an acquaintance of Jaye's through people at work. Bill had a beer in hand, and a goofy grin on his face. "He's finally old enough to vote!"

"Close," Jaye replied. "You're close, man. Haven't had the chance to vote in many elections thanks to the fine print and circumstances, but I'll get there one day."

"I swear he gets younger while the rest of us get older," smiled Grant. He came in for a hug, which Jaye gladly returned. "Happy birthday, kid."

"Thanks, Grant," Jaye said, clapping him on the back. He'd never had a father figure in the slightest, but something about Grant had begun to fill that void a little. He had plenty of years on Jaye, as well as the wisdom and patience Jaye had always imagined in fantasy fathers or uncles that didn't exist. Even the hug was a good one — solid and committed, like he wanted Jaye to really feel that the sentiments behind it were genuine. "You and Brek really didn't have to do all of this."

"Yes, we did!" Brekken cried, bouncing over as Sesi cranked up Paula Abdul's Opposites Attract to full volume. She threw herself into a hug of her own with Jaye, which felt like she was trying to squeeze the negative energy right out of him.

Laughing, Jaye allowed it while Dixon caught his eye with a calm, proud gladness.

"You're twenty-two! The world is yours for the taking!"

"As long as you pay for it first," Dixon whispered in Jaye's ear. He threw an elbow into Dixon's side for that one. Dixon just laughed and kissed Jaye's cheek.

"Dance with me," Brekken said eagerly, taking Jaye's hands after Dixon peeled the coat from Jaye's shoulders.

Grant and Dixon backed steadily away as if afraid to be reeled in by her next. Jaye was happy to go, though. He let her take him into the middle of the crowded living room. Most people had drinks in hand, and were friends, co-workers, or friends of friends. He knew them all by sight if not name. They moved along with the beat to Material Girl as the track changed. Brekken squealed with joy, throwing her hands up. Feeding off of her good mood and lively spirit, Jaye couldn't stop smiling and danced.

Colorful paper streamers draped from the ceiling, doorways, and furniture. Hand-made Happy Birthday signs were taped to the walls. To someone else, it might not have seemed like much, but to Jaye it was mind-blowing how much effort he was beginning to glimpse went into the planning and preparation for the party.

He bounced, moved, and gyrated to the beat, feeding off of Brekken's huge, happy grin and easy laughter. The other dancers — all women plus one elderly gentleman Jaye thought helped run the post office — surrounded them. The collective good energy quickly made Jaye high. He'd never been to clubs or anything of the sort, but he began to see their allure.

"Dixon!" Brekken yelled. "Get your ass in here and dance with your boyfriend!"

Jaye smiled so wide his cheeks hurt as Dixon bashfully relinquished his position as chatty wallflower and slowly made his way into the shifting, wild collection in the dance-floor area — created by shoving furniture out of the way to clear the center of the main living space.

A few of the women let out cries of delight as he moved up close to Jaye and started to move his hips. Dixon blushed and Jaye let out a belly laugh. Not missing a beat, he hooked a hand around Dixon's hip to keep him close.

"Loosen up, Trooper Rowe," Jaye teased as Dixon's blush deepened and his dancing remained somewhat rigid. "I've seen the way you can move your hips. Don't pretend you can't dance."

"Where the hell would I have ever danced?" Dixon challenged, probably to cover over his sudden shyness.

"Come on," Jaye lured, fitting their hips together and slinging his arms behind Dixon's neck.

A wolf whistle went up and Dixon's glance snapped around to try to identify the whistler. Jaye dragged his lover's attention back where it belonged with a strong grip to Dixon's chin and pecked a kiss to his lips.

"Whatever makes you happy," Dixon said with a glad sparkle in his sexy blue eyes. "Love seeing you this happy."

Jaye saw some of the women pairing up together as Lionel Richie's Say You, Say Me came on next, beginning to slow dance together. A few bravely tried to pull their men in as well, and some were even successful.

Brekken sang loudly along to the stereo and Grant looked like he knew just how lucky he was, with only eyes for his wife as she swayed in his arms.

His attention pulled in all directions. He wanted to stop time and study each couple, the freedom and life in their eyes, the absolute lack of tension or guardedness in their bodies, the way they lived in the moment without a thought for the next. At the same time, he wanted to focus only on Dixon. To be only in his arms, dancing, surrounded by countless people from their lives. He wanted to let everything else go, but he also knew, way down deep in his heart, that it was the contrast with his time in Sheridan, and Anchorage, that made the night that much more special.

In that moment, in that little house tucked into the wild of Zus, Alaska, none of those people were afraid for their lives, sanity, or future. They carried no demons. They held nothing back out of fear.

It felt like heaven.

It took his breath away.

They danced for a long time, until the sentimental feelings bursting from him caused Jaye to follow Brekken to the kitchen when he saw her duck away.

"Hey," she said, blocking his path when she noticed him behind her. "No peeking!"

"All right. I just..." He nodded toward the hall leading to the bedrooms. She let him pull her aside into the relative quiet of an empty room. He set his back to the door and cleared his throat. He felt the letter hanging over him, and everything he could only guess it implied. He sensed the torment of the Disciples who had years to go before they got to have any peace, if they got out at all. He understood the absence of his parents, and all of the people he'd left behind. He was who he was because of all of it. There was no pretending otherwise.

"What's up? You've got a look," she said, paying close attention to his expression as only a family member could.

"I just need to say thank you."

"Jaye..."

"I need to."

"The party's barely started! Just enjoy yourself," she urged tenderly.

"I am. Believe me. I just need you to understand how much this means to me," he said, voice breaking and eyes watering.

"Oh, honey." She pulled him into a tight hug. Somehow, it helped him breathe. The ache eased as he hugged her back.

"It's not just because of how nightmarish my past few birthdays have been, or how my life was before Dix. It's all of it. I never... I never thought I'd get to have this."

"You're welcome," she replied with an extra tight squeeze before letting go and searching his eyes. "Who knew you could be such a softie? And over a lame little house party, too?"

"It's an amazing house party," he assured her. She wiped his eyes dry with the pads of her thumbs and he almost lost it again.

She saw it though and warned him with a pointed finger. "Nope! Don't even think about it. We're going back out there, right now."

"I love you, Brekken Rowe."

"Aww. I love you too, Jaye Larson."

It was like there was a light made up of nothing but nurturing, warmth, and goodness inside her as she looped her arm through his and led him back out to the action. Jaye caught Dixon's eye right away, and saw a flicker of concern cloud his expression. He quickly came over, excusing himself from a conversation with Sesi and a few others from the station.

"Hey," he said, glancing between Jaye and Brekken.

"Get him back out there. Have a drink. Get some snacks. Have fun. I've got top-secret work to do."

She snuck away to the kitchen again. Dixon whispered by his ear.

"Everything okay?"

"Yeah. Just saying thanks."

Since it was Dixon, who knew Jaye inside and out in literal and figurative ways, he read between all of the lines and kissed the side of Jaye's head, then drew him in for a quick hug.

"Come on. I'm starving and I need a beer. How about you?"

"Sounds incredible."

Dixon led him through the throng by the hand. Jaye called hello and waved to some others he hadn't had a chance to speak to yet. He smiled and said thanks whenever he heard a Happy Birthday shouted in his direction. They rounded the corner and stepped into the dining room where the food was laid out. He spotted some slow cooker roasted caribou for sandwiches and some bacon-wrapped duck breasts. While he decided what to try first, he heard Oki ask, "What're you gonna wish for?"

"Nothing," he called back. "All of my wishes have already come true."

Almost greedily, Jaye soaked in each and every moment, burning them into his memory, etching them into his bones. There had been some long, cold nights in his short life, and he knew how precious the little miracles were. They demanded reverence and rapt attention.

When Grant brought out the huge chocolate cake, decorated in icing in a rainbow of colors, scrawled with his name and his age, Jaye studied each second that ticked by as if his life depended on it.

He noticed some looks that indicated people thought he was acting out of character. And he was. There weren't any jokes or cockiness. There was no effort put into pulling himself up and acting the part in order to impress or convince, threaten or intimidate. He was himself in a way he'd just begun to allow. The past was there, with all of its experience and hard lessons. But he had hope and contentment too, in such huge quantities, he could only stand in awe of it.

They sang to him, and he blew out the candles, asking only for it all to not end before he was ready.

There were cards stacked on a table. There were some small gifts he'd open and cherish later. There was hot food and plenty to drink. He shook more hands in one night than he'd done in his whole life.

Out back, some people were challenging each other to some friendly Inuit sports competitions like kneel jump, Musox push, and back push. The few eager challengers were in the center of the pool of light cast by the floodlight on the back of the house, with plenty of others holding drinks in a circle around them, cheering them on. It wasn't at all like anything Jaye had seen growing up or in Sheridan — everyone was laughing and encouraging each other, keeping spirits up and helping anyone that stumbled. He knew part of that was due to the many Alaskan Natives present and the way they constantly influenced life in Zus. Fitness, strength, agility and camaraderie were vitally important to survival. No one faced anything alone, but always with the support of ancestors, family, and friends. Everyone was needed. No one was disposable.

Jaye talked to Sesi and some of Dixon's friends about the past winter and the upcoming summer, comparing plans and activities people were excited to do. He asked about their families and their health. He deflected most questions about his past, but eagerly shared his desire to go hunting, fishing, hiking, off-roading and every other outdoor activity he could think of. With how much more established and stable he and Dixon were compared to last summer, they'd have much more opportunity to get out and explore. If they could do it with friends, it would be even better.

As the night wore on, and people's energy became more subdued, Jaye became more tempted to express to Dixon in a more personal way just how grateful he was.

He saw his moment when Brekken and Grant were settled with a large group discussing plans for a camping trip a few months down the road. Jaye nudged Dixon and escaped down the hall. Dixon followed.

Jaye took him into the bedroom which used to be his and closed the door before locking it. Turning his back to the door, he took a long look up and down the man he was about to climb, or devour, or both.

Dixon's chest looked muscular beneath the t-shirt pulled tightly over it. His arms bulged. His pants were filled out in all the right places. His vivid coloring made him seem like living candy designed to lick and suck for hours.

"I'm so hard right now."

Dixon gave him a crooked, wicked grin and manhandled him onto the bed with arousing ease. He pinned Jaye's arms and gave him a hot, passionate kiss. Then he stripped off Jaye's shirt and yanked open his fly. The sounds of the party filtered easily through the door, but Dixon seemed to have only one thing on his mind.

He pulled Jaye's boxers down and swallowed him whole.

"Fuck," Jaye moaned, probably too loudly, then laughed. His thighs fell open and he gently rocked into each suck. Dixon rolled Jaye's balls in a hand and that only made him moan louder. "Good present, Dix," Jaye panted. "Just what I wanted. Nice, slow ride on your tongue."

Dixon pulled off with a wet sound. "Thought you'd like it."

"No, no, keep going. Unless I have permission to fuck you. Because I totally will. You think it's still in here?"

"Only one way to find out."

Dixon got up and went to the closet. He reached up inside, behind the doorframe, and smiled. When he withdrew his hand, it held a small bottle of lube.

"Your sister's either not a thorough cleaner or very considerate."

"No talking about my sister when I'm about to get fucked. New rule."

Jaye chuckled and climbed out of bed only to push Dixon down into it. He gleefully stripped Dixon's clothes off until he was completely naked, then spread him wide and licked him from thigh to neck.

The sense of people lingering nearby was impossible to ignore, but after two years in Sheridan, public sex was no big deal at all. In fact, that they had a closed, solid, locked door between them and everyone else seemed a luxury, allowing a private oasis to enable him to get exactly what he wanted without worry of what anyone else might think or do about it.

Of course, Dixon's take on the situation might have been a little different.

"Seriously, don't take your time," Dixon panted, raising his hips and tipping his ass up to receive. Jaye fed him two wet fingers that went in with a little resistance. "Maybe we should barricade the door somehow."

"It'll be fine. I'll protect your modesty, Trooper."

"Everyone I know is out there right now."

"Small worlds are kind of my specialty, you know. Still not an issue. Plus, my birthday, right? My rules."

He withdrew his fingers, having spread lube as deeply as he could reach. Knowing how Dixon liked it didn't mean some precautions didn't need to be taken first, for Jaye's peace of mind at least.

Spread, ready, and ass-up on the bed, Dixon waited for it. After taking one more moment to enjoy the view, Jaye lined up and applied gentle pressure to enter him. Patience was key. He'd barely stretched him at all. Lube and the slow stretch of his rim widening around Jaye's cockhead were what made it happen. Jaye loved the soft moans from Dixon and the little shivers through his muscular body as he struggled to bear it.

Even the party noise around them brought Jaye a weird kind of comfort. Though he loved solitude, he'd grown strangely accustomed to being surrounded by others at all times. In Anchorage growing up, the urban setting meant being in the thick of it day and night, constantly. Sheridan only intensified that reality. Being out in remote Zus had its appeal, but it was nice to be around lots of people for a little while at least.

Dixon might have noticed Jaye's enthusiasm because he glanced back over a shoulder, his skin flushed pink, his blue eyes peeking out from beneath golden eyelashes. "Guess you're not shy, huh?"

Jaye chuckled and finally bottomed out. He sighed and caressed the curve of Dixon's ass.

"Dix, if there's something I never was or will be, it's shy."

"So if someone accidentally walked in here right now?"

"Wouldn't even break my rhythm," he replied, setting a slow, easy pace to give Dixon more time to adjust. "Might ask them to get me a beer, though."

Dixon laughed, but Jaye saw the strain in his face, too. He bit his lip, frowning slightly. His breathing stayed rough. Reading the cues, Jaye gave it harder. Dixon's mouth fell open. His frown deepened.

His hand reached under his hips for his cock. Jaye let him tug a few times, then said, "Hands off."

With a groan, Dixon obeyed, bringing his arms up by his head. One rubbed hard over the back of his head as his breathing got even rougher. Holding Dixon's hips steady, Jaye pounded his hole as hard as he dared. The sound of Dixon's panting and quiet whimpers were the sweetest music. For a fleeting, private moment, he wondered what it would have been like to top Cash and if it would have been as thrilling as it was to top a cop like Dixon.

Up on his knees, riding the snug heat of Dixon's pale ass which was bent over in offering in front of him, Jaye held on and took the ride. He pulled out just before he came, shooting up through Dixon's cheeks.

"Let me see you."

Dixon turned his face to the side, trying to catch his breath. Jaye reached between Dixon's thighs to gently caress his straining erection. Feathering his fingers along its length, he watched Dixon fight not to thrust like he wanted. Instead, he gave over completely to Jaye, giving him all of the power and control. It was exhilarating. Jaye knew the high of getting to dominate a strong, capable, sexy man like Dixon would never wear off. With proof of the world carrying on without them only steps away, Jaye savored every quiver and flinch, each jagged breath and quiet grunt. Dixon held out a while, but he finally came, his breath choking off completely as hot come dripped through Jaye's fingers.

"God, I love you," Jaye marveled.

"Love you too," Dixon panted.

"No, I mean it. I know how rare it is to get to have someone like you like this. I've been trying to trust people my whole life, in the worst circumstances. I never dreamed I'd have someone trust me as much as you do. You're my treasure, Dixon. Thank you."

Pretty blue eyes flashed back at him. "You're welcome. Happy Birthday."

"Yeah, it is, isn't it?"

Chapter 9:
Disturbed

The party went late, and Brekken offered to let them stay in the guest room after most of the citizens of Zus filed out, seeking their beds and various hangover cures. But Dixon knew enough of Jaye's mindset to insist on taking him home for some privacy.

A few hours shy of dawn, they were finally back in their snug little cabin. The fire in the hearth blazed high.

It had been one hell of a long day. Jaye was clearly exhausted and absolutely wide awake.

"Good thing we're both off tomorrow," Dixon commented. "This is gonna catch up, hard."

"Go to sleep. You're tired. I can tell."

"No way. I'm not leaving you to deal with this alone."

"I'm not dealing. I'm just…" He sighed. Gave up. His face turned slightly away, avoiding eye contact. Instead, he watched the flames twist.

Dixon went over to the bed where Jaye sat cross-legged in only a pair of cotton sleep pants. He imagined the longer, dark curls Jaye used to have, hanging in his eyes, adding to his mystery. But they'd been gone a long time. Jaye kept his hair short now. It was part of the new normal.

"Talk to me about it. Are you afraid to sleep?"

"No. I just don't. I don't sleep on my birthday. In Sheridan, I tried." He shrugged. "Just laid there all night, listening to the guards do their rounds. Listening to Cash snore." He pushed hair back over his ear that had been cut away and gone for almost a full year. The horror on his face at that little slip made Dixon's heart ache.

He took Jaye's hand and held it.

"You know no one's going to hurt you here, right?"

"Logically? Sure. My world doesn't always run on logic," Jaye told him. "I do get it, you know. I know if I hadn't been sleeping, it still doesn't mean I would have been able to stop them from doing what they did. It wouldn't have changed much. But..."

"I know. I wish I'd been there with you, to protect you."

Jaye looked over at him, his light, smoldering eyes searching. "Me too."

Dixon caressed the side of Jaye's face. "You look so tired," he lamented. "Just sit back with me and get comfortable, okay? If you're not going to sleep, at least try to rest."

Jaye relented and let Dixon pull him up to the headboard where he propped pillows for them to lean on. Then he drew Jaye to lay back with his head resting against Dixon's chest. He smoothed the hair back from Jaye's temple in a repeated light petting motion. The fire popped and crackled. Outside, the wind blew. After a while, rain began to fall, pattering against the roof.

Dixon became aware of the steady rise and fall of Jaye's breathing. Craning his neck a little without moving much at all, he saw Jaye's closed eyes and the utter lack of care or worry on his sweet young face as peaceful sleep carried him out of the reach of bad memories and persistent fear.

For hours, they stayed just like that. Dixon fought off his own urge to sleep and sat guard of his precious love so that nothing could hurt him. Nothing at all.

During the course of that week, Dixon saw the effect the letter continued to have on Jaye. It took a couple of days before he identified it. It was the look of someone who had been through Hell itself, come out on the other side, had a taste of peace and healing, then got news that he'd be paying Hell a visit once again, whether he liked it or not. It was the same look Jaye would have had if he'd been sentenced to more time behind bars.

It didn't seem to matter that Dixon had no intention of letting Jaye get anywhere near the place again. In Jaye's mind, it was all the same.

Lynn Kelling

The typical life and fire Jaye had in him since they'd met seemed to have been snuffed out, or at least allowed to die down to a low smolder. Dixon hated how old and tired Jaye seemed over the course of that long week. He'd catch Jaye staring out of windows with a hopeless gravity in his eyes, or drawing something while curled up in a corner somewhere pretending away reality like a desperate man. His appetite shriveled to almost nothing. He went on long walks alone. When he got home from work, he'd sit outside in the car until Dixon came knocking on the window to snap him out of it.

After one of these instances, Dixon asked Jaye as he finally got out of the car, "Why are you giving him this kind of power over you? You can decide to not let him have it, you know. It's all in your head."

Jaye gave him a long, weary glance. "There's a shitload of awful that's all in my head. Be glad I'm not medicating it away anymore. Or bashing my head against concrete walls."

It felt like a punch to the chest. "Jaye..."

"I don't know how to be his and yours at the same time."

"You are not his!"

Jaye sighed. He gathered his coat tighter around his neck and headed to the cabin.

"Talk to me, damn it."

Jaye flapped his arms a few steps from the door and turned back around.

"What do you want me to say? He's got your number! He knows where you are, who you are. The hook is already caught. I can't pretend it's not there. I can't pretend I'm the same guy I was when I got out, because I'm not. Being with you, living here, with my job and my friends and our life... it's everything I've always wanted, but I can't have it without taking all of that shit with me for the ride. I can't set it down and walk away."

"Why not? Why the fuck not?"

"Because it's who I am!" He jabbed a finger at the inked tear on his face. "I did shit in there, and promised shit in there, and it has consequences! I had that asshole torturing me to death and I needed him to die. I needed someone to kill him for it. And they did. They did that, Dixon, because of me. I'm responsible. And I'm not sad about it, or regretful, but it's a lot, okay? It's not just Burt anymore.

70

It's Burt and Ecker. And I have to pay for that shit. But how? What's the cost gonna be? How do you pay for a life?"

He looked backed into a corner, like he might bite or lash out if Dixon got too close. But Dixon was responsible for helping to fix this, so he approached Jaye quickly and with determination. He gathered him up in a hug against his chest before he could fight back or pull away. And Jaye let him.

Some of his tension melted away.

His breathing quieted.

"I'm sorry," Jaye murmured.

"Don't you dare apologize." Dixon looked down into Jaye's eyes. "I know you're dealing with a lot. You don't have to have it all figured out. You don't have to pretend you're not scared. You don't have to be strong. You're not doing this alone anymore. You don't have to shut us all out in order to keep us safe. You're allowed to make mistakes. You're allowed to feel bad about what happened. You're not responsible for what Cash or the Disciples do. You don't have to do what they want you to do. All you have to do is be here with me and take care of yourself and do the best you can. That's all."

Jaye took a deep inhale and let it out fast and hard. He came to lay his head on Dixon's shoulder. His slender arms wound around Dixon's back. He was shaking a little.

"You're doing the best you can," Dixon whispered, caressing the silky tumble of Jaye's hair.

More tension fled, softening his edges, quieting him down.

"Thank you," Jaye said urgently.

Dixon kissed him and took him inside.

The call came at mid-morning on a Tuesday, while Dixon was in the office doing paperwork. Most of the time he was out driving high and low across their territory, so it felt like the fates planned for the call to go through.

At the time, Dixon's thoughts were focused on the forms laid out in front of him, demanding a full account of an incident where a trespassing hunter and a landowner pulled guns on each other in a heated argument. He'd managed to talk them both down, and cited both for some minor offenses, but there were a lot of details to capture.

The phone rang at the desk as he was trying to remember the exact sequence of what had gone down the day before. He answered briskly. "Yeah, Trooper Dixon Rowe here. Zus State Patrol Office. How can I help you?"

"Do you accept the charges for a collect call from the Federal Corrections Institute of Sheridan, Oregon?"

Dixon froze, all tidbits about who was holding the shotgun and who had the pistol, and who had been drunk, who had threatened someone's mother went right out of his head. For an odd moment, he feared a slip-back in time, that it was Jaye on the other end of the line, back in prison like the past year had never happened and he needed Dixon to help him get released.

When he realized it wasn't Jaye, and who was waiting to talk to him, Dixon almost forgot how to speak. The words short-circuited on the way from his brain to his mouth.

Man up, pussy. This guy is as cold and hard as they come. You give him an inch and he'll take a mile.

"Uh, yes. I'll accept," he replied long after the question had been asked.

He can hear you. Man the fuck up, Rowe. If you have ever been capable of intimidating and acting like a man, do it now. Do it for all of those moments with Marcus when you caved like a coward.

The call was connected.

A gruff, growly voice straight out of Dixon's most vivid imaginings of what Cash might sound like came through.

"This Rowe? Trooper Rowe?"

"Yes," Dixon replied lamely, his thought process still gumming up. Too abruptly, he asked, "What do you want?"

There was a cold chuckle. "Hit the nail on the head, don'tcha? There's lots of things I want, Trooper. Gettin' a letter from you wasn't one of them, that's for damn sure."

The longer he listened to Cash speak, the more connections were made, way back in the more subconscious layers of his awareness. Stories that had once only found life through Jaye's words and actions now blossomed with new vibrancy. He envisioned the thug who was speaking into his ear being alone with the man he loved. A criminal caged up with a helpless boy. A monster force-fucking that poor boy over and over and over again, with no one to stop it.

You keep thinking about that shit, and you'll fuck this up for Jaye. Get over yourself, Dixie. This ain't your problem, is it? This problem belongs to that underage-looking piece of ass you killed me over.

He hated that the voice warning him off sounded like Marcus.

Shaking his head and clearing his throat, he tried to snap out of it.

"Trust me, I never thought I'd be writing you either," he said, feeling a little surer of himself at last.

"He with you?"

It was briefer than he'd expected, and the true meaning behind the question only registered after a long moment.

"In all the ways that count," Dixon responded.

Cash breathed out a sound that was half grunt, half laugh. There was no humor in it, but many things besides anger as well, like sadness, exhaustion, and resignation wrapped around an iron will and concrete certainty.

"I wanna talk to him. Johnny."

"I get that. But I'm the closest you're gonna get."

Passing that right over, Cash said, "It's funny, him being with a guy like you. Been trying to figure it. First thought was he's playing you for a sucker, giving it up to the law to keep his ass covered. Good strategy, I admit. Some of the guys wouldn't believe it, but I do. I know that kid better than anyone."

Dixon bristled at many parts of that.

Before he could figure out how to respond, Cash kept talking.

"But the more I thought about it, and how you sent that fuckin' letter to me, balls out, the more I realized how fucked over Johnny is. Cause this ain't about some deal anymore, is it, Trooper Rowe? You owe him, don't you? Enough that you couldn't keep him away from me. You had to cave, just a little. But I can't figure what you owe him for."

Tell him he's full of shit. Tell him to climb back in his hole and die.

"Drugs? Sex? Did he break some law for you? Help you skirt a few legal lines?"

"What the fuck do you want?" Dixon cut in, his anger showing.

Cash laughed again. "Damn. No, I hear it now. I do. Good on you, Johnny, wherever this lawman's got you spread in high style. Got him wrapped around your cock like the clever piece of ass I know you to be. You fucking love that kid, don't you?"

"Don't talk about him like that."

Cash laughed even louder. "God damn. Okay. How about I tell you what I know?"

"About what?"

"You. Johnny."

"His name is Jaye."

"Yeah, J for Johnny. Johnny, who had no one. Who got locked up for shitty reasons, and who fought like a wildcat in a sack the whole time he was in here, except for the days when he was too fucked up to function. When he was skin and bones and not a glimmer of sanity in his fucking green eyes. You know who he had then? Not his momma. Not his pops. Not a lawyer or a friend coming to visit. You know what he had?"

"You."

"That's right. See, you ain't so dumb, Trooper. He had me. I'm his goddamned family. You would never have met that kid if not for me, and tell me I'm wrong."

Dixon sighed, biting down on his back teeth nearly hard enough to crack a crown.

"So, the way I figure it, you owe me too. Can I make another guess? See, I've had more than my fair share of thinking time the past few days, and I know a few more things, in addition to how you feel about the kid. I know how he is, biblically and otherwise. I know how he gets when he's on his meds, when he's off his meds, when things are great, and when things are shitty. I know that about two hours after he downs a pill, I can ask him any old goddamned thing I want, and I'll get the ugly truth right back. He might not even remember the conversation after, with being so fucking stoned. I know he comes faster when you hold him down and ride him slow and deep. I know the way that scar on his side looks when it's been sliced open. I know one hell of a lot of things about that kid. This is how I see it. Again, you tell me if I'm wrong. He's fucked up over this, isn't he? Ain't eating much. Ain't sleeping well. Runs hot and cold. Grumpy like a bitch on the rag."

Dixon said nothing.

"You there?"

"Yeah."

"Are the ghosts fucking with him?"

"No," Dixon answered, not sure if he should have or not.

"Good. That's good," Cash said, some of the cockiness being subtly replaced with a more muted form of triumph, because he knew he had Dixon. Sure he did.

Cash continued, "I saw it happen, you know."

"What?"

"What he couldn't get over, or get away from. I'd been getting the story from him on the regular when he was soaring up in the clouds. He just needed a nudge and he'd talk a while about it. So, I knew, but then they went the extra step and showed me. They held me, chained, gagged, beat the piss out of me, and made me watch from the next room. I saw the light go out in his eyes when those fingers went down his throat. I heard the meaty sound of the baton hitting him over and over again. I heard him cry when it went up inside him. He wasn't a man. He was a fucking *kid.*"

Dixon stood, began to pace.

"Saw him in shackles, bent over a counter, as a night stick was jabbed up his ass. He was pale as one of his fucking ghosts, muttering his thank you's like he prayed it wasn't a knife going up there next."

Dixon kicked a trashcan across the room.

Debbie poked her head in with a concerned expression. He waved her off.

"He never told me you — "

"Because he doesn't know. I swore to myself I was keeping a lid on that shit until a solution was found. So I'm telling you again, Trooper Dixon Rowe. I need to talk to Johnny. I want to see him. I want to see there's some meat on his bones, and life in his eyes, and that he's not still in that fucking room night and day, praying thank you to a sadist piece of shit. You're gonna give that to me, because I gave him to you. You're fucking welcome."

The line went dead.

Dixon dropped the phone with shaking hands. It clattered on the ground. His hand went to his mouth and he panted like he'd just run five miles.

Chapter 10:
Dixon Dominates

Dixon's early shift and frazzled mindset led to him getting home early, and well before Jaye. He used that time to prepare a meal with some fresh caribou steaks he purchased from a hunter in town on the way back to the cabin. He set the meat to grill, then went to check how he looked in the bathroom mirror.

Standing at the sink, leaning heavily on the counter, Dixon stared at his reflection.

He saw the Trooper who'd submitted to his lover's abuse for far too long.

He saw the man who'd fired the gun to kill Marcus.

He also saw his unending devotion to Jaye, who'd taken over Dixon's whole life with his irresistible seduction and the fragile, sweet heart masked by his breathtakingly deceptive appearance.

He knew how Jaye had felt lately, wondering how all of his pieces added up under their current conditions and challenges. Dixon had some mismatched fragments of his own, but he'd made his peace with those. It was Jaye's conflicting sides which were still in question.

After talking to Cash, a lot had become suddenly clearer to Dixon.

More of Jaye's pieces made sense, and Dixon felt certain he knew what to do.

His reflection looked steady, alert, and a little restless. He felt energized, the way he did after getting a call to investigate a possibly dangerous situation, knowing he could handle it, no matter what way it went down, but preparing himself for anything.

Reassured of what he thought Jaye would see once they were face-to-face, Dixon returned to his culinary preparations.

A little later, when the door opened, Jaye came inside, head down, coat buttoned to his chin.

"Hey," he said, still sounding like a dial in him had been turned way down low. His gaze stayed lowered and his natural spitfire energy was dulled.

Ecker had done that.

Fear and torment had done that.

As he began to shed his coat and set down his car keys, he caught the scent on the air and frowned a little, looking up.

"Steaks?"

"Yeah," Dixon smiled. "They're ready if you want to take a seat. I've got some wine, too."

"What's the occasion?"

"No occasion. I just know things have been tough lately, and I wanted to make you feel good tonight."

Jaye watched him, masking his reaction. Dixon hated it, that right now Jaye's instincts had him building up walls he hadn't needed to hide behind in a long time. It made it seem as if Jaye was miles away, alone in the frozen tundra, instead of safe in their cozy home with him.

Without a word, Jaye sat at the table, picking a seat that allowed him a view of the kitchen area where Dixon plated their food and poured the wine. Sitting with his back to the wall, Jaye rubbed his hands as if to warm them up, but his gaze stayed locked on Dixon.

In a way, it was like they were all the way back there, on that first morning. Dixon had brought breakfast and coffee to break the ice with the kid who'd tried to rob the Stop and Shop. Jaye was dragging his finger through the sugar, licking it up, daring Dixon with a sultry look and a crooked smile to defy temptation, while behind his eyes there was nothing but screaming.

How had they come so far and found themselves back at the start again?

"If this is a way to try and get in my pants, you know it takes a lot less to get there, right? No steaks necessary. Just tell me to drop 'em and spread, and I will, Trooper Rowe."

Dixon shot him a look, but refused to rise to the bait. Steady and steely-eyed, he carried the plates to the table. Setting one down in front of Jaye, the other across from him, Dixon circled the table and gently caressed the side of Jaye's jaw as he went. For just a second, Jaye's gaze dropped. A smile threatened the side of Dixon's lips, but he fought it down.

Dixon fetched the wine, then sat across from Jaye.

"What if I'm not hungry?" Jaye asked, as if testing the waters.

Pushing back, Dixon gave him a no-nonsense response. "You need to eat, so eat. It can be an order if you want it to be."

They each picked up their silverware and dug in. The silence around them felt thick and charged.

After a while, Jaye asked, "What comes after dinner?"

With a heated, upraised gaze, Dixon replied, "You'll see."

"You seem different."

"Maybe I've had enough of you trying to fuck yourself over, mentally or otherwise. You don't have to worry about anything. I'll take care of what you need, whatever it is."

"That's a big promise," Jaye warned, sounding like he was turned on in a big way and trying not to show it.

"Oh, I know."

They finished their meal in silence, but the way Jaye watched Dixon's every move, not letting his thoughts turn completely inward, told Dixon that Jaye might have guessed where the change of the mood came from.

When Dixon took their plates to the sink, leaving the refilled wine glasses behind, Jaye stood, hands going into his pockets.

Keeping his back turned, Dixon said, "Take your clothes off."

He thought he heard a quiet laugh, but when he turned back around, Jaye's expression gave nothing away. He was in the process of peeling his shirt off. After it fell to the ground, he reached for his fly and toed off his shoes.

"You like to watch, Trooper Rowe?" Jaye asked, starting to play it up a little, keeping his seductive movements subtle enough to let Dixon question if it was natural sensuality or an intentional seduction.

"Like to watch you, sure."

"That what this is?"

Dixon bit his lip and walked up to Jaye, caressing one bare hip as Jaye dropped his pants. At the touch, Dixon saw goosebumps raise on Jaye's skin. He dropped his hand a little more, letting the pad of his thumb barely skim over Jaye's cockhead as he lowered his boxer briefs. In response, the flesh twitched, swelling. Closing his eyes, Jaye stayed still, his briefs barely lowered, his chest rising and falling, his hands hanging at his sides. Dixon caressed the silky skin of the crown a little longer, watching him become erect. He lifted Jaye's cock, letting it fit in the junction of his thumb and forefinger. Jaye's expression seemed serene, patient.

Softly, Dixon told him, "I know what you want. Should I give it to you?"

A smile, there and gone, moved over Jaye's full lips. His gaze rose, eyes blazing.

"Yes, sir."

Dixon considered him, and his body, for a long moment.

"Okay." He turned toward the bathroom and switched on the light. Stepping up to the shower, he turned on the water, letting it run hot, and began to undress. To Jaye, he inclined his head with a faint smirk and said, "Come on."

"Watersports?"

"Not exactly."

Jaye began to lose the ability to suppress his smile the more naked Dixon became. He also lost the ability to keep his hands to himself, rubbing Dixon from chest to thigh. His fingers scratched through Dixon's golden chest hair. When steam began to rise, Dixon pulled the curtain aside to allow Jaye to step under the spray.

As soon as the water hit Jaye's skin, he let out a moan. Dixon got in behind him and began to lather up a sponge. As Jaye enjoyed the hot spray, Dixon lightly scrubbed Jaye's body, starting with his neck and back.

Relaxing into the touch, Jaye let his lips part around a blissful sigh. "I like your style, Trooper."

"Good."

Taking his time, Dixon lathered up Jaye's body, running the sponge over every line and curve, watching him lean into every touch. His cock stayed hard and his eyes closed. When he finished, Jaye took the sponge from Dixon's hand without a word and set to work repaying the favor.

He lingered with the sponge in washing Dixon's cock and balls, so much so that Dixon was quickly erect, despite his best efforts to spare himself the discomfort. He was trying to hold off, having planned how he wanted things to progress, but when Jaye sank to his knees, he knew there was no use.

With a hard moan, he watched Jaye swallow him down. Humming, suckling, Jaye slowly pulled back. The rapt pleasure on his face was the main thing that stayed Dixon. Caressing Jaye's jaw and the back of his head, Dixon rode his tongue for a few indulgent pushes. It took a massive rally of will to let Jaye pull off before finishing, but he did. Jaye took one last lick up from Dixon's root, kissed his tip, then allowed Dixon to help him back to his feet.

"I'll go and let you finish. Be thorough and be quick."

Jaye knew what that meant. The douching bulb was in arm's reach and he glanced at it. There was a fascinating inner battle then, which Dixon scrutinized happily. Jaye's protest was right on the tip of his tongue, but he bit it back.

Asking for certain specific sexual favors wasn't just difficult for Jaye, it was almost impossible to get him to mention them at all. Maybe he thought it too selfish. Maybe he was still finding his comfort level in submitting to his own pleasure. Either way, Dixon was determined as ever to get what he wanted that night.

"And that is an order," he added, grabbing a towel and stepping out of the shower.

He had Jaye lie face down on the bed. His hair was still drip-drying. His skin smelled fresh and felt damp under the caress and nudge of Dixon's hands.

"Dix."

"Mmm." Dixon pushed Jaye's legs farther apart, settling between them. He cupped Jaye's cheeks and pulled them apart. His nose nudged Jaye's crease and his knot.

"Dix." Jaye's voice gained an edge, his breath catching hard at the first touch of Dixon's tongue.

After a firm lick, Dixon said, "Relax."

He saw the tension throughout Jaye's back and legs. He was propped up on his elbows, and Dixon would have bet that his fists were clenched.

Deliberately, he pressed the pointed muscle of his tongue at Jaye's opening, which was also clenched tight. Determined, Dixon forced it through.

Jaye let out a breathy gasp. Bowing his head, body trembling, Jaye visibly fought the sensations.

Dixon dug his fingers in harder to spread Jaye's ass wide and pressed his tongue deeper. An arm shot out to grab at the headboard and a whimper broke through Jaye's defenses. Dixon let his lips kiss Jaye's rim and moved his tongue in shallow pulses. Jaye tasted clean and felt incredibly warm. The grip of his inner muscles was incredible and Dixon had a lot of fun working him gradually looser.

The longer it went on, the more Jaye lost the battle. His trembling intensified. Then he collapsed to the bed, lying flat for just a moment, until finally tipping his ass up in invitation for more. Dixon could see him frowning, panting, his hand restless as it rubbed over the bed.

Dixon withdrew only to dart his tongue back inside, over and over again, licking along the way.

Becoming frantic, Jaye struggled to remain still. Dixon noticed him trying to thrust against the bed, rocking back into the inward thrusts of Dixon's tongue. When Dixon finally stopped, climbing up on the bed to lie on top of Jaye, there was a pleading, primal moan.

He didn't waste time, but fit his cock against Jaye's saliva-wet hole, then entered him with a firm push. He felt the crown pop through Jaye's rim. Quivering, Jaye pushed back into the thrust almost greedily.

"Easy. Nice and slow," Dixon whispered. He kissed Jaye's neck, found his hand and wove their fingers together. "Don't want to hurt you. It's been a while."

Jaye's mouth opened, as if he was trying to speak, but his eyes rolled in ecstasy and the sound choked off as Dixon fed him more of his cock. Once he was fully seated, he brought Jaye's arms up to rest circled above his head. Holding them by the wrists, holding him down, Dixon began to ride him. Jaye did his part though, meeting each push and hurrying every pull, rubbing off on the bed below them. When he whined and convulsed slightly, Dixon shifted his angle to drag right against Jaye's gland, triggering him as he came with a rough gasp.

"Dixon…"

Letting go, Dixon caressed up and down Jaye's body, scratching lightly as he kept moving, taking his time and giving Jaye slow, deeply penetrating thrusts. His goosebumps remained and when Dixon came with a moan, it was while marveling at the boneless, sated vision of Jaye's body beneath him.

"I'll help clean up," Jaye rasped, not moving a muscle nor opening his eyes.

"No, you won't. I'm not done with you yet."

Jaye raised an eyebrow at him, glancing back over his shoulder.

When Dixon stayed sheathed in Jaye's ass and began kneading Jaye's shoulders in a massage, Jaye laughed a little.

"Man, you must have done something really bad," he guessed. "Or I've died and gone to heaven."

"Or you're just proving that I need to do more of this so it's not so novel to you. You deserve to feel this good."

"It does feel really good," Jaye moaned almost deliriously.

For a long while, Dixon kept massaging Jaye's back. He lightly caressed Jaye's arms, causing shivers to run down his spine. Once in a while, Jaye would clench up on Dixon's cock, intentionally or reflexively.

Eventually, Dixon began to get hard again.

"Too tired?" Dixon asked, half-joking.

Jaye gave him a disbelieving glance. "Yeah, right."

Chuckling, Dixon pulled out. He climbed up the bed beside where Jaye lay and sat back against some pillows. Taking instant advantage of the opportunity, Jaye climbed up to Dixon and straddled him. He reared up to allow Dixon to line up, then sank down with a happy sigh, coming in to kiss Dixon's lips.

They kissed the whole time, breathing each other's air, brushing against each other's lips. Jaye wrapped himself around Dixon in every imaginable way and they moved together, crashing and receding like the tide. Jaye ran his fingers through Dixon's hair and clasped to his shoulder or back. Dixon pumped Jaye's shaft as best he could with how tightly Jaye was holding on. He drank down Jaye's whimpers as he came, flooding Dixon's fingers with hot come, wringing the orgasm from Dixon as he did.

Setting his head down on Dixon's shoulder, Jaye tightened his embrace even more, winding his legs around Dixon's back, and his arms, too. Dixon caressed along Jaye's spine and kissed his hair.

Soon, Dixon felt the slow, even breaths as Jaye slipped into sleep. Holding on to his cherished one, his heart soothed by Jaye's peaceful rest, Dixon knew he had everything he could have ever wanted, right there in his arms.

Chapter 11:
Johnny for Cash

Dixon made the coffee and carried the steaming mugs back to bed where Jaye was curled up on his side beneath the blankets. A new fire was banishing the morning chill. Soon, they would have to get ready for work, but there was some time to talk first. Jaye was glad. There were things he needed to know.

With his head nestled in a pillow, and most of his drowsiness shaken off, Jaye mentally shuffled the stack of notes he'd privately taken while scrutinizing Dixon's behavior since he got home the night before. He'd already pieced together some of what Dixon was about to say, but was eager to learn how the pieces would fit together.

"He called you, didn't he?"

"Yeah," Dixon admitted.

"And what's the verdict?"

"You don't want to know what he had to say?"

"Not really. I know him pretty well. You don't. This was more about you and him than me. But I do want to know what you plan to do next, because I can tell you've decided."

Dixon sat heavily on the side of the bed and cupped his hands around his favorite porcelain mug. It had a hand-painted moose on the side and a chip on the handle. Jaye steered clear of using it if there was a chance Dixon might need it. But if Dixon had already gone to work, sometimes Jaye used it specifically because he knew how much Dixon loved it.

"He was different than I expected," Dixon muttered, like he would have rather been getting a root canal than talking about this.

"And not. I don't know. I mean, I get the whole doesn't-take-any-shit thing. He's gotta project an image, after all. But I didn't think he'd..." Dixon shifted restlessly, tucking one leg under the other.

"What?"

"He needs to talk to you."

Jaye breathed out a laugh and sat up. "I fucking know that. Yeah."

"No, I mean the whole thing. I'm sure there's a favor involved here somehow. He didn't get into it. But I'm pretty sure that to him, getting to talk to you and making sure you're okay is the whole point. He was..." Dixon exhaled heavily and rolled his head on his shoulders. When he started to talk again, he gestured with his hand, getting more agitated. "He really laid into me so I understood I would never have met you without him. He says I owe him for that. And what he wants to even the scales is to talk to you."

With wonder, Jaye guessed, "And you're going to let it happen, aren't you?" If the tables were turned, Jaye would have never relented like that.

Dixon glanced sideways at him. Jaye still felt flushed with a happy glow from the night before, followed by a solid night's rest at last. It had been over a week since he'd slept so good.

Dixon took Jaye's hand and brought it up so he could kiss the knuckles. The tenderness in the gesture touched Jaye in ways that reminded him who Dixon Rowe really was — a sensitive soul who questioned himself more than he should, because of assholes who'd taken advantage of him for too long, and a man who knew the true value of the good things in his life and would never be too proud to show his appreciation.

"There was something panicked in his voice," Dixon confessed. "Not for your sake. He doesn't think you're in trouble. It's more... he loves you, Jaye. I could tell. I think he really just needs to see you're doing better."

Jaye sank back into the pillows. Brushing the soft, thick, golden hair on Dixon's forearm, Jaye said with a downturned gaze and remorseful feeling, "Yeah, well. Like I told you, we didn't part well. That's probably part of it. It's hard to accept something's over when there's no closure."

"Tell me more about it."

"He was afraid. And you heard the guy. He's never scared of anything, but leading up to my release date, Cash was fucking scared. And they knew. They saw it. So, they set him up with the stashed drugs. Threw him in ad-seg a solid week before I left, just so we couldn't have those last few days to say goodbye to each other. I heard him... screaming... when they carried him off. The sound of that? The helplessness? After everything he'd done for me when he never had to do a thing? It killed me." He made eye contact, showing Dixon some of the hard-earned wisdom his youthful face sometimes masked. "I didn't love him back, okay? It was always just a deal to me. At most, I was thankful he was nice to me in private. He was a means to an end, but he deserved to get to have goodbye. And I was too much a coward to be able to go back and see him in there once I was out."

"After everything you endured in there? Of course you didn't want to go back. It's a miracle you survived at all. Don't blame yourself for that. You earned the right to be selfish for once and make your own decisions."

Jaye picked up his coffee from the nightstand and sipped it.

"I trust you completely," Dixon told him. "You know that. I'll leave it up to you whether you want to get on the call or not. You've more than earned the right to make that choice, too. I can't tell you what to do here, and I can tell my judgment is clouded. I still fucking hate that guy."

Jaye smiled, but Dixon didn't.

"I'm serious."

"Oh, I know," Jaye assured him. "But there's always that whole 'the enemy of my enemy is my friend' thing with Cash. There are worse guys who've had me in their sights. And Cash goes to war with those bastards every bleeding day."

"You hated Marcus. You should know how hard this is for me. You would have never volunteered me for a sit-down with him."

"Marcus broke your fucking nose on purpose by slamming your face into a wall just to get out of a holiday party. That's who Marcus is. Was. May he rot in Hell."

"Oh yeah, tough guy," Dixon said quietly. "You look me in the eye and tell me Cash never did just as bad to you. Directly or otherwise."

Jaye started to speak, but then his memory coughed up a gem from the gang rape in ad-seg, filmed for the sexual pleasure scumbags, as well as the way Cash had fucked him later that night too, like clockwork, even though Jaye was in agony and sobbing uncontrollably. He remembered trying to play mental gymnastics to get through it, while he had guy after guy going to town on his shackled and helpless body from both ends. He remembered Hax threatening in a dead voice to break Jaye's jaw if he felt any teeth, and feeling certain he would have done it, Cash be damned.

A hand folded over his. "Hey... I'm sorry. I should know better than to make you go back there and remember that shit. Let's just stop talking about it, okay? The whole point of last night was to help, not hurt, I — "

"Dix, you can't save me from my past, anymore than I can save you. And last night was incredible. You're right, okay? There's plenty of reason why you should want to keep me away from Cash, and why you should hate him. I won't lie about that. But where's the harm in some closure? I mean, really? What's he gonna say that could hurt me more than I already am? Especially if you got the vibe that he just wants to check in for sentimental reasons."

"You don't owe him that."

"I know. But I know how much it fucks with you when people you care about are just suddenly gone, forever."

Dixon tugged him by the hand, pulling him into a loose hug that Jaye melted into.

Staying in the warm hold against Dixon's chest, Jaye heard him murmur by his ear, "That's another thing I hate. So, if you need some closure there too, I won't keep you from it."

"Thank you."

"So you do want to talk to him?"

"Yeah. I think I need to, not that I totally want to. I'd rather not have to reopen that door, but it's not just about me. Plus..."

"What?"

Jaye thought about how to say it. "There's no way he's doing this only for sentimental reasons. That's not the kind of guy he is. But something tells me he pulled the emotional card in order to get me on the phone, like he wants to tell me what's going on instead of telling you. I want to know why."

"Just promise me you're not going to fall for his shit or guilt trips. He doesn't get to tell you what to do anymore."

"Promise."

The second call came later that day, around the same time. Dixon had been out on the road, but made sure he came back to the station, just in case. If that was when Cash had access to the inmate phones, Dixon would plan to be there to facilitate them figuring this out once and for all. He was sick of seeing the worry in Jaye's eyes.

The call didn't last long.

"Hey, Trooper," Cash said in greeting.

"Cash."

"You thought about what I said?"

"I did. I don't like you. I trust you about as far as I can throw you, but if you want to talk to him, and he's okay with it, I won't stand in the way. But that's all it is. Talking. I hear a word of threat in what you say to him, you're done for good."

"Why the fuck would I threaten Johnny?"

"His name isn't Johnny. It's Jaye. Like the bird."

"So you threaten me to keep me from threatening him? That's how this works?"

"If it has to. Helps that I've got the law on my side, too. I know the kind of shit you did to him. Maybe not all of it. There's some he won't talk about, even with me, but I know enough to know what kind of man you are, deep down. He's not your property anymore. He's a man with his own fucking life and he doesn't need you."

"Ain't that the truth. But he needs you, Trooper Dixon Rowe?"

"We need each other."

Cash breathed out a laugh. "How nice. So, if I call tomorrow, same time, he'll be there?"

"He'll be here. But so will I."

It turned into a late workday for both of them, with Dixon out on a call in the far northern end of their territory, and Jaye also out on a call, fixing the wiring for a couple living on the west end of town after a tree fell and severed the lines running from their solar panel array and their home.

By the time they both got home, after eating dinner on the run, all they wanted to do was sleep. Crawling in bed together, they cuddled up close and drifted off. The following morning they made their plans. Jaye was ready for it, anticipating the arrangement before Dixon said a word about it. In fact, he'd even shifted his work schedule that day, so he wasn't due in until afternoon.

For the morning, he went with Dixon, tagging along on a call and his usual patrol loop in the Expedition. There was no flirting for once. He didn't think it would have been appropriate or appreciated, even if he'd had the stomach for it. Psychological echoes from so much constant whoring in Sheridan kept Jaye quiet and withdrawn, especially without being able to anticipate what the real task was going to be. He'd been trying to guess, and couldn't.

Once in a while, Dixon would stop the car and look over at Jaye, curled up in the passenger seat with his knees to his chest, trying to tuck into a ball and deflect anything that came his way, shutting out the whole world. Dixon wouldn't say much, or try to take Jaye's hand, but he would ask, "What can I do?"

"Just be here."

"Okay."

Maybe he was finally growing up, but Jaye did feel shame for how he'd hooked both Cash and Dixon, using his body as a weapon or tool. For so long, he'd wanted to be more than that, but survival had to come first. Now, he was past surviving. The danger of death was more remote than it had ever been. He had a job, a devoted lover, a family, friends, community, and home. He didn't need to turn it on as strong just to ensure he would make it through the day. He could relax, and be himself. And the fear of the unknown chewed his gut, causing any sort of seductive act to seem highly distasteful. He also wanted to make sure when he did talk to Cash, that he didn't get the wrong idea. He didn't want to send any signals to indicate he could still be treated the way he used to be. Jaye wasn't anyone's whore any longer, and he never would be again.

They returned to the station well before they needed to. Dixon sat Jaye at his desk and fetched him some coffee to sip. When Sesi and Debbie tried to come over to make conversation, Dixon diplomatically headed them off, asking for a little time and space until the call was done. Jaye appreciated it more than he could say.

Hunched over by the phone, clasping the paper cup half-filled with bitter, weak coffee, Jaye stared at the phone, daring it to ring.

When it finally did, his mouth was completely dry. He let Dixon answer to accept the charges. Then Dixon said, "Yep," and passed the phone over.

Jaye took it, letting it hang by his side for a long moment before gathering his wits and chewed guts for a conversation he'd been anticipating since the day they'd carried Cash away, screaming.

He felt cold and thin as he answered, "Yeah. It's me."

"Damn good to hear your voice, kid. You doing well?"

"Yeah."

"You got a job?"

"Yeah, I'm an electrician."

"Good. That's real good."

"Look," Jaye said, taking a breath to help feed his courage, feeling the creeping touch of old, unwanted ghosts begin to caress over his thighs. "I'm sorry it ended the way it did. I truly am. But it's way too late to make up for that now."

"You don't think I know that? You think I'm stupid?"

"No. Of course not."

"I know you've got someone new to watch your ass. You've got the law and a guy who isn't too much of a pussy to talk to me on your behalf, even if his name is Dixon."

A small smile curled Jaye's lips, but he kept his head down, leaning on the desk.

"Dix for short."

"Well, see, that makes more sense."

Jaye laughed. He could feel the force of Dixon's stare, boring into him.

"I bet he's pretty, too, huh?"

"He's not bad."

"Anything's gotta be an improvement on me, huh?"

"I wouldn't say that."

"He treat you good?"

"Yeah. Better than I probably deserve."

"Ahh, kid..." Cash sighed.

Jaye rubbed his eyes, keeping his head low, trying to control his breathing. He hadn't had enough goodbyes in his life to be able to appreciate how much they could absolutely suck, but now he was starting to get the picture.

"It makes it easier, knowing you're safe and protected."

Yeah, but you're not, are ya, boss?

With a voice too thick with emotion, Jaye blurted, "Why? Why did you send it? Why are you saying this shit to me? Can you just tell me already, because it doesn't make any sense and — "

"I know you're a realist, kid, but fuck. You really think that little of me? You think I'd just forget you after they walk you out those doors? That I'd stop worrying who's coming for you next, now that you've got no look-out? My crew is my family! My — "

"What the fuck happened in there, Cash? Why are you being like this? You're freaking me out. Why — "

"Fine." A heavy breath. "Fine."

"Tell me!"

"It's Jinx, okay?"

"What about Jinx? What the fuck happened to Jinx?"

Tony 'Jinx' Jaconelli was the youngest member of the Disciples, not counting Jaye. A chill went up Jaye's spine as previously unrealized possibilities flooded his imagination.

"Well," Cash started, sounding worn down, "we don't call him that no more. Tony. Not Jinx. And, with you gone, he was the youngest, right? They still wanted to go after me through the backdoor. Same as always. Same as they did with you."

"They didn't... they didn't fucking..."

Fingers down his throat, up his ass. Piggy, piggy, piggy... You like that? Say thank you...

"Tony was stronger than you, to start with. He held his own. Tough as nails. You can't just go for someone like that without a little muscle. A little extra force. You've gotta break 'em, right? Then, while they're down, you keep hitting until they're nothing but a smear of blood on the concrete."

Jaye couldn't breathe. Dixon had crouched down beside him, was gripping Jaye's shoulder like he was panicked too.

Jaye tried to speak, but an awful, pleading sound came out instead.

"He only had a year left on his sentence, when they started. He was so damn close."

"Cash, I swear to Christ!" Jaye screamed, his naturally soft voice shattering.

For a full minute there was nothing. Absolutely nothing. And Jaye nearly had another meltdown thinking they'd been cut off.

"He's, uh… he's alive, but…"

Jaye said a prayer, pressed the heel of his hand into his eye.

"I think that sadist was pissed you left. I think he went a little nuts without you to ream out on the regular. Then there was the fight. You remember the fight? Before he was transferred?"

Jaye did remember. Kett and Tug had staged a fight in order to get Ecker in trouble, to get him transferred out of their unit so Jaye would be able to recover from the constant attacks and have a little peace. If Ecker knew they'd done it on purpose to get rid of him, of course he'd want payback.

"Just tell me, please?" Jaye begged.

Anything that had happened to Jinx could have happened to Jaye, or should have happened to him, or happened to Jinx because of him. He had to know.

"Got him in the exercise yard. Held him down, stuffed a shirt in his mouth to muffle the screaming, and dropped weights on both of his hands until they were like… fucking pulp."

"Oh Jesus," Jaye moaned.

"Then in… in recovery, after they'd tried to piece the bones back together as best they could, they still came for him. They raped him, regularly. They weren't even trying to get him to talk or nothin'. They just wanted him to hurt. They wanted to hurt us. I went to O'Neill, filed a report, but I didn't have any other names. I knew that piece of shit had help, but Tony wouldn't talk, not even to save himself." Cash cleared his throat. "So when we heard that something had happened to him, we weren't surprised they were investigating everyone. They thought it might be the blacks, targeting him to clean house, sweep the board of dead weight. That's, uh, that's what we think, too. But there's been no official ruling."

Jaye slowly began to breathe again, understanding that Cash couldn't talk about it anymore than that, or explain their part in it, whatever it was. They monitored the calls. He couldn't implicate himself.

"Did it stop? Did they stop?"

"Yeah, but kid... It was too late."

Jaye punched the desk. Sesi and Debbie were there, listening, but he didn't look at them, or Dixon.

"He's getting out soon?"

"Yeah. Yeah, he is, but he ain't got no one, and he can't do for himself. He's out of the life, you get me? He don't talk much anymore. They've had him on suicide watch for months. He needs... he needs someone to... he needs someone."

Jaye took a deep breath and blew it out. He sat back in the chair, eyes closed and let it settle down on him.

"Maybe he could push a mop someplace? Earn some money to rent a room? He don't need much. I think, if we told him he'd be near a familiar face, it might get him through this. I wouldn't ask if I didn't have to, kid. You think it over, okay? I've gotta go. You take care of you."

The call ended. Jaye let Dixon take the phone, then covered his face and moaned. Dixon pulled him into a hug and Jaye held on as tight as he could.

Chapter 12:
Giving What's Wanted

Jaye explained to Dixon, with Sesi and Debbie overhearing the whole thing. He spoke in monotone, stating facts, giving a rundown of the history. He didn't know how to explain why it was so horrible, and was sure his explanations didn't touch the heart of the issue.

"So, wait," Sesi said, once Jaye had stopped. "You're telling us a gang had this Ecker guy murdered? Like a professional hit?"

"I have no idea who did it," Jaye told her. It was the truth. He didn't know who Cash had hired, but he was content to let her think it was the one of the black Sheridan gangs who'd done it, following Cash's lead. One glance at Dixon's face told Jaye he also had no misconceptions about what had really gone on.

"Tony was a friend of yours, then?" Debbie asked with an apologetic expression.

Jaye dropped his gaze, unsure how to convey the truth.

Jinx wasn't a friend, but for a while, he'd been family. Why did it upset him so much, knowing what they'd done to break him? He'd been one of the guys holding Jaye down during the gang bang porn shoot. He'd watched plenty of times while Cash gave it to Jaye hard and dirty, making it look like force, like rape. He hadn't done a thing to stop any of that.

At the same time, he'd been there for everything with Tio. He'd had Jaye's back in plenty of ways that counted. There was no blaming Jinx for being a witness to other people's crimes, or even for following Cash's orders and holding Jaye down to get taken from both ends by guards and brothers alike. It had all been survival. If Cash gave the orders, Jinx had to obey, the same as any of them.

But there was no escaping that small, private certainty that what had happened to Jinx after Jaye had left could have easily happened to him instead, had his sentence been a little longer. But no matter how he looked at it, Jinx's fate was Jaye's fault. He hadn't been there to keep Ecker satisfied, so the sadist's attentions had found the next best target.

And for all of his spirit, courage, and grit, Jinx hadn't been able to cope.

Even without seeing Jinx, and just hearing from Cash the little he had, there was no question Jinx was a broken man. And it had done something to Cash's mind, to see the youngest member of his crew taken apart physically and mentally, in ways that would probably never heal.

He tried to imagine the foresight needed to plan the hit the way they had, while everything had still been going down with Jinx, the desperation in the play. Cash had been thinking of the long game, even then. He knew he would need to send Jaye a message he couldn't ignore, and he'd done it.

It had been effective.

Because here they were — the bulk of the Zus, Alaska law, waiting to hear Jaye's decision. Waiting to help a thug they'd never met and never should have needed to.

It hadn't hit Jaye before as hard as it did then. But he got it. He really did.

Jinx was family. Cash was family.

That didn't go away.

The ties didn't break.

Looking right at Dixon, Jaye said, "I need to see him. I need to see him for myself."

"You're talking about going to Oregon. Going back to Sheridan," Dixon replied, like he wanted to make sure Jaye understood. Which pained Jaye to hear, because it just proved how Dixon didn't really get it, and never would. All of the things Jaye had held back out of fear for Dixon's remaining shreds of innocence and purity — those were the things that would always live deep down in Jaye. They were the dark. They were truth. He'd been through things with those men, his crew, that no one else would ever understand. If it had been him, instead of Jinx, they would have been there. No question.

95

Jaye had to pay the same respects. It had nothing to do with what he wanted anymore. Now, it was duty.

"I won't know how to help him until I see him for myself. I need to see how bad it is."

"Jaye, we need to talk about this. Think about this," Dixon urged.

"Dix. I get it. I appreciate that you want to protect me. I do. But this isn't about me. Think about what I went through in there. I'm the only one who can help him. They're trying to make sure he stays safe. In there, once you're marked as that kind of a target, everyone knows. Everyone. I'm talking guards, rival gangs. Hell, without Jinx being under Cash's personal control, guys within the Disciples might be going for him too. It'll be the same on the outside. I'm sure Cash could ask someone in the Disciples to take him, but what then, huh? Tony becomes someone's bitch in exchange for shelter and food? He'd kill himself, no question. Cash is trying to get Tony someplace safe. He's trying to save his life. Who else can help him the way we can? Who else is gonna understand this? Or care?"

"Dixon, we've gotta help this Tony guy," Sesi said, frowning.

"Jinx — Tony. He's a good guy. He knew his place. Loyal. Strong. He was always…" Jaye blew out a breath, wiped a hand over his eyes. "Always laughing. Always in good spirits. But I need to see how far gone he is. I need to see how much hope we have of saving him."

"Either way, we should still try," Sesi told him. "Hasn't he earned that much?"

"This isn't your problem, Sesi."

"Maybe it is. Maybe I'm making it my problem."

Jaye looked over to Dixon, who seemed to be running it over and over in his mind. He waited for the decision.

"Okay. I'll think about it," Dixon said, sounding like it was the last thing he wanted to do.

Sitting forward, taking his hand, Jaye gave it a squeeze and said, "Thank you."

That night, Dixon looked purely miserable. He was a thousand miles away, off in his head in bad places. He frowned constantly and kept going over to the chest of drawers by the window where he stowed his duty belt and holster. Standing there, he'd finger the pistol's grip, staring off into space.

Jaye wondered who he wanted to shoot. Who he needed to get his hands on.

Dressed in jeans and a tight gray shirt, barefoot, his hair mussed, Jaye walked over to Dixon. His sleeves were tugged down over his hands. Taking a shy, uncertain stance, he played up his best helpless, innocent act as best he could, knowing it always made Dixon weak.

Softening his voice, letting it break and tumble over the words, draining the strength from them, he said in imitation of the uncertain young man he might once have been, "Sometimes I pretend I met you first, back in Anchorage, when I was seventeen. That you were my first real boyfriend, instead of Kris."

He pushed his hands into his pockets, tugging them lower to flash the bare skin of his pelvis where the tribal tattoo sprawled out above his cock, letting his shirt ride up a little. He kept his head bowed, but gave Dixon a bashful, flirty glance.

Dixon sighed, his thumb running over the Glock's grip, over and over again. He was trying to resist, to act like he wasn't listening, wasn't going to play along, but Jaye saw his gaze drift down to that little bare strip of skin, again and again. Temptation was a funny thing.

"Can you see it? So close to being legal. Horny as fuck. Wanting so bad to get fucked by a hot guy who just needs to get inside me. I'll beg, you know. Actually love to beg. I'm good at it."

It was all true. Jaye had done his fair share of both begging and lusting.

Dixon rolled his eyes, biting his tongue.

When Jaye hesitantly pulled his shirt over his head, Dixon looked. Of course he did.

His nipples stiffening, Jaye rubbed a hand over his chest and up around the back of his neck. He felt Dixon looking more steadily, so he kept going.

"I know I'm probably not your type, Mr. Rowe, but I swear I won't tell if you want to fool around a little. No one has to know about it."

He slowly unbuttoned his fly, inched down the zipper.

"I've dated a couple of guys. Some of them liked to jerk me off, or let me play with them. One liked to spank it while he sucked me, but none of them were ready to go... you know. Farther. But I am."

He pushed the jeans down. He wasn't wearing anything underneath. Jaye got them low enough for Dixon to catch a glimpse of the base of his cock, the short, dark curls of his pubic hair. He turned around so Dixon could see the crease of his ass, acting like he was nervous as hell.

"It's okay if you wanna finger me, or... try to give me your cock. I know it'd hurt but I think I'd like it."

"Jesus fucking Christ, Jaye," Dixon breathed. "Why do you do this shit to me? Why do I always fall for it?"

Jaye took a step forward, bent over the table and let the jeans slip down farther, to show his whole ass. The energy coming off of Dixon was charged and dangerous. Letting his hands tremble a little, Jaye reached back and spread his cheeks.

"Just be gentle? Please?"

He wasn't sure if Dixon would actually take the bait, and if he would, how, but Jaye was ready to take it as far as he needed to in order to get Dixon out of his head and back where he belonged.

The wooden floorboards creaked.

A warm touch caressed the underside of his ass. A fingertip brushed his knot, tickling.

The question was a short, abrupt growl. "You want it?"

"Yeah," Jaye pleaded. "Just don't hurt me."

A dry finger entered him, pushing to the last knuckle. When a hard shiver ran up his back, stiffening his cock, that wasn't an act at all.

"How's that? You like that?"

Jaye whimpered.

"You should be more careful who you give this up to," Dixon warned. Twisting the finger around inside Jaye's ass. "Save it for someone special." He pumped the dry finger in shallow pulses. "You like that?"

"Mmm."

"Is it making you hard? Let's see."

The jeans were pulled down farther. A hand wrapped Jaye's swelling cock. He kept spreading himself, panting against the tabletop.

Dixon's finger twisted again, finding his gland and triggering it. Jaye made a startled noise and quivered. Dixon kept massaging the spot and Jaye's cock dripped in response. Biting hard on his lower lip, Jaye convulsed a little with each rub, and he didn't hold in his pleading, breaking cries.

"Does that hurt? If you want me to stop, you're gonna have to ask nicely. Beg. Go ahead and try. Cause see, I think I like those sweet little whimpers too much to stop. And I like to feel you drip. You gettin' wet for me? Gettin' hard? Answer."

"Y-yeah."

The finger withdrew quickly. His pants were yanked to his ankles. He stepped out of them, shifting his legs wider.

"Get on the bed. Now."

Jaye kept his head bowed, his breathing quickened. Nude, he climbed up and lay down on his stomach. Dixon was in a white undershirt and dark pants. He stood at the foot of the bed.

"Turn over."

Jaye rolled.

"Grab ankles."

Jaye drew his legs back, holding them by the ankles as directed. The pose spread him wide, showing off his rigid, soaking wet dick, his balls drawn up and swollen.

Dixon grabbed the lube, working it over his hands as he stared at Jaye's exposed body, his eyes dark as storms gathered behind them.

"Do you l-like my body?"

"Yeah," Dixon said heatedly. "I do. And I like that I make you hard."

He grabbed Jaye and drew him down the bed, so his ass was right on the edge. Then he twisted three lubed fingers through Jaye's rim, drawing a very real moan. He clenched on them, his head thrown back, his cock twitching.

"Yeah, you can take it, huh?"

A glance showed Dixon staring down at Jaye's hole taking the fingers, stretched wide around them, his rim shining with the lube, and pink.

"Please…"

"Please what?"

The fingers pumped deeply, and Jaye started to rock against them, riding them. Dixon palmed Jaye's cheek with his left hand,

99

guiding his movements as he took him deeper, rubbing hard from within to stretch him from the inside. Jaye cried out, panting.

"Please don't tell anyone, Mr. Rowe. I don't wanna get in trouble."

Dixon breathed out a laugh, incredulous. Then he mastered it, giving Jaye a dark look.

"Okay, this is our secret. Get comfortable now. I wanna take my time. Watch you take my hand a while. That hurts a little, huh?"

"Mm-hmm."

"But your cock's still stiff. That's good. You like it a little rough?"

"Yes, Mr. Rowe."

The squelch of Dixon's fingers continued with each slow, deep push. He withdrew them completely, rubbed over the pink of his rim as it closed back up. He got a squirt of extra lube, then pushed all four fingers through.

Jaye gasped, shaking, spine arched and mouth fallen open. His whimper was genuine.

Dixon squeezed Jaye's ass, gave it a hard slap, watching the fingers get swallowed by his hole. Leaving them buried, he wrapped his free hand around Jaye's dick and tugged.

"Good boy," Dixon grinned. "Just stay nice and still for me. I just want you to feel that."

Jaye was panting again. Dixon's four fingers moved shallowly, the stretch from them so intense, Jaye had trouble thinking around it. Dixon's left hand steadily pumped Jaye's dick, squeezing from root to tip. It took enormous effort to not move, to not ride the tugging to completion. The struggle left him trembling constantly.

When he got close to orgasm, he whined and shuddered.

"Good. You gonna come? Lemme see. I wanna watch you shoot."

Dixon wrung him out, squeezing tight with complete tugs and Jaye came. Semen arced from his slit. Drops landed all the way up his stomach and chest. Dixon leaned down and, humming with hunger, took Jaye down his throat all the way to the base. He swallowed and Jaye cried out, moving finally as he rode Dixon's lips in small pushes.

"Fuck," he panted, rasping. "Oh fuck."

Dixon pulled off with a slurp, not missing a beat as he climbed higher, yanked his pants open and replaced his hand with his cock.

It sank in easily, without pain or resistance. Wrapping Jaye in a tight embrace, he rolled them so Jaye was on top and Jaye went for it, humping Dixon with little bounces.

"Fucking crazy, beautiful, irresistible pain in my ass," Dixon moaned, rubbing a come-soaked thumb over Jaye's lower lip. Jaye licked it, then sucked it clean. Dixon palmed the back of his head and drew him in hard for a passionate kiss, licking the salty taste of Jaye's spend from his tongue.

Frowning, Jaye rode him faster, bouncing with sharp slaps onto Dixon's cock. The thrusts were wet and welcome, and Jaye's cock tried to stiffen again from loving it so much.

"Mine," Jaye growled, weaving his fingers through Dixon's and pinning his hands down above his head. Dixon's gaze was slipping everywhere, seeing everything. He started to whimper too and shuddered as he came.

Once Dixon was through the aftershocks and his cock slipped, softened, from Jaye's ass, Jaye lunged sideways to the nightstand. He opened the drawer and pulled out a large dildo.

"Here. Fuck me 'til I come again," Jaye demanded, slapping it against Dixon's chest.

Dixon laughed. "Yes, sir. That might take a while."

Jaye shifted over, ass up and ready. He flashed a look full of triumph and pure, lustful need and said, "I got plenty of time."

"Where'd that innocent virgin go?"

"I'll always be your innocent virgin, Dix. Over and over and over again."

Dixon moved up behind Jaye, feeding his ass the dildo. Jaye felt delicious anguish move through his expression as he was stuffed full once more and the steady, slow ride began again.

"So, I'm your first?" Dixon asked, kissing him from over his shoulder, chasing his heavy exhales and small cries.

"First, last, and only."

"Likewise," Dixon smiled.

Chapter 13:
Dixon, the Bad Guy

After kissing Jaye goodbye, Dixon left early the next morning. With a mug of home-brewed coffee in hand, he parked the Expedition at the station, then went for a walk through town to clear his head.

He'd told Jaye not to come in for the follow-up call he assumed would be coming that day. The less contact Jaye had with Cash, the better. Though it was a relief to know what form Cash's hook was taking, the truth was it still dug gruesomely into Jaye and Dixon had little hope of dislodging it.

He understood the strength of the ties Jaye must have to the Disciples after everything they went through together, but it didn't mean he had to like it. Witnessing Jaye's anguish after receiving the news about Tony had been maddening. Just in waiting by Jaye's side during that call, Dixon felt it getting away from him. It was all so far out of his control. He couldn't stop Cash from luring Jaye in, he couldn't stop Jaye from feeling responsible for Tony, and it seemed he couldn't help inviting a member of the crew to Zus that had made a cold, calculating thug out of sweet young Jaye, sexually traumatizing him, making him a target for assault just from being close to Cash, and nearly breaking his mind. He didn't accept that the Disciples should only be praised for saving Jaye's life. They'd done a fair share of their own damage.

And now they'd never be free of them. If Tony came to live in Zus, it would be a permanent reminder of that part of Jaye's life and identity. He'd never get away from it, or be able to forget about it.

Though Jaye didn't like to talk about it, Dixon knew the kinds of things he'd suffered. He knew Tony had been there for some of the forced sex. He'd stood by, watched, and done nothing to help. He'd probably gotten off on it.

That wasn't someone Dixon was eager to welcome into his town.

However, he wasn't heartless. He appreciated the hopelessness of Tony's situation. Being an ex-con was hard enough without adding in a lack of support or family on the outside to help in finding their feet. Most companies flat-out refused to hire convicted felons, so adding in Tony's likely limited physical abilities, it just made things that much harder. All of those factors did appear to equate to a dire existence for him, giving him plenty of reason to hurry his exit from the world, by his own hand.

Dixon knew he had to think of it in terms of Jaye. It had been the same kind of thing when they'd met. Jaye had been desperate. He'd needed help, but was almost too proud to ask for it. Tony was even worse off, from what they were hearing. Tony needed help too. Dixon just wished it wasn't them expected to give it.

Marcus's brutal treatment and mind games with Dixon had always happened in private, away from others. The isolation had been a tool in his weaponry, making it seem that much more impossible for Dixon to reach out to anyone else for advice or assistance. Still, he tried to imagine some of Marcus's buddies witnessing several incidents between them, standing there off to the side in their bedroom while Dixon was sexually humiliated and verbally and emotionally abused. Maybe he'd be on his hands and knees on the bed, a leash around his throat, getting fucked and whipped, being called every degrading name under the sun, and Marcus's buddies watched, touching themselves a little, egging him on now and then, telling him to give it to Dixon harder. Then he imagined one of those buddies falling on hard times, coming to Dixon for help.

He stopped walking, tried to slow his breathing, closed his eyes as a cold gust blew against him, like nature itself was trying to cool his temper.

He wanted to hit something.

If Tony moved to Zus, every time he saw Jaye, would he see him only as Johnny? As the teenage kid who'd sold his ass for the privilege of getting to wake up the next day, locked in a hellhole? Would Dixon be forced to bear witness to Jaye's mental torment for the rest of their lives, without any hope of peace?

He had to talk to someone. Someone who would sympathize. Sesi was out. Sesi had likely already talked to Brekken about everything, which meant...

He dug out his phone and rang the number.

"Dixon? What's up?"

"You busy, Grant?"

"Nah. Brekken's out on a flight up north for a tour. I'm holding down the fort here."

"Good. I think I need to talk to you, if you have a minute."

"About what?"

"It's kind of you to pretend you don't know."

"Ahh. I see. The kid with the unfortunate name. Jinx."

"Right on the money."

"So? Fill me in. What're you thinking?"

"What am I thinking?" he echoed, then let out a cold laugh. He was walking down the middle of a little-used side-road. The near-permanent white of the winter snowfall was finally melting, but the grass hadn't started to grow yet, which made for a muddy, colorless landscape. He was impatient for spring and the signs of life renewing itself. "I'm thinking this asshole is guilty by association. I'm thinking he was in prison for a reason. I'm thinking every time Jaye interacts with him, it's going to be a blatant reminder that he agreed to let some thug piece of shit rape him every day as a show put on for his buddies. I'm thinking I'm more likely to strangle this kid than help him."

"But saying no makes you the bad guy? Right?"

"What the fuck am I supposed to do here, Grant?" Dixon asked with real desperation. "I think out of anyone, maybe, you know how hard it is for me to say no to something when everyone else expects me to say yes, for appearance's sake or whatever the fuck."

"You get a say, Dixon. You get to say no. You can say no."

"But it's fucking..." he laughed again, sounding even more crazy. "It makes me the bad guy."

"No, it doesn't."

"Yes, it does! To Jaye it does. To his whole fucking gang. To this merciless dick, Cash. To this guy I want to never meet, who had his hands smashed to a pulp with weights and now probably can't even wipe his own ass without help."

"Dixon..."

"He's more than Johnny, okay?! He's not Johnny! And if this kid moves here, and becomes his responsibility, he will fucking *always* be Johnny! He will always have to live in the shadow of that, and..." He blew out a breath. He growled and yelled out his anger.

Grant fell quiet, and it felt like an opening. Dixon took it because part of him had to.

"If this was a friend of Marcus's, expecting me to help him out, I'd tell him to go fuck himself."

"No, you wouldn't."

God, it hurt. Because it was true.

Dixon dropped the plastic thermos holding his coffee in the gravelly mud. He crouched down in the middle of the road and held his head in his hand. Nearby, an elderly woman came out of her raised mobile home, looking over at him with concern.

"Okay, first off, you need to talk to Jaye about this. You need to tell him everything you just said, if not more. Let it all out. You can't filter this shit to spare him. He's a tough little brat. He can take it. You believe me?"

"Yeah." Dixon sighed, feeling a little less likely to implode.

"And second, if your answer is no, let it be no. You can't lie and say it's yes and let this happen if you're against it, because it will tear you two apart. I see how much you love him, Dixie. I do. Don't let this be the thing that kills that. What was Jaye's mindset like last night after hearing all of this?"

Dixon laughed again, but in a more heartfelt way, because it really was ridiculous.

"He, uh," he cleared his throat. "I think he was concerned about me."

"Why?"

"Grant..."

"Come on, I'm not a child."

"It's hard to explain. We have this thing." Dixon stood, putting his back to the older woman who had started to approach. He waved her off and gave her a polite smile. Then, he started to walk again. "Sometimes, our situation, it's stupid. We know it's stupid. The age difference. The whole ex-con/cop thing. So we make fun of it by, uh, role-playing."

"Okay."

"And I was in a mood. A bad one. And he came onto me in this really insane way, acting like he hadn't met Kris yet, or gotten locked up, that he was just an innocent kid who liked me, and I don't know, Grant. I don't know what that's supposed to mean. But he was trying to pull me out of it. He was trying to get me to stop worrying about everything and — "

He stopped talking as the emotion choked him.

He fought it down, using everything in him, all of the tricks he'd picked up thanks to Marcus, to hide from Grant that he was as upset as he was.

"I know how much you love him, Dixon. I know that. And I know how much he loves you. He would do *anything* for you. Including saying no to Jinx, or Tony, or whatever his name is."

"Saying no is selfish."

"You get to be selfish! This is *your life*! You've been sacrificing yourself for other people for years. Don't sacrifice yourself for someone you don't even know. Hell, maybe Jaye would be grateful if you insisted he say no. Maybe this is something he doesn't know how to say no to without you to back him up. Jaye hasn't said one way or the other yet, or is he totally in for helping Jinx?"

"He wants to see Tony before he decides. He says he wants to go back to Sheridan and evaluate the situation. I think he wants to see how far gone Tony is before committing."

"Good. That's good, right? That buys you time. Even if he goes, that gives you plenty of opportunity to talk this out more. It means Jaye is still weighing his options. So breathe, brother. Breathe."

He did. He let out a breath and took a deeper one.

"I'm a fucking mess, aren't I?" Dixon asked.

"No, you're a good man who survived years of abuse and is still learning to stand up for himself when the time comes. You're allowed to have a hard time with this. You're allowed to need help, and time, and understanding."

"Okay."

"You better?"

"I am. Thank you. Thank you for letting me rant, and lose my shit and everything."

"Just remember, there is no right or wrong answer here. All you can do is what you're able to do. Know where your boundaries are. Track down and guard those sons of bitches."

"Okay. You're a lifesaver, Grant."

"Go get 'em, tiger."

Dixon smiled and hung up.

Three hours later, his phone was ringing. He sat there, looking at it with his hands folded in front of his mouth, while leaning on the desk. He almost didn't pick it up.

He accepted the charges.

"Cash."

"Trooper Dixon Rowe. Thought I'd check in, see if anything had been decided. He there?"

"No."

"All right. And?"

"And no decision has been made, but..." Dixon pulled himself up straighter, spoke a little louder. "He thinks he wants to pay a visit, see things for himself before he makes the call."

"I thought he might. Hoped he might, actually."

"Why?"

"Selfish reasons of which you probably wouldn't approve."

"You don't fucking touch him."

"Oh, I know. Always was easy on the eyes, though. I ain't trying to be a dick to you, Trooper. I'm really not. But put yourself in my shoes for a minute. Pretend you did something in your life, made a rash decision the courts deemed unacceptable, and landed in here. Imagine you had someone who made you smile, made the shit you waded through daily a little less awful. Imagine you had a chance to see them, one last time."

"You're fucking playing me. I wish you'd knock it off."

"Am I, Trooper? You think this is me being insincere?"

The bitch of it was, he didn't think that. He actually suspected Cash was letting on to sides he might not show any other person on the face of the earth, just in the off chance it helped his case.

"You're fucking crafty, man," Dixon said. "I'll give you that. Jaye's sharp. More common sense than I've seen in anyone his age, but you? No wonder he turned out the way he did."

"Look, I'll make an offer, okay? Since I saw this coming. No bullshit. I've got funds to cover your airfare and hotel costs. Yours and Jaye's. Pay the visit and see."

Dixon took a moment to think about that.

"Okay."

107

"I'm gonna say one more thing, before we wrap this up. Just hear me out. You don't need to respond. Just listen."

The water ran in the pipes in the ceiling. In the next room, someone was on another call and he picked up bits of what they were saying about a bear on someone's property.

"Jaye, Tony — they're out of the life. We get it. But that don't mean we don't still have their backs if needed. You know what I'm talking about, right? Keeping my boys safe? Making sure people like Marcus Slater don't get the upper hand no more. More than evens the playing field, don't you think? Ain't about favors. It's about looking out for your own. You need some help, say the word. Don't need to bother Jaye about it at all. Keeps him safe, right?"

A chill ran up Dixon's spine. At first, he was too stunned to speak.

"I think it's good for him, you know," Cash added. "To need to step up and watch out for his own, too. To be the one kicking ass for a change in a way that builds him up, keeps him on the right side of the law. Makes him the hero."

"How the hell do you know about Marcus?"

"Oh, come on, Dix. You think I'm stupid or something? You know, the way I see it, I saved him. He saved you. Maybe it's time to man up and do for someone else. Pay that back a little. Help out a guy who's got nothing and no one. Don't cost you nothing, really. Think about it."

"The hell it doesn't."

"I'll send information along on those tickets, all right? You know where I'll be."

Chapter 14:
The Heart of It

Idling in the lot outside of Jaye's office, Dixon had the engine on but the radio off. The sound of the wind blowing against the side of the vehicle was lulling enough for his strained state of mind. Once in a while, a good hard gust shook the Expedition, making Dixon feel even more like an unwanted surprise tucked inside some perfunctory wrapping lying in wait to be opened. The jostling was nature's way of trying to figure out what he was really up to in there.

Jaye came out of the entrance, coat bundled, head down, hands pocketed, eyes sharp as he watched his step and made a beeline for his sedan. He got right up to it and stopped, key in hand. After a three-count, he turned around and squinted right up at Dixon.

Pushing the button to lower his window, Dixon gave a lame greeting of, "Hey."

Some surprise he was.

"But I..." Jaye pointed to the car with confusion. "I drove today."

"Yeah, I know," Dixon said apologetically.

"So," Jaye looked around, as if for a clue. "Why are you here? Is something wrong? Was there a call, or emergency, or — "

"No. No, nothing like that. Sorry. Didn't intend to freak you out or anything," he said, knowing how he sounded suspiciously glum.

Jaye's hands dropped to his sides. "You look like someone ran over the dog, but we don't have a dog."

He opened his mouth to say something else, then shut it, then walked around the Expedition. Dixon pressed the button to raise the window again. A moment later, Jaye was seated beside him, facing him with a profoundly expectant expression. He even folded his hands in his lap.

"Spill."

"It was just nice to sit here, knowing you were inside. I don't know."

"What does that even mean?"

Dixon groaned and let his head fall back against the headrest. He closed his eyes and said, "Grant said I should talk to you."

"Grant. Said you should talk to me," Jaye parroted back. "As if you previously planned on not talking to me?"

"Cash wants to pay for our airfare and hotel costs to go to Sheridan."

"Oh-kay," Jaye said slowly, still squinting at Dixon. "And that's good news, or...?"

Dixon sighed heavily and gave up.

"I hate Cash."

"For offering to pay for shit?"

Dixon shot Jaye a sideways glance but didn't respond.

"For making me ride his dick every day? For existing? D, all of the above?"

"And this Tony guy is like a part of Cash, so..."

"You hate Tony."

Dixon made a groaning noise to express his resistance to admit that much.

"It's like if one of Marcus's accomplices came expecting favors from me."

"Does Marcus have accomplices?"

"I'm not saying it right."

"Tony isn't gonna hurt me."

"Physically? Of course not. Mentally? Emotionally?" Dixon shrugged, hands turned palm up. "I'm trying to be a realist here. I am. But this is going to mean someone seeing you as 'Johnny' all the time, forever. It won't go away."

"But I am Johnny," Jaye told him. "I'm Johnny right now. It's just a name, Dix. Tony being nearby wouldn't change who I am."

"Oh, come on," Dixon said with some anger. "That's a fucking line. Don't bullshit me. You know what I mean. You know there's a difference between when I was the guy who didn't even think of leaving Marcus after getting his fucking nose broken for daring to ask to go to a party, and the guy sitting here right now. I mean, I hope to hell there's a difference. I don't ever want someone to see me as that delusional coward again. That guy was ashamed and small and worthless and a mess."

Jaye dropped his gaze and shifted closer. He reached out and took Dixon's hand.

"Look at me." Dixon did so, feeling defensive with the last person he wanted to feel that way with. Jaye's eyes were bright, clear, and unconfused. "You're not that guy. You'll never be that guy again. Ever. But when we change, people notice. They change with us. Tony isn't Jinx anymore. So what makes you think he's going to assume I'm still Johnny?"

"I don't know how to protect you from this," Dixon confessed, getting to the heart of it at last. It raced up on him and he had to look away. He bit down hard on the inside of his cheek. Jaye grabbed him behind the neck, dragging him in and resting their foreheads together as if determined to narrow Dixon's focus whether he liked it or not. "You knew instinctively how to protect me from Marcus, but now I'm fucking it up, and — "

"Dixon Andrew Rowe — yes, I'm going there. I'm using the middle name — I'm not expecting you to turn into some other guy in order to fill this weird role you think you need to fill right now. You're not me. You're not Cash — and thank fuck you aren't. You're you. And I love you. You give me things without even trying that I've been searching for and not finding in everyone else in my life since I was born. You don't even have to try. It's just who you are, and that's a fucking miracle," he laughed. "You're so worried about caring for me in the perfectly right way as soon as you detect I might get upset, that you turn yourself inside out, twisted up like a crazy gymnastic pretzel on acid, just to try to manage it. Just to try to become this vision in your head of the impossible, exact right thing, when all I've ever wanted was just to have someone who cared *at all*. Who stuck in to the end, through the hard shit without diverging off on their own path along the way and consequently leaving me alone again. I don't need a thug protector in my life anymore. I need you. You're perfect just the way you are."

"Fuck," Dixon hissed. "I made it about me, didn't I? You're going through all of this with Cash and Tony and I'm the whining bitch again, aren't I? I — "

"Dixon. Stop," Jaye pleaded softly. "I'm not worried about Tony. I haven't even decided if I'm going to do it or not yet. But he's a friend, and I feel I owe him a visit just to see how he is, okay? That's all. I'm okay. I really am. But I know you're not. That's why I did what I did last night, trying to distract you and all."

"You really did distract me. That was incredible."

"Good," Jaye smiled. "It's okay to not be okay. This is all out of your element. It's not for me. This is expected. This is easy. Of all of the things Cash could have wanted from me, he's just asking me to give a shit about a guy who's so bad off, he's suicidal. And I can do that without him asking me a thing."

"You can't really be totally fine with going back to Sheridan," Dixon pressed.

"Okay. I'm not. I admit it. But I think it'll be good for me. Facing a fear and all. Plus, I'll have you with me. You can keep reminding me they're not gonna cuff me and throw me back in a cell."

"I can. I can totally do that."

"See? We've each got our specialties. That's why we fit together so nice," Jaye grinned.

"We do, don't we?"

"You okay to drive home? You can take a hot bath, drink some wine?"

"God, I don't deserve you," Dixon lamented.

"Likewise," Jaye said, more sincerely than Dixon was prepared to process. He hopped down from the passenger seat, shut the door and gave Dixon a little salute before heading to the sedan. It was time to go home.

Jaye took one last peek through the door into the bathroom at Dixon sprawled out in steaming water fizzing with Epsom salts, given to him by his sister as a way to help reduce stress in situations just like the one they were currently in. It said a lot to Jaye that Brekken knew enough to give him those types of things to have on hand just in case.

An mp3 player had some mellow meditation music playing and Jaye had stoked the fire to get the cabin nice and hot. Dixon leaned back against a rolled towel placed behind his head, wearing a subtle frown that creased his brow, but he looked a lot better than he had earlier.

Jaye inched the door shut, then closed it completely as soundlessly and unobtrusively as he could.

Without wasting a moment, he palmed his phone from the tabletop and went to sit on the floor on the far side of the cabin with his back leaned against the side of the bed, facing away from the bathroom door.

It wasn't a number he'd dialed often. There had only been a handful of instances of needing to track down Dixon that had warranted him using it at all.

It was picked up on the third ring.

"Hello?"

"It's Jaye, Sesi."

"Oh, hi, Jaye. I should really add you to my contacts. I keep forgetting. How are you?"

"I'm fine. Look, did you mean what you said before about Tony?" He kept his voice as lowered as he possibly could, speaking barely above a whisper. "About helping him out if you could?"

"Yes, absolutely," Sesi said with what sounded like genuine enthusiasm. "Maybe you already know this, but back when you came to town I tried to take over taking care of you from Dixon, but he wouldn't let me," she laughed.

Jaye grinned. "Can't imagine why he'd do a thing like that."

"Yeah, he had this totally obscure excuse of, 'he's real pretty,' if I'm remembering accurately. But that's the truth. I knew he was already dealing with a lot in his personal life at the time. He's got this good guy streak in him that he can't get away from even when it lands him in a lot of trouble, so I figured that was what was happening again. Zus — we're a community, you know? We're a big family. We have to take care of each other, whether it's making sure the elderly folks in town have enough food during the winters, making sure they're stocked with firewood, or giving the young people reasons to stay, finding them work or ways to take care of themselves — it's what keeps us going."

"I get that. It's one of the reasons why I've grown to love this place so much. It has a welcoming aspect that's really hard to find everywhere else. But at the same time, the people already living here have to be willing to accept a new person for it to work."

"True. There's definitely a trial process that happens. I know you're a guy who lives free of bullshit so hopefully you won't mind me saying this, but it happened with you, for sure. Some of my people think doing anything taboo or risky is only inviting bad luck, and when one bad winter can mean the end of an entire community, they don't want to take a chance. But at the same time, they recognize the importance of each spirit they encounter, and respect it. When you worked at the truck stop, you dealt with a lot of different folks every day. They were feeling you out same as you were trying to adjust. And, no offense, but someone with your record probably wouldn't be working for the municipality as an electrician the way you do."

"Oh, I know that for a fact. I saw it in Anchorage, with people my mom knew who had done time. It follows you like a bad smell. That's why I feel like I need to give this a shot for Tony. He's damn loyal and he's got a good head on his shoulders. If anything, I think following orders too well is what keeps getting him in trouble. And I'm not saying this is happening for sure. I want to see what we're working with first. He has to be a little bit self-sufficient. We can't provide him with nursing care or anything like that way out here. But if he can tackle some basics, I think he'd be more likely to thrive with our support. And maybe he could help out the town, too. Like you said, we need to give young people reasons to stay, or else it'll be a ghost town. It'll die. I don't want it to die."

"How about this?" she asked. "I'll do a little digging, see if anyone has a room they'd like to rent out for a small fee. That way, he wouldn't need to cover the cost of a full rent payment, and he wouldn't need to take care of a whole place on his own either. He could help out the owner in small ways, or just provide company. A lot of the older Native folks can't read or write — they're hunters trying to provide for their families, not scholars looking to grow their minds — so if Tony can manage some reading, he'll have plenty to do to help. There are a few people springing to mind who simply go nutty if they don't get some regular conversation with others. If we could line him up with a job doing as much as he can manage with his current physical challenges, it won't pay much but it should get him by."

A surge of energy shot through Jaye's arms, legs, up his back to his neck and right to the top of his head. He sat up straighter, leaning forward eagerly.

"That sounds perfect, Sesi. It really does. I'd be grateful if you could."

"Is this something I should keep to myself?"

Jaye glanced back at the bathroom. The door was still shut.

"Yes, for now. It's all up in the air anyway."

"What about Dixon?"

"Yeah." Jaye used the edge of his nail to trace a groove in the floorboard below him. "That's trickier. He's not really okay with any of this yet. I don't blame him. I know trust issues can be hard to shake, and he's got some doozies."

"Is it just because Tony has ties to the gang?"

"Kind of. That's part of it, but he blames Tony for being there for... things. And not trying to stop them."

"Do you blame him for that?"

Jaye blew out a breath and thought about how to answer.

"If you need anyone to talk to about that stuff, Jaye, I hope you know I'm here. I'm a good listener, and I'm not actually family, which can be a bonus."

"Thanks, Sesi. I appreciate it. I don't know, really. It's complicated."

"Was Tony there for things he should have stopped? Or objected to, at least?"

"Oh yeah."

"How bad?"

Thinking specifically of the gang bang porno, Jaye felt the old weight of those emotional hurdles sag down on him once more.

"Bad."

He kind of wanted to tell her. Saying the words out loud might help give them less power. Funny how he never felt that way with his prison counselor.

"If I," he said hesitantly, "tell you something, would you swear not to tell Dixon, or Brekken, or anyone?"

"Of course, Jaye. Brekken is my friend and Dixon is my co-worker, but I can be discreet. It's part of being a cop. It's also how I was raised. You keep things close when it's called for."

115

"Okay. Well, there was this one thing I keep coming back to. There was a lot that happened while I knew Jinx — Tony — but this was the worst, for me. It's something I've struggled to get past, just on my own."

He gave her the basics, about why Cash had found it necessary to pay the debt, and how it went down, without giving any gory details.

"So, I'm pretty sure he was just one of the guys holding me down, that he didn't actually... rape me. But still. He was there. He didn't say a word. He helped it happen. But he was following orders. There would have been no way for him to say no to Cash without fucking up his own life in awful ways."

"Oh my god, Jaye. That's just horrifying. I had no idea. I'm so, so sorry. That must have been so traumatic for you. Have you been able to talk to a therapist about any of it?"

"No. Not really. They gave me one. A counselor. But I've got my own trust issues and it just hasn't worked out. It's not something I dwell on. I don't dwell on any of it, really. Not anymore. But just with all of this stuff about Tony — Dixon doesn't know about that part of it at all, and it just makes me hesitate, I guess."

"Of course it does. And I can't really know what you went through or how this is for you, but I do have experience with needing to fulfill a role in order to do my job and keep people safe. Even if there are other factors going on, you should always listen to your gut and your conscience, first. You know?"

"Yeah. I know."

"What's your gut telling you?"

Jaye shifted position, drawing his knee up to his chest.

He thought about Cora, lying on her couch, doped out of her mind and unresponsive. He thought of Kris waving goodbye on a darkened street outside a diner when he should have been heading home with Jaye to help keep him safe. He thought about Dixon, crouched on the floor in his childhood bedroom, crying and about to lose his mind over Marcus's continued abuse and threats. Then he thought about Tony, sitting in a cell, his hands near useless, surrounded by men who knew he took cock and would again with little complaint, if they could get away with giving it to him again beyond the notice of the Disciples or Cash. He thought of Tony wanting to kill himself, facing a world that didn't want him or had a place for him.

"It's telling me it's nice to be needed."

There were sounds in the bathroom. Water was running down the drain. Dixon was walking around.

"I've gotta go," he told Sesi.

"I'll get to work on this, okay? Call me whenever you need to, or want to."

"I will. Thanks, Sesi. He's not a bad person, okay? I know he's not. Just because you've done bad things doesn't mean you're worthless."

"I know, hon. Believe me. Take care, okay?"

"You too. Bye."

He set the phone aside and sat there a while longer. When the door opened, and Dixon asked, "Hey. You all right?" Jaye smiled at him and said, "Yeah. I'm good. Just thinking. Did the bath help?"

"It did, actually," Dixon replied. He wore a towel around his waist and nothing else. His wet hair was tousled and his skin flushed. Seeing him like that made Jaye want to just curl up in bed beside him, but other things had to come first.

"Good. Help me make dinner?"

"Love to," Dixon smiled.

Chapter 15:
Old Times

Jaye was on his knees on the bed, with Dixon on all fours in front of him. They were naked and Jaye was balls deep in Dixon's ass, which was flushed pink with slight welts from being repeatedly slapped by Jaye's hand. Jaye hadn't started to fuck him yet. The perfect, snug heat of him, gripping Jaye's aching erection, and the way his posture cried out for more of anything Jaye wanted to give, was invigorating. It made it seem like Jaye could do anything, like all power in the situation was his to take. Dixon arched his back and clenched briefly on Jaye's cock, so Jaye slapped him again. Hard.

"Relax."

The clenching stopped and goosebumps pebbled Dixon's skin. Jaye felt his subtle shiver through their connected bodies. He glimpsed Dixon's duty belt over on his dresser and he felt again the pleasure of having an officer of the law get naked, offer up his ass and beg for Jaye to fuck him hard and slow. For someone with Jaye's history, there really was nothing better. It was a more exquisite opiate than he could have concocted in his wildest imaginings.

And it wasn't just that Dixon was a cop. His body was strong, thick with muscle. His shoulders were broad, his legs toned, glutes firm, arms bulging. Physically, he far outmatched Jaye in any and every sense. In a wrestling match between them, Jaye's only hope would be in playing the crazy wild card and breaking some rules to win.

Jaye traced the raised welts on Dixon's ass with his hand, feeling heat bake from the tender flesh. Then he let his fingers quest over to Dixon's rim, stretched out around Jaye's shaft. Rubbing it lightly, feeling the slick of lube there, Jaye heard Dixon's breath catch. Lowering his head, Dixon surrendered to the intimate touch. He stayed loose, open, so Jaye pulled back, letting his cock withdraw until the head caught on that stretched rim. He pushed back in, all the way, and heard Dixon's grateful moan of pure bliss. There was no pain in it. No fear or anxiety. He only, purely, wanted. He had given himself over, with trust and reverence.

Jaye spanked him again, watching Dixon's ass jiggle with the impact, feeling Dixon's inner muscles tighten in reflex while he withdrew again, causing the friction to intensify in the best kind of way.

Rubbing over Dixon's inner thigh, then rolling his balls in a hand, Jaye heard him give a yearning sigh, pushing back greedily into the next thrust. When Jaye's fingers found Dixon's cock, it was soaking wet from being so damned hot for it. It throbbed in Jaye's grip. He watched Dixon muffle a hard groan in a pillow while he fought to be still and obey Jaye's previous requests to not do a damned thing without permission.

"Do you even know what this does for me?" Jaye wondered aloud. "I mean really. Do you?"

He traced Dixon's dripping crown with the pad of his fingertip and heard him swallow a whine. His hips stuttered slightly as he fought to be still and take it without trying for more.

He wasn't sure that Dixon could answer, he was so far gone into a place where words had no meaning, and only physical reality had any power. Jaye was well familiar with it himself.

He let go. He pulled out. Dixon's ass expelled his lube-slick, reddened shaft. It sprung up between Jaye's legs as he shifted back for a good look at his prize. Dixon shivered and kept his head bowed, shoulders down, ass up and spread wide. He didn't clench, his hole stretched looser and shining with wetness.

"Please," Dixon begged. He shifted his legs even wider and sat back to spread his ass more in invitation. "Please."

Jaye thought of Kris, who had been more than content with blowjobs and hand relief. He thought of Cash, and Dorrance, and every other guy in Sheridan who'd gotten incredibly familiar with the inside of Jaye's ass while keeping him in his place, keeping him tamed and using him purely as the whore he'd been, through and through. Not one of them had given him anything close to what Dixon had. None of them had been strong enough to be weak.

"My first," Jaye said with awe, slipping his thumb into Dixon's opening, pushing it as far as it would go, then pivoting his wrist to feather his fingers over Dixon's sac.

Dixon let out a gruff moan.

"No wonder my offers in Sheridan had such appeal and value. There really is nothing better than this. Keep your drugs, your cigarettes, your booze — all of it. Doesn't compare." He rubbed the insane softness that was the inside of Dixon's sphincter, liking the way his hole puckered around the thumb, liking the sight of such a strong cop, and a smart, good man with an incredible heart, desperate to be taken and tamed only by Jaye.

Quickly, Jaye replaced thumb with cock, driving hard into Dixon, causing him to grunt and tense up. Holding him by the hip, Jaye pounded him, knocking the breath from Dixon's lungs. Dixon reached for the headboard to brace himself as the force of Jaye's thrusts knocked him repeatedly forward. He didn't hold anything back and grit his teeth together as he poured all of his emotion and energy into fucking Dixon dizzy.

He didn't stop until he came, a wash of tingling and euphoria crashing through him as he did. Gasping, Jaye came down, riding out the aftershocks more slowly.

Dixon was growling, panting. It woke up some deep-seated animal instincts in Jaye. Ones he hadn't known he possessed until Dixon found them.

He pulled out, his cock softening, and picked up the huge phallus waiting and ready by his side. Spreading Dixon's hole with the fingers of his left hand, Jaye fit the massive silicone head at Dixon's hole and slowly fed it through, being careful with the stretch to prevent tears. A glance up showed Dixon grabbing at the hair on the back of his head. His panting had gained an edge, his pitch climbing. The head passed through and Dixon's ass began to swallow the rest, taking it in with little effort on Jaye's part to hurry it inside. Bracing his palm back near the fake nuts, he guided the phallus along and kept Dixon's hole pried open with his left hand.

Dixon struggled to take it and his cries said as much. The toy was much bigger than Jaye in both circumference and length, and he didn't stop pushing until Dixon had taken the whole thing, every inch. When the plastic sac was resting flush against Dixon's body, Jaye heard how hard he was breathing, saw him tremble, smelled the sweat on his skin and the sex in the air around them.

"Relax. I'm not starting until you do. I know you can."

"Keep — keep talking," Dixon stammered breathlessly. "H-helps."

Maybe, for Dixon, it had become too easy to imagine it was Marcus back there instead of Jaye. Jaye knew what a nightmare that would be, if the tables were turned, so he complied.

"Okay. I was just thinking how no one else I've been with has been man enough to submit to me like this — submit to anyone, actually. I think it takes an impressive kind of man to own himself, his body, his pleasure, and his sexuality, to this extent. To be capable, intimidating, and powerful in every other facet of life, but to let himself be this vulnerable in bed. No one else ever let me fuck them, period, let alone let me have them like this. So I never realized how much I loved it, until I had you, Dix."

It had helped. He could tell. Dixon's body had unclenched completely. He was lax, hugging the pillow under his head and chest, staying open for when Jaye decided Dixon was ready for the huge phallus to begin moving.

When Jaye did begin to move the toy, slowly withdrawing it. He heard Dixon's happy sigh and saw Dixon's cock jump.

"You want to take care of me, Dix? Help me feel strong? Like I can take care of myself, and you, and everything else I need to, no problem? Make me feel like I don't have a care in the world? That the past and future don't matter one bit?" He pushed the toy back into Dixon, drawing a shuddering moan, and kept it moving, pumping in and out of him. "This is all I need. Just this. Do you understand why? Can you? I've had a lot of scary guys intimidate me into giving up my body to them. They made me cry, made me bleed, tore me up emotionally, psychologically, and physically. But none of them could do what I can do. None of them can make a real man beg like I can."

Dixon was taking the ride, oh-so-subtly pushing into each thrust, pulling forward to hurry the withdrawal. When Jaye lightly stroked Dixon's still-dripping cock, so hard it jutted up tight to his pelvis, Dixon let out a desperate cry.

"Oh please... please don't stop... please more... Jaye..."

Jaye smiled and rolled onto his back, sliding up between Dixon's widely spread legs. Once he was lying there, beneath Dixon's pelvis, Jaye began to fuck him harder with the huge phallus, slamming it into him. At the same time, he gave Dixon's delicious cock a long lick. Dixon cried out and reached to weave his fingers through Jaye's hair. Jaye felt him playing with it as he swallowed Dixon's down, humming with triumph, savoring the taste of pre-come as it coated his tongue. He relaxed his throat and swallowed, feeling Dixon convulse, his breath choking off. Jaye felt come flood his throat and took it right down too. He kept the phallus moving constantly, taking Dixon over the edge. Dixon never stopped shouting, never stopped touching Jaye's hair.

Jaye let him roll over onto his side as his legs quivered with exhaustion. He also let Dixon manhandle him, easily, up into his arms, burying his face against the side of Jaye's neck, winding his arms around Jaye's back and hooking his legs behind Jaye's body. Engulfed, Jaye held his love and knew he had the answer to everything — to Cash, Tony, Sheridan, Burt, Earl, Anchorage, Cora and all of it — right in his arms.

"Thank you, Dixon," Jaye whispered. Dixon sought his lips and kissed them. He didn't dare let go, not for a moment.

"I'm so lucky I get to love you," Dixon told him, "and have you love me back. Whatever you need, you can have it, okay?"

"Okay," Jaye grinned.

"But what I need right now is a nap," Dixon chuckled.

A hush blanketed both of them, broken only by the wind screaming outside of the tiny cabin.

Jaye thought of his call with Sesi, and the growing certainty in his gut that he would go to Sheridan even if Cash didn't pay their way. He'd go for Tony, and his own need to see that part of his life was in the past, and wasn't going to follow him any longer. He thought of the way he'd needed to walk and be alone the day the letter came, and how part of him still had that impulse — to leave everything in Zus behind and go hide even deeper in the world, somehow, to cut all ties and just escape the threads that led to Ecker, the Disciples, and all of his ghosts. He thought of the hell he'd lived in, not so long ago, and how eager it must be to have him back one way or other. He thought of a federal prison full of men who saw him as a thug whore, and of bringing Dixon willingly into that world. He thought of

Dixon finding out every single thing Jaye had done while in Sheridan, all of the gory details. He thought of bashing his head on concrete just to try to make it all stop, and of taking meds to silence his own mind until he was a drooling mess. He thought of all of the times he'd pretended to fight back and washed away real tears in the shower's spray. He thought of...

Piggy, piggy, piggy... time to play. Say thank you.

Chained in an unused room with all the lights out and his pants around his ankles, the repeated blows to his head making it ring and ache, the hard thwacks to his testicles making his stomach cramp sickeningly, his insides burning with dry friction and sharp pain as the nightstick kept raping him, and not fighting back at all, but only saying, 'yes sir' and 'thank you, sir' so they wouldn't add onto his sentence and ruin his one chance at escape.

Gonna pull your guts out. Make you watch.

A brutal man's finger pushed through a slash in his side, hooked around a loop of his intestines, one fraction of a second away from yanking them out, hand over hand, until they were spilled around him in a bloody pile and no way to ever shove them back inside.

You got this coming, faggot. Tell Cash, he steals from us, we steal from him.

Raped bloody in a bathroom stall, pulled up by his hair, beaten unconscious and left on the tile with the piss stains.

Screaming.

Carving out a man's eyes with a plastic spoon. Watching one of them pop and ooze down the bloody side of a face twisted in pure agony.

"Hey. Hey, you're shaking. Jaye? Jaye, look at me."

"No. No, no, no..."

He huddled down, buried his face against Dixon's shoulder, shaking his head. Fingers twisted down his throat, up his ass, into his guts.

Gonna snitch you out, Johnny. Gonna tell. Come on back inside with us. You'll never, ever leave. We'll sink our hooks into you, pull you apart, piece by bloody piece. It'll take a long, long time...

Jaye retched. He scrambled out of Dixon's hold and ran for the bathroom. He slammed and locked the door shut behind him. He got to the basin, crumpling to his knees just as his dinner came rushing up for a second visit.

Just like old times.

Chapter 16:
Burning

When he'd continued to refuse to open the door, Dixon had gotten a screwdriver, removed the handle completely, and got inside anyway. When Jaye hadn't responded to demands to come sit down, to get up, Dixon had lifted him off of the bathroom floor and carried him to the couch. He'd used a cool washcloth to clean Jaye's face and gave him a glass of water to sip.

The ghosts were laughing.

Dixon wrapped him in a blanket to try to stop the shaking.

"Jaye, talk to me," Dixon demanded. "You were doing so good! What is this? What's wrong?"

Jay grunted, then shook his head, pressing the heels of his palms into his eyes.

Faggot.

Piggy.

You fucking worthless trash.

You had this coming.

We're coming.

At the top of his lungs, he screamed, "Shut up!"

"God no," Dixon groaned. "Jaye, listen to me," he said with the cop's voice, trying to cut through. "Listen. They're not here. No one else is here."

"I won't. I won't go. I won't go back. They can't — "

"Jaye, no one is making you go back, okay? No one. You're home. You're safe. I love you. You're okay, I swear. No one touches you. No one hurts you. They don't even get close."

"They'll find me. They always find me."

"Jaye!"

"NO, Dixon! No," Jaye yelled."You don't understand! You don't know, okay?"

"I'm trying," Dixon told him tenderly, taking his face in his hands. "I'm doing my best. You went off in your head, started to think about things that are better off forgotten about, right? You don't need to take it all on. You don't. You're doing so much better, but you still need to cut yourself some slack. Okay? Please? You can't let it all in. You need to let it go. Leave it behind. You need to try."

Jaye held onto Dixon's arm. His heartbeat was finally slowing down, but he still wanted to puke. He kept spiraling back there, to that alley, to that cell, to that dark, secret place, to that bathroom stall, to that bloody storage room. Then it all started to overlap, to smother him.

"Fucked and fucked-up. That's me. That's Johnny. That's all I'll ever be," he whispered. "They used to tell me that and it's true. It's really true."

Dixon sat beside him on the couch and pulled him onto his lap. Curled up there, huddled in the blanket, Jaye felt Dixon's arms come around him again.

"You're not Johnny anymore. You're not that guy. You're home. You're safe. No one is forcing you to go back there. You're okay, babe, I promise. I have you."

But it was all as good as done. Jaye knew it was. Cash would buy the tickets. Sesi would find the place. Jaye would have to go to Sheridan and he'd never leave. They'd rat him out about what he'd done to Tio and keep him there. He'd never see Dixon again, because they'd dissect him before he ever got the chance. Maybe they'd take his eyes first, like he took Tio's. What would they take next? His hands, so he couldn't fight back? His feet, so he couldn't run? His cock and balls, to prove he was nothing but their bitch? They'd tear him apart, piss on the remains.

"I can't," he muttered. "I can't do anything right. Can't even do this right. I'm fucking it up for Tony. It's my fault. My responsibility. Everything… everything he's gone through — "

"Jaye, stop."

"They should have crushed my hands. Took my eyes."

"Stop!" Dixon held him tighter. "Just stop. Please."

"I can't say no, can I? Couldn't say no to Cash. To Hax or Dorrance in solitary. To Ecker in the secret place. To the fucking film crew, watching me cry. To Tony."

"You can say no. You're allowed to say no. I want you to say no," Dixon said urgently.

Jaye started to cry.

Dixon hushed to him and kissed the top of his head.

Warmth and exhaustion took him before the pain and fear ran out. He cried himself to sleep. Hours later, he woke in bed, in Dixon's embrace. Then, he lay there, wakeful, the rest of the night watching the cabin's door, listening for voices, wanting to run.

—◻—◻—◻—

When Dixon woke at five a.m. and went to roll over to his other side, he saw Jaye sitting up in bed, staring out into space. That startled him enough to banish the vestiges of sleep.

"You're awake," Dixon said drowsily, rubbing his eyes clear. "What's wrong?"

Jaye shook his head. Dixon realized Jaye had a pad of paper in his lap, his knees drawn up to block Dixon's line of sight. He reached for the pad and Jaye didn't move to stop him.

He hadn't been drawing the cabin, or Dixon, or anything else Dixon might have guessed. It was a view of the inside of a cell. The cinderblock, the combination sink and toilet, the small desk and small window.

"What are you doing, babe?" Dixon pulled himself upright, facing Jaye.

Jaye dropped his gaze and chewed on his lower lip a moment.

"What do you need?" Dixon asked, changing tactics. "Coffee? Massage?"

"A walk?"

"In the dark?"

"Sure."

"You're not going to work today." It wasn't a question. "But I do have to go, unless you need me to pull some strings."

"Can I go with you?" Again, he didn't make eye contact as he said it. Dixon felt him pulling away, almost like they were back in the muddy snow outside the Stop and Shop, and Jaye was just hoping

127

not to be charged with petty theft for taking some potato chips to sate his ravenous hunger, but didn't believe his luck would spare him that much.

"Of course you can."

Dixon sat on the edge of the bed and stretched. Jaye stayed where he was. How long had he been like that? How many hours?

After making the coffee and taking a quick shower, Dixon dressed in his warmest clothes. Jaye was already dressed and waiting by the door once Dixon was ready. Thermoses of coffee in hand, they went out for a walk under the moonlit, starry sky.

Before taking his first sip, Dixon called in to Jaye's office, saying he was too sick to come in that day. When he hung up and tucked away the phone, Jaye shot him a glance.

"Can we just not talk for a while? And just walk? Please?"

Dixon didn't like the beaten down, broken sound to the pleas, so he capitulated. "Yeah. Yeah, that's fine." He did take Jaye's hand though. "Is this okay?"

They both wore gloves, but it was nice to feel the life in Jaye's hand as it grasped onto his.

"Mm-hmm."

There were so many questions, and Dixon knew that was why Jaye didn't want to speak. He wasn't ready. It was painfully clear. Still…

Dixon consulted his mental checklist of frightening things Jaye had referenced without thinking during his episode the previous night. He couldn't even decide what was the creepiest one: the taken eyes, the film crew, the secret place.

Their footsteps crunched on gravel as they followed the road heading west. There wasn't a cloud in the sky and some meteors shot through inky space. Dixon made a wish on one, hoping for something good to come out of all of their pain, somehow. Their breath fogged the air. Now and then, they took a steamy drink from their mugs. Dixon liked the way the coffee heated him up from inside.

What had gone so wrong the night before? Their lovemaking had been mind-blowingly good. After, as they lay together, something had happened. Jaye had slipped off in his head to somewhere bad. Could it have been prevented? Should it have? Had it just been overdue? Dixon knew from experience that some demons needed facing, one way or another. They were patient, but persistent. Maybe all of Jaye's triumphs and victories just meant it was time for a stumble.

Dixon glanced over at Jaye's beautiful face as often as he dared. Jaye's eyes stayed focused on the path ahead, his coat's hood drawn up to shield him from the wind and most of Dixon's snooping. He was an enigma, so young and so old at the same time. His body seemed fresh and new, untested by the world, but his spirit had seen too much and been worn down dangerously, over and over again.

They walked for a few miles, then doubled back. Jaye's pace never slackened but kept Dixon urging himself on, even as his leg muscles began to ache, his lungs chilled from the frigid, early-morning air.

When they got in sight of the cabin, Dixon broke the silence.

"I've got to trek up north today, but we can wait until after mid-morning if we want to take the call and make a decision one way or another. If not, we can blow it off and head up earlier."

"I can't deal with it today. I need some time," Jaye told him.

"Do you want me to tell Cash to back off and let you think about it longer? So he doesn't reach out in other ways?"

Jaw clenched, hands shoved down deep in his pockets, Jaye stopped. He strolled away from Dixon, eyes on the horizon line where the sun was beginning to rise.

"Yeah, I guess you should. Make it official."

"I can always have Sesi take you out on one of her runs if you don't want to be there."

A muscle in Jaye's jaw twitched at that. "Nah."

Dixon pulled out his keys and unlocked the vehicle. "Look, I know you think you need to keep things from me. You have your reasons, but I want honesty here, Jaye. I want you to be real with me, like you always have been. I can take it. I can take a lot. Whatever it is isn't going to make me stop loving you, or love you less."

"It's ugly," Jaye breathed, and Dixon heard the pain in the words, the way things from his past still ate at him, chewing away from the inside, carving holes. "It's real damn ugly."

"You think I don't know ugly? When my ex mouth-raped you while holding a knife to your throat? When I fucking shot and killed him for doing it?"

"It's not the same. That was noble. You were my hero when you did that. None of this is fucking noble — "

"What are you really scared of, here?" Dixon demanded. "Just tell me. Is it Cash? Is it going back there? What?"

"They..." Jaye gestured with one gloved hand, but his voice wavered, then broke. He cleared his throat and tried again, his soft, sexy rasp lending an eerie flavor to the words. "They could rat me out, Dix. They could tell someone what I did. Get me charged. Get me..."

"For what?" Dixon asked with exasperation.

Jaye hardened up even more, taking on more of the shell of the ruthless criminal and leaving behind all of the softness of Dixon's sweet lover. Seeing the transformation sent a shiver up Dixon's back that had nothing to do with the cold. He took a step toward Jaye, but Jaye took a backward step to maintain their distance.

"For taking his eyes," Jaye said, staring right at Dixon when he said it. "I took Tio's eyes."

It was more quiet, but it was different this time. It wasn't filled with the rush of morning wind, or birdsong, but only the soft rumble of the Expedition's engine and the ticking of the turn signal as they rounded into the parking lot. They soon found a spot and the vehicle stopped.

Dixon hadn't looked at Jaye once the whole drive, and Jaye felt the rejection like another form of creeping madness.

Fucked and fucked-up, eh Johnny? You piggy whore. You fucking come-rag.

The voice sounded like Cash. Just like him.

It had been months since he'd heard the ghosts.

Months.

One of them caressed up his inner thigh and he swatted it away, feeling pure frustration and shame burn its way into his gut.

Dixon grabbed Jaye's hand — the one that had done the swatting.

"What film crew?"

Jaye shook his head, tried to pull free. A finger slid down his throat, tickling his gag reflex and, squeezing his eyes shut, he wished he could bite it off.

Dixon refused to let him pull away. He didn't let go.

"Tell me, right now."

"You should have set me on fire. Burnt me up like that poor fucking bastard whore. Burnt to a crisp in — "

"Stop it!" Dixon raged, loud enough to make Jaye's ears ring.

In Jaye's memory, he heard the door in ad-seg slam shut, locking him inside. He saw all of those men — too many of them — waiting to take him apart. He remembered the panic, the pain, and telling himself to role-play his way through it, even though it felt like the worst kind of betrayal and like there wasn't a safe place left in the whole world.

"I won't tell you that, Dix. No way."

"You think I can't take it? You think I'm so fucking fragile? You told me earlier you took a man's eyes out of his head with a goddamned spoon! How is this worse?!"

"Because it is. It's worse than Tio. Worse than anything. It was the moment I knew there was no coming back from any of it. Ever." He gave a miserable, hollowed-out laugh. "And I was right."

"Do you regret it? What you did to Tio?"

"No." Jaye looked Dixon in the eye. "I'd do it again. They would have kept coming for me. First it was bloody rape and a beating in a bathroom stall. Then it was a shiv in my gut. They would have kept poking new holes in me. I know it. They would have let me heal up again, after, and come again. Slow death. Torture. Just to send a message. Just to spook Cash. Look at what they did to Tony, for fuck's sake. He's crippled for life. I had to protect myself. No one else was going to do it."

"I thought it was Cash's job to protect you."

Jaye laughed again, but it turned on him fast, shifting into something closer to a sob.

"It was a deal, Dixon. My body in exchange for some security, but debts needed to be paid. Cash couldn't fuck me without a dirty guard in his pocket, paid to look the other way. Who do you think payment was?"

Furious, eyes blazing, tensed and charged, like electricity was arcing off of him into the air around them, Dixon seethed, "He gave you to the fucking dirty guard?"

Jaye gave a cold smile. He shook his head. "You're really not going to let this go, are you?"

"You can't carry all of this shit anymore alone. Please, just tell me."

"Okay. Okay, fine. So, Cash was a long-term arrangement, right? Dorrance would have to look the other way for years. So he wanted a favor that would pay off for years too."

"What favor?"

"Porn." Jaye looked down at his lap and wished Dixon would let his hand go. He felt dirty. Disgusting. "A gang bang rape scene in administrative segregation. Guards and inmates, all having a go while I was shackled and pinned down. They... they filmed it. Let go. Dixon, let go!" He gave a hard, desperate yank at his hand, but Dixon was determined. His grip was painfully strong. "Let me go!"

"Never. I never will," Dixon swore, pulling Jaye into a hug. Jaye fought it at first, but then he felt it as the familiar scent of Dixon's skin got in Jaye's head, and the feel of him against Jaye's body lured him as no other intoxicant could. It was home, right there in Dixon's arms. So Jaye let it wrap around him, breathing like he'd just run five miles to get away from a pack of wolves, nipping at his heels. "I'm so sorry. I'm sorry. I've got you. No one is ever going to hurt you again. Ever. I swear it. I swear, okay?"

Dixon's strong hand wrapped behind Jaye's head, the fingers twining through his hair, sending shivers as the fingertips moved against his scalp. Lips brushed kisses over Jaye's flushed skin. Where had this love been when Jaye had needed it? Why had it been so damned hard to find?

Chapter 17:
Sucker Punch

"Here," Sesi said, passing Dixon an ice pack.

"Thanks," he muttered, setting it against his aching hand. Jaye's eyebrow was raised in judgment, but Dixon didn't care.

After they'd come into the station that morning, Jaye had gone to splash cold water on his face and pull himself together in the bathroom. Meanwhile, Dixon headed to the lockers and punched a few of them as hard as he could. Sure, he was paying for it now, but he was happy to. He hated making the mental connection between paying for his anger with physical, self-inflicted pain, and Jaye's willingness to pay for security with his participation as the victim in a gang bang rape scene, filmed for posterity and being sold even now to vile scum all over the world to beat off to.

"Calm the fuck down," Jaye told him, low and steady. "Or we're going home."

"I need to take this call," Dixon argued, wanting to punch some more things. At least the agony in his hand helped cloud out the imagined sound of Jaye's pleading sobs coming from inside a crowded, locked prison cell.

"The fuck you do. I'll talk to him."

"No, you won't. Over my dead body will you ever talk to that piece of shit again," Dixon warned.

Sesi was there, lingering, as if she wasn't sure if she needed to step in, or how to do it. Dixon couldn't figure it out. She hadn't asked a single thing. It was almost like…

"No. You've gotta be kidding me."

"What?" Sesi asked innocently.

Turning to stare at Jaye, Dixon said with astonishment, "She knows?! How the hell does she know?!"

Jaye looked up at the ceiling, guilty as sin. His cheeks began to color. "I just thought — "

"You told her about this before me?!" Dixon yelled. "I'm the one who fucking loves you, Jaye!"

"Don't blame him for wanting to confide in someone, Dixon. He's dealing with a lot," Sesi argued.

"You stay the fuck out of it!" Dixon raged.

"Knock it off," Jaye snapped. "She was helping me. You should appreciate that there are people willing to do that. I get that you're pissed, but this is exactly why I didn't want to tell you."

"Dixon, take the day, all right? I'll cover what I need to here. Go cool off."

"We'll take the call," Jaye chimed in. "Tell him the answer is no, and leave. If you need to go to the gym and get some of this out, you can do it there instead of punching metal doors like a dumbass."

"I wanna wring his fucking neck," Dixon said with wonder. "I really do. That he put his hands on you, every single day, after putting you through *that*."

Only he'd done a lot more than put his hands on Jaye. Dixon had never been a jealous person, but the absolute cruelty of the relationship between Jaye and Cash left him flabbergasted. It didn't help that Jaye didn't seem to possess any anger over it towards Cash, but only continued to suffer the consequences of the brutality directed towards him.

"Rowe, you need to stop dwelling on it. Do some work. Some paperwork or something. Field calls from the main line for a while. You're driving yourself nuts and it helps no one," Sesi told him, taking control in ways he was unable to at the moment.

"I'm..." he deflated a little. "I'm sorry for snapping at you."

"No sweat. I can take it, can't I? You gonna listen to me?"

"Yeah," he admitted, shifting in his chair and gazing at the stack of files on his desk.

"You need to walk it off first? Cool down?"

"Thought I did all the walking I needed this morning, but... yeah. I guess."

He stood and asked Jaye, "You'll be all right here?"

"Safest place in Zus, right? Anyone messes with me, I'll sic Sesi on 'em." Jaye smiled. Dixon wondered how he managed it, how he had ever been able to smile again after Sheridan.

With that thought, he turned and walked out, trying to make sense of madness.

—▭—▭—▭—

"You okay?" Sesi asked Jaye once Dixon had left. He was sitting in a chair beside Dixon's desk — the one usually reserved for citizens and criminals coming to report a crime, or answer for one. Strangely, he liked sitting there, straddling that moral line. It fit.

"Me? Sure," he told her. "Never better."

"Bullshit, sunshine."

Jaye sighed. "Yeah. But what am I supposed to say? Shit doesn't let me go. I don't know if it ever will, so I force myself to smile and keep going."

Quieter, she asked, "I understand that. I do. But you're giving up on Tony?"

"I have to," he said reluctantly. "I wanted to do this. The moral thing. The good guy thing. I wanted to be that guy for once. But I've got enough trouble getting myself straight, let alone taking that on. And going to Sheridan? Everything in me says that's wrong, that it's the worst thing I could do. I don't know. I just have to own it when enough is enough. I've just started to make a life here. The last thing I want is to ruin it all."

Sesi looked at him a moment, then nodded. "Let me know if you need anything."

"Thanks. I will."

Ten minutes later, Dixon was back and dove right in to his files. Jaye watched him work, focusing on and frowning at the pages, scrawling in his tight, slanted handwriting. The texture of it was alluring. Jaye wished he could have a page full of it to run his fingers over, feeling the condensed ridges of Dixon's words, flowing right out of his hand.

He didn't do anything else but watch. Maybe someone else would have been bored, but Jaye had been given plenty of time to adjust to days filled with limited stimuli. To be somewhere he knew he was safe, with his lover at his side and friends nearby, it was the closest thing to heaven he had.

An hour later, the phone rang at Dixon's desk.

Intuition made Jaye's heart jump and he bit down on his back teeth.

"He's early," Dixon commented warily, looking at the phone like he wanted to pull his gun on it.

After two rings, he answered.

That's when everything went wrong. When everything changed on them, permanently, for better or worse.

The voice was unique in its eeriness, full of empty rooms and barricaded doors. Wind swirled between the sounds, suggesting nightmares and the faded, trampled remains of a man who used to be full of light and energy. Dixon heard and believed all of it, with every single one of the hairs on his body standing on end and a queasy knot in his gut.

"Trooper... Trooper Rowe, sir? Sorry. Sorry to bother you, sir. I'm sorry."

Dixon was barely aware of Jaye sitting forward, mouthing a question. Most of his mind was taken up with hellish comparisons between the way he sometimes heard Jaye's torment in his voice, and the way he suddenly understood why Cash had sent the letter. Now, it all made sense.

His mouth dry, Dixon opened up to speak, but the words wouldn't come.

"I shouldn't have called. I shouldn't. Sorry, I — "

"Tony? Is that you?"

It happened quickly. One moment, Dixon was flailing for the right thing to say. The next, the phone was yanked right out of his hand.

"Hey!" he protested, but Jaye's eyes were blazing and he wouldn't be stopped. Dixon knew it wasn't his place to even begin to try.

"Jinx? Sorry — Tony? You there? It's me. It's — "

"Johnny." There was gladness in the realization, but so much else too. Tony had been draped over life's grinding stone and worn down paper thin. There was no doubt about it. "No. Jaye. You're Jaye now. Cash told me. He warned me. I... I'm sorry."

"Talk to me, man. Tell me how you are. What you need. Anything. Is someone watching out for you? Cash? The crew?"

"I-I," There was a clatter, then silence. After some rustling, Tony's voice came back. "Sorry. Dropped it. Hard to, uh, hold things."

"I know. I heard. Who's helping you, Tony?"

"I was, uh, protected custody? Sometimes? But then... No. No good. Came back and the blacks. The blacks, they... So Hax. He. He's my... He keeps me."

A surge of anxiety and sympathetic panic swept through Jaye, along with bits of the memory of Hax mouth-raping him in ad-seg at Cash's command, and the disturbing way he'd turned himself off to go through it. "Keeps you the way Cash used to keep me?"

"Yeah, that's it," Tony said almost cheerfully, but it was fake. An act. The tremble in the words betrayed his real feelings on the matter. "And they backed off, you know. They did. And he only... when there's people watching. People watching..."

Cold. The blood ran out through his feet and he was left freezing. A hand gripped his shoulder and he saw he was standing, that Dixon was next to him and Sesi nearby with her hands on her hips, eyes alert.

"Tony, you got any people outside? Any at all?"

"Well, you know, my fiancé . But she broke it off a year after I got locked up and I heard through a guy that she... she got married," Tony chuckled, in that scary, false way. "Two years ago, maybe."

"Family?"

"Nah. You know how it goes. We make our own family."

"Yeah. We do."

Jaye closed his eyes. He heard some of the sounds echoing through the line, the voices ringing off the linoleum. The footsteps and bangs. He knew that place so well.

"I get out real soon, Jaye. Two weeks! I've been marking off the days. It's real close."

"Is Hax good to you, Tony?" Jaye cut in. "Does he — "

137

"Oh yeah," Tony said with hollow enthusiasm, in the voice of a man who'd gladly take a knife, gun, rope, a pill, you name it, and be done with all of it in a second, no hesitation. "It don't really hurt no more. They told me not to talk about it, but it's so nice to have someone who gets it. You get it, don't you, Johnny? Fair trade. He makes it look good. Tells me to play it up, but I usually don't need to, cause I always... I get real scared, you know? I didn't never wanna be this, Johnny."

Jaye ran a hand over his mouth. His knees were shaking.

"I'm getting you out of there, okay? Me. I'm doing it. I'll give you a place, okay? A place to stay. To belong. No one'll touch you. It's real pretty outside here, with the mountains and all. I can give you rides to the parole office. Find you a job. All of it. You're getting out, man. You're gonna get through this."

"I can't ask you to do that, Johnny. You got your own life now and I see how much of a hassle I am these days. I don't wanna be a hassle anymore."

"This shouldn't have happened, Tony. None of this. You're not a hassle. You're my friend. You're family."

"You... you're... but I can't... I can't pay you, unless. Well, I guess I could." He trailed off at the end, like a roadway crumbling into a bottomless ravine, soaring into the blackness.

"No. No fucking way is anyone going to do that to you again, okay? We just wanna help."

"No one just wants to help," Tony laughed.

"I do. We do. It has to all be for something, doesn't it? No bullshit here. It has to mean something. Maybe it means we help each other. Start fresh. Do something good with our lives."

There was quiet. Breathing.

"You really think that?"

"Just make it through the two weeks, okay? Can you do that?"

"I'll try, man. I'll try."

"Good."

"Oh, uh, the boss says your tickets are on the way. You gonna visit us, Jaye? If you did that," he sighed, sounded stronger, more like himself for just a moment, "I think I could do it. I really do. Something to look forward to, you know? Something real."

Jaye blew out a breath. He was trapped, but he didn't struggle. He just gave in. "Okay. Yeah, okay."

"Thank you. Thank you, sir."

Just like that, Jaye was losing it. Vision blurred, gasping for air, chest burning, fist clenched, he looked helplessly at Dixon, at Sesi. He tried to keep it silent. He really did.

Somehow, he managed to say in a choked voice, "You're welcome, Tony. Take care of yourself now. That's an order."

The call ended. Jaye dropped the phone and covered his face with his hands, crying, "Oh god, Dix. *Oh god.*"

Chapter 18:
The Follow-Through

Jaye drank some water, given to him by Sesi. He was sitting again, trying to process everything, but Dixon and Sesi were both pacing restlessly.

"I don't understand why," Dixon said, sounding riled again. "Why would they allow that to happen? Why would they hand Tony over to continue getting sexually assaulted by a member of their own fucking gang?"

Jaye looked up at him, wishing he didn't understand these things as well as he did. "You don't know what it's like in there. It's a cage full of sharks. They sense blood and they're all over it. With Tony's hands mangled, I'm thinking he was unable to fight back in a hand-to-hand combat situation. Easily overpowered, and it would have been a huge blow to Cash. Hit him where it hurts. He always liked Tony. Like he was his kid instead of a peer. And Tony's straight, but it doesn't matter. All that matters is they could, so they did, and once someone had him, he was a bitch. He was fair game for everyone. The only way to stay safe is to be protected. Hax handles Cash's dirty work. Always has. He's a scary guy when he needs to be. Good deterrent."

"Why wouldn't Cash take him, then, if he needed protection so badly?"

Jaye shrugged. "I can't tell you, Dix. I don't know. Maybe he just couldn't go there."

Dixon kept fingering the butt of his gun, which kind of made Jaye smile. Who the hell was he going to shoot? Ideas? Ghosts?

"You told him you'd be there," Dixon said almost in accusation. "I thought we'd agreed that was a bad idea."

"You didn't *hear* him. He's at the end of his rope. He needs something to get him through this last stretch, or else we won't need to worry about his living arrangements once he's out, because he'll be sleeping in a pine box instead. Yes, it's that bad. Trust me. I know."

Letting out a crazed laugh, Dixon said, "He's good. He's really good. Clever. He put that kid up to that." He jabbed a finger at the phone. "He had Tony call in his place, because he fucking knew, didn't he? He knew we'd second guess it all."

"He's the boss for a reason," Jaye said tiredly. His gaze strayed to Sesi, leaning against a doorframe with an unsure expression and furrowed brow. "So you're back on the job, I guess, if that's still okay with you."

"What are you talking about?" Dixon asked.

Jaye explained, "I asked her for help."

"When?"

"Before."

"Before," Dixon echoed.

"With finding a room and a job for Tony," Sesi supplied with a hushed voice. "I said I'd be happy to help and I am. This shouldn't all be on you two. We're a community. A family. We can share the load. The town needs people. Good people. Jaye says Tony is good people."

"He is," Jaye agreed.

"So you're just fine with this now," Dixon said, his fiery temper lighting up his eyes, surging through his body in a way that made him look like he wanted to lash out. "After everything from last night and today?"

"Of course I'm not fine!" Jaye yelled. "I don't know if I'll ever be fine, Dixon. But I don't have a choice. I'm not a heartless asshole. I actually give a shit about people. What Tony is going through is Hell itself and I've fucking been there! I'm the only one who can show him the way out. What kind of person would I be if I left him there to hang? Maybe this was the point all along — to know how to get through that shit, so I could help other people get through it too. Maybe it wasn't all for nothing."

141

For a long moment, no one said anything. Then a phone rang in the next room. Someone walked in the front door and went over to the front desk, looking for help.

"We'll be right with you, sir," Sesi called. To Dixon, she said, "We still need to investigate the reports of looting and trespassing up on Mr. Samson's property. You need me to handle it?"

Dixon groaned and straightened his shoulders. "No. I'll go. I'll get it done. Jaye can come along for the flight. It'll be good to get out, get some air."

"Okay. Keep me posted."

"Yeah, I will. You don't need to do this, you know. This isn't your problem."

"Now it is. No arguing. Go on. Get your air. Do your job," Sesi told him, using enough force to make Jaye smile.

"Yes, ma'am."

-o-o-o-

The plane tickets and hotel reservation paperwork came two days later via express mail. The trip was scheduled for two days after that. The urgency and speed mirrored the harrowing call from Tony and the way it impacted both Dixon and Jaye.

They borrowed luggage from Brekken and Grant, since neither of them owned any, and luggage stores were not exactly plentiful in Zus. Jaye claimed Brekken's purple bag, and Dixon was happy to let him have it, taking Grant's black one instead.

Those four days were quiet ones. Dixon chose not to press Jaye at all, on anything. Though Jaye receded and mostly kept his mouth shut, he didn't show any outward signs of hearing his ghosts. He stopped fighting off invisible enemies and barking protests at people who were either dead or damned. But Dixon knew all still wasn't right. Jaye flinched whenever Dixon touched him, fairly consistently. When Dixon stayed away in reaction, he found Jaye coming over to cuddle up at his side while watching TV or reading in bed. Dixon tucked Jaye's slim body under an arm and measured his breathing, just glad to have him near.

The morning of the flight, Dixon kept a close watch over Jaye. Something about him seemed lessened or weaker than it should have been. The years fell away and he was only a boy again, in over his head and afraid of facing what he knew he had to do. He stood by the dying fire, rifling through his packed bag to check its contents. The golden-orange light warmed Jaye's pale skin and sparkled in his green eyes. The tattoo ink seemed too heavy and garish on him, painted on rather than part of him. He tugged constantly at the ends of his sleeves to pull them longer. He even seemed thinner than he should have been, with hollower cheeks, the clothes hanging from his shoulders and narrow hips, like the ghosts had been claiming half his meals.

Jaye dressed in layers for the trip, wrapping a scarf around his neck and slipping on sunglasses which hid his tear. All of the fabric piled on him made him seem younger still, taking him from twenty-two to fourteen in the blink of an eye. Without any visible tattoos, there were no hints of Jaye's darkness.

They packed light, easily fitting everything in their pair of carry-on bags. Dixon was fascinated to see how much Jaye brought, stuffing his small bag full of clothes, supplies, and drawing gear.

He didn't need to ask why.

Last time Jaye had made this trek, it had been without anything but himself. The popular saying about material possessions and how you can't take it with you had strange connotations for those who'd been forced to leave it all behind against their will. Dixon sensed how it was a comfort for Jaye to have his things close, to feel weighed down by it all like an anchor of home and belonging. Maybe he just needed to remind himself that he wasn't a ghost, too.

They woke at two a.m. to take a puddle-jumper south, piloted by a friend of Dixon's who worked out of the local airfield. Jaye spent the flight staring raptly through the window at the scenery below and the clouds around them. The lights far below weren't plentiful, but they were beautiful to see in little scattered starbursts stretched out over the pristine Alaskan countryside. He held tight to Dixon's hand the whole time.

Their tickets from Cash were for coach seats on a flight out of Anchorage International Airport. When Dixon caught sight of their reflection in some of the huge, gleaming mirrored walls inside, he was struck by how easily they could probably pass for father and son rather than romantic partners. There was something in the fearful grip of Jaye's hand to Dixon's, and the resigned set of Dixon's shoulders. He could see how wide-eyed Jaye was behind the sunglasses, which he'd been wearing whether they were out in bright sunlight or not. They were part of his armor, Dixon knew, keeping the world around them back, just a little more.

Once they were seated and waiting at the gate for their flight to begin boarding, Dixon turned to Jaye and asked, "You doing okay?"

Their fingers wove together and Jaye was pressed up to Dixon's side, as closely as the seats — divided by unmovable armrests — would allow.

"Fuck no," Jaye answered with his face turned to gaze through the massive windows showing planes arriving and leaving in a steady stream. "We never went anywhere, you know. Couldn't afford it. If we could, I'm sure Cora would have moved us to the lower forty-eight. There was nothing about Alaska in particular that she loved. Too few opportunities. Too much poverty. Too little action. I think even the beauty of nature around us pissed her off, like it was taunting her with how grateful she should have been to have it so nice."

"Yeah, I wasn't a big flyer either. We went down South once when I was eleven to visit family. It was like going to Mars. It was so damn hot," Dixon laughed. "I mean it. Surface of the sun. Felt like I was dying. Couldn't wait to get home."

Jaye's knee bounced. Now and then, it would twitch, too.

"Those bastards bugging you again?" Dixon asked under his breath.

Jaye shrugged.

"It's so different," Jaye said with amazement. He nodded to people seated around them, fixated on their cell phones. "Somehow I slipped through into the real world. How'd I even get here? It's so normal."

He cleared his throat and hummed a little. Dixon saw a guy a few rows in front of them giving them his unwavering attention, so he stared the guy down until he looked away.

"No one fucking touches you, okay? No one. You're fine. You're doing an amazing thing for Tony."

"Corpse or whore. That was my choice. They'd either kill me or take me apart in other ways, whether I wanted it or not. I would have never been this way if it wasn't for Sheridan. I was a dumbass kid who worked at a store and liked to look at hot guys. I became everything I swore I never would — a prostitute, a junkie, a bad person."

"You've never been a bad person," Dixon argued gently. "Ever. You've been fighting for yourself. It's noble. It's necessary."

"Look," Jaye sighed, "I get it if you don't trust me anymore."

"What? What are you talking about?"

"Because of Tio, and the things I didn't tell you. I get it if it's a deal-breaker. I know you think you need to support me through this Tony shit, but if you want to be done afterward, I get it."

"J-bird, I'm planning to be with you for the rest of my life," Dixon whispered, leaning in to speak right by his ear. "I would never fault you for things you did trying to save your own life. I may not understand, but I'm trying to. I'm on your side, always."

Barely audible, Jaye said, "The things I did for Cash, with Cash — still make me feel disgusting. Especially with how easy it all became. I had no reason to think I'd ever have a better life than just surviving, so I didn't hold myself to any standards. I debased myself with that guy, constantly. I wasn't a person, I was meat. A hole."

A sickly feeling twisted Dixon's stomach, hearing that. "But you made it through. And we found each other. And you saved me. And now you're going to save Tony. You're the hero, Jaye. You're the strongest man I know. Look me in the eye and tell me even a guy like Cash could have survived what you went through in there."

Dixon took hold of the sunglasses and gently slid them off. Jaye was searching Dixon's eyes, holding nothing back. He was bare, needing, all emotion right on the surface. No wonder he'd been hiding behind the dark glasses.

"I love you, Dixon Andrew Rowe," Jaye told him. "I don't know how you've forgiven me for so much, but I'm so grateful you have."

Soon, they called for the passengers to board. Jaye fell back, happy to follow Dixon's lead, handing over his pass, then trudging through the passageway to get onto the plane. Their seats were about halfway back. Dixon let Jaye go into the row first and claim the window seat, for which he was thankful. Much more was visible as they took off, now that the sun was up. The ground fell away. Jaye's ears popped with the pressure change. He let himself dream he was headed anywhere else rather than where he was actually going.

It was three and a half hours to Portland. He kept flashing back to his first encounter with Cash, which had been arranged on his last flight to Oregon, hearing Cash laugh in his ear and ask if it hurt, if he could feel how he was still fucking that hole, seeing Dorrance watching and the rest of the Disciples. So, Jaye closed his eyes and fell asleep on Dixon's shoulder.

He woke as they were landing, the pressure in his head increasing for external reasons rather than internal for once.

Feeling like a zombie as sleep was slow to be shaken off, Jaye grabbed his bag to deplane and walked beside Dixon through the airport to the rental car area.

Jaye sat cross-legged on the floor by a wall as Dixon arranged for a car, eating a sandwich purchased at a stand on their way down.

The car they wound up with smelled vaguely of smoke, but in every other respect it was like new. Settling into the passenger seat, Jaye curled up for the quick ride to the hotel, located near the airport rather than in Sheridan. Maybe that was because Cash guessed Jaye wouldn't want to be in Sheridan itself longer than was absolutely necessary. Or, maybe it was just cheaper. Either way, he was glad to have some breathing room.

"Can we swing by a store on the way? Get some supplies?" Jaye asked.

"Sure. What kind of supplies?"

He shrugged.

They spotted a store two blocks away and swung into the lot.

Jaye got out before Dixon cut the engine. "I'll go in. You can stay. You want anything in particular? A drink? Snack?"

"Yeah, get me whatever looks good, I guess."

"Okay."

Jaye shut the door and jogged inside.

Thinking of his first time meeting Dixon, following the theme of the day, Jaye smiled as he recalled shoplifting in the Stop and Shop, pocketing things that appealed to his appetite rather than heeding any rational voice telling him to get something healthy. At the time, he'd figured if he was going to go for it, it was going to be for something he actually wanted to eat.

Picking up a basket, Jaye went to toss in some soda and iced tea. Then he got some trail mix, dried fruit, jerky and a few other things before heading for the thing he'd actually gone in for.

Once he'd paid, bag in hand, he returned to the silver sedan where Dixon was gazing at him suspiciously.

"Good to go?" Dixon asked.

"Yep. Let's find this place."

"You wanna go out to dinner first? A nice restaurant or something?"

"Nah, let's check out the room."

"Okay. You're the boss," Dixon told him, pulling back onto the road.

Dixon could see Jaye's impatience as they checked in and got their keys, but he couldn't figure it out. No matter how hard he tried to put himself in Jaye's place in order to try to imagine what he was going through, he failed to guess at the reasons for the ways Jaye was acting.

In the elevator, Jaye jabbed the button, then stared at the red floor read-out, almost bouncing on his heels as they slowly ascended.

Once they'd gotten to their floor, he surged ahead of Dixon, getting to the room first and popping his key in the slot. He swung the door open and flicked on the light. Without even looking around, Jaye yanked off his sunglasses, his scarf, and his coat. He pulled his shirt over his head, then worked at his fly.

"Hey…"

"Shut up, Rowe," Jaye rasped, shucking out of his pants and briefs. He palmed something from the shopping bag. Naked, he climbed onto the king-sized bed on his hands and knees. Tipping up his hips, parting his legs, he spread his ass invitingly. Dixon heard the snap of a cap. Jaye reached behind himself and pressed a finger through his hole. The sight of it made Dixon hard, right away.

Jaye pumped his finger, purring, "You want it?"

"Fuck yes, I want it."

"Then take it. Make me feel like I'm yours and no one else's. You're always going to be more real than they are."

"Damn right I am," Dixon answered, also shedding his clothes and making sure the door was locked from inside.

He could see Jaye wasn't hard. The need came from a different place. Dixon wasn't one to question such things. He hadn't been where Jaye was, but he had been in similar places, where the physical outweighed the mental and emotional in every way that mattered.

Walking to the bed, Dixon took the lube Jaye had brought over to it. He spread some over his hand, warming it before touching and watching Jaye's wet finger work. It had been a while since he'd received. He was tight.

Dixon spread Jaye's cheeks with one hand, then rubbed his rim with the other, tracing around where Jaye's middle finger was buried. A shiver shook Jaye, his skin pebbling. When Dixon pushed his finger in below Jaye's, Jaye moaned. Once he was buried to the last knuckle, Dixon watched Jaye fuck himself a few more times. Dixon's cock was swollen thick and red. Then Jaye pulled out, breathing harder. He braced the hand on the bed, settling in, his back a sexy curve, his cheeks firm and round. Dixon gave him a second finger and went right for his gland.

Jaye whimpered as it was triggered, his hips rolling. Dixon chased him, palming Jaye's pelvis to steady him, feeling every quiver. When he went to stroke Jaye's cock, he found it wasn't soft anymore, or dry.

"Feels nice?" Dixon asked, rubbing over Jaye's dripping cockhead, grazing over his gland with each push of his fingers.

Panting, head bowed, Jaye pushed back farther onto Dixon's hand. His cock jumped under Dixon's touch.

"Yes, sir."

"Who makes you feel nice? Who makes you hard?"

"You. Just you."

He pulled out, got more lube and re-entered him with three fingers, causing him to moan heavily as they sheathed in him.

"Any pain?"

"No, sir."

"You feel any pain at all, I order you to tell me."

"Okay."

For a while, Dixon just watched him take the three fingers, moving in long, slow thrusts into his gorgeous ass. Jaye's toes curled.

148

His cock stayed rock hard. Soon, he was restless and began to bounce against Dixon's hand, riding it. Allowing it mainly because of how fucking hot it was, Dixon stroked himself. Jaye reached for his own cock, jerking off with panting little breaths. He came with a sigh and a shiver, slowing down.

Dixon withdrew his fingers and lined up. All it took was a slight push and his crown popped through Jaye's rim. Jaye's ass swallowed the shaft slowly and he groaned, pushing back onto Dixon's dick. Dixon held him by the hips, guiding him back.

"So fucking nice," Dixon breathed. He savored the view of Jaye's slim young body, spread before him, as he stuffed that pretty ass full. Caressing up Jaye's spine, scratching lightly over the skin, kneading his ass, rubbing along his thighs, Dixon took deep breaths. He felt Jaye clenching around the cock and his undulations in response to the caresses. Dixon looked at the scar on Jaye's lower back, at his ink, at every line and curve he'd memorized so well over the many months they'd had together.

Before Dixon was ready to begin to thrust, Jaye began to move. It started subtly, pulling forward, pushing back. But he picked up speed, moving more and more with each bounce. Soon, he was riding Dixon hard, fucking himself back onto him while letting out alluring little rasping cries, his fingers splayed on the bed, his whole body relaxed, open and taking every inch he could.

Waves of pleasure raced up Dixon's back, from his feet to the top of his head. He never stopped touching Jaye, massaging and stimulating in ways that only seemed to drive Jaye on.

But Dixon wanted to see him. He wanted to kiss him.

So he pulled out, manhandled Jaye over onto his back, hooked his arms under Jaye's knees, folding his legs back and sinking back into him where he belonged with a heavy sigh. Chasing in until his lips kissed Jaye's, his panting breaths heating Dixon's air, Dixon groaned. They rocked together, moving ceaselessly until Dixon shot, coating Jaye's passage with his come. The next thrusts were wet and squelching.

"Don't go," Jaye begged, keeping Dixon close and holding him behind the neck. His lips brushed kisses to Dixon's jaw and below his ear.

When Jaye fisted his own cock again and leisurely, lingeringly, brought himself off for the second time, Dixon tuned out every

Lynn Kelling

single thing in the whole world other than Jaye and the heat of his skin..

"Don't ever go," Jaye whispered again, kissing, breathing, his feet hooked behind Dixon's back.

"I swear I won't."

Chapter 19:
Squeal

They showered together, washing each other's backs, kissing in the water's spray. Jaye could tell Dixon was confused about why Jaye had instigated sex, and he wasn't ready to explain, so he was glad for Dixon's trust. He knew Dixon was able to read Jaye's cues to interpret situations when Jaye wasn't feeling chatty. Part of that came from being a cop, but it was a handy aspect of their dynamic, helping them find balance when things got skewed. Neither Cash nor Kris had ever been much for reacting to Jaye's moods or trying to help him feel better if he fell into hopelessness. But Dixon never stopped trying to do the right thing, and be everything Jaye needed him to be.

There had been a particular speed to Jaye's existence with Cash. It had been high gear, with things flying at him night and day without rest, as if life was spent entirely inside a car without brakes, careening down a steep hill in the dark, with any possible obstacles or the bottom impossible to anticipate or see. Life was all about reacting and finding comfort in the ways certain things never changed, ever — like their schedule, their surroundings, the rules, and their cell. The sameness offset the chaos and wild, clawing danger.

It had taken a while for Jaye to drop his guard and stop constantly bracing himself after he'd left Sheridan. Now that he had the luxury of almost a year's time away from it all, Jaye wasn't sure how he could ever get his guard back up as high as it had been, not that he would ever want to try.

The person he'd been with Kris in Anchorage was even more alien. He'd been stuck in low gear with no way to shift out of it. There had been the struggles with Cora and the striving to take on more adult responsibilities, to cling to optimism when there was no reason to believe his hopes would ever be fulfilled. He'd been a fool, a child, and highly delusional. He'd been with a guy who was absolutely unable to give him what he really needed, but if he'd been told so at the time, he would have gotten defensive about it and clung even tighter to Kris in reaction. Age and experience finally lent the benefit of hindsight and hard-earned wisdom.

Now, with Dixon, it felt like things finally ran smoothly. If he became overwhelmed, he could adapt and cope as needed, mostly because he had help, a support system, and a community. He also had the freedom to take time off, to go back into his head or the expansive wilderness of nature to pause, step out of the rat race entirely and gain fresh perspective on where he was with it all.

Jaye wanted the things he'd never been able to have. He wanted to be able to take charge and ask for intimacy when the mood arose, with a partner who was only too happy to comply and give him the tenderness or passion he required. Just being in Oregon threatened to unravel his progress and security. The ghosts kept trying to bully him, jabbing all of his weak spots. They were a many-headed beast, their collective voice constantly shifting to mimic various enemies. It was Cash calling him piggy, saying he was the prettiest come-rag he ever did see, even though it was Ecker and Dorrance who'd actually said those things. It was Ecker, not Cash, asking if Jaye could still feel it, how he was still fucking that hole, how that was their deal. It was Dorrance, not Ecker, wondering if he was gonna squeal, gonna cry. The overlapping acted as a blender, making Jaye feel like he was losing his grip on sanity, that reality was getting chewed, digested, and turned to shit.

The way he fought back was through choices, testing what he knew he had won for himself, proving how far he'd traveled.

The nuances built Jaye up, making him feel stronger.

He heard noises from the hotel's hallway, and distant thuds or chatter from other, neighboring rooms. Through the gap between the shower curtain's edge and the wall, Jaye looked into the huge mirror on the opposite side of the room, at the colorful glass tiles surrounding it and the elegant vanity beneath with carefully rolled white towels stacked beneath on a wooden shelf. The gloss and modern fixtures of the bathroom were nothing like his old cell, or the creepy, bug-infested showers with their greasy soap, fluorescent lighting and lack of privacy. They also weren't like his old apartment with its water-stained ceiling and leaky pipes, cracked porcelain and persistent sense of desperation.

He was there at the hotel as a guest, a normal traveler along with his lover. They were welcome. No one was coming to throw them out, incarcerate or threaten them.

Feeling the pleasant ache in his ass from their lovemaking, along with the lingering tingle and happy flush from climaxing twice, caused a faint, honest smile to linger on Jaye's lips. He'd had his lover on his own terms, without pain, fear, or doubt.

Dixon kissed the side of Jaye's neck from behind, fingering through his hair to hurry out the shampoo bubbles.

"You've been quiet today," Dixon noticed.

"Just sorting things out. I'm okay."

"You could have told me what you wanted to stop for."

"I was still deciding if it was something I needed or not. I just wanted to have the option."

"Still, we can talk about stuff like that. I won't ever pressure you."

"I know," Jaye smiled. He closed his eyes and moaned a little, bending into Dixon's touch as it caressed around Jaye's hips to palm his abdomen and Dixon's larger, muscular body pressed up from behind.

"We should go out to dinner. They actually have restaurants here with things like steak made from cows, handmade pasta with fresh vegetables, fresh baked desserts…"

"Mmm, now we're talking," Jaye chuckled. Dixon nipped at his earlobe, sending a thrill shooting down to Jaye's cock. "I've never been to a nice restaurant. Couldn't afford it." The memory raced up on him, the hateful stares and comments from the hunters at the diner in Anchorage who'd later raped and tried to murder him, and the vision of Kris waving goodbye for the last time. He tripped over the words. "My last — last meal with Kris had been at a fucking diner. That's how they found me."

"Who?"

"Burt and Earl. My monsters. They saw Kris and I together, could tell we were a couple. I guess they followed me home after Kris left to get his bus. You know, it's the dumbest part of the whole damned day, but I'm still mad they didn't have the kind of cake I wanted. It was my birthday, after all."

"I'm so sorry," Dixon told him, giving him a hug. Jaye held on to Dixon's strong arm, crossed over his chest, feeling the warm water run down through the golden hair. "If you don't want to go — "

"No, I do. I just don't really have anything nice to wear. I don't want people to… you know. Stare."

"If they do, it'll be because of how beautiful you are. I'd stare."

Jaye laughed. "Well, I know that."

"We'll swing by a store. They have those here, too."

"I remember stores," Jaye said thoughtfully. "The overpriced jeans and crowded dressing rooms. I used to be a good dresser, you know. I had good taste, but I'd only get stuff on clearance, with my employee discount."

"Aww, baby Jaye the fashionista," Dixon teased. Jaye elbowed him for it.

"It seems so stupid now, to worry about clothes like that. I was so stupid."

"You were a kid," Dixon reminded. "Kids are only supposed to care about stupid shit. That's all they should have to carry."

"Yeah."

They got out of the shower, dried off and began to put their clothes back on, picking up all of the discarded pieces from the floor between the door and the bed. Sitting on the bed, Jaye slipped on his shoes.

Dixon glanced his way and asked, "You ready?"

It was an innocent question. Jaye didn't know why his brain made the connection it did. Maybe it was just a fragment from his mental blender, rising to the top of the foamy, rotten stew of memory.

The hotel room fell away.

He was in darkness, his pants around his ankles, the shackles on his wrists tightly attached to the ones on his legs by a couple of zip ties Ecker had pulled from a pocket. Ecker crouched over him, baton in hand. Another guard was there too — one of Ecker's lackeys, a dark-skinned guy named Thompson who had always targeted the whites and the Disciples in particular. When Jaye fought back as they'd hogtied him, Thompson kicked Jaye in the head until he'd stopped. The ringing and throbbing in his skull made it hard to focus, to listen. They'd ripped off his prison-issued underwear and stuffed it in his mouth to muffle his cries.

"You ready?"

Jaye yelled, sobbed, but the fabric soaked up the sound.

Thwack.

The baton struck his testicles.

He couldn't breathe to scream, but he bucked, writhed. They held him down, struck his balls again.

"Come on and cry for me, piggy," Ecker taunted. "That's it. Come on and cry."

His empty stomach cramped up, making him want to puke again. A guttural choking sound was all he could make as the baton caressed his sac like a promise. He coughed, retched, and Ecker hit him again. Whining, Jaye let out all of his terror and pain, willing to be as pathetic as Ecker wanted if only he'd stop. He knew Ecker would stop before rupturing Jaye's testicles if only to avoid the questions and inquiry that would come via the medical staff afterward, but absolutely anything that wouldn't leave a noticeable mark was fair game.

"Go on and squeal," Ecker invited, rubbing the baton over Jaye's sac again. Thompson held Jaye by the chains on his upraised ankles, yanking his legs back to expose him for Ecker. Jaye couldn't stop shaking, his body in a type of agony he'd never imagined could exist. "Piggy, piggy, squeal for me now."

The baton began to tap, tap, tap where Jaye's balls hung, hitting them squarely, the force increasing with each touch.

So he did. He squealed.

"Louder."

Harder tapping. He sobbed again, pleading pathetically. His whole body tensed, his thighs clenched, but Thompson pushed down on Jaye's bound feet as hard as he could, forcing his knees farther apart. Ecker slid his palm under Jaye's balls, raising them, and continued to smack them lightly with the baton.

Jaye shuddered uncontrollably, grunting. He bore down on the pain and made himself squeal again, and again, and again.

"That's it. That's nice. That's my piggy. Ain't you mine?"

A finger jammed up his hole, all at once, no warning. He tried to close his thighs, to writhe away, but Thompson held him, kept forcing his hogtied limbs down to spread his ass for Ecker.

The finger pulled on his hole, hooking in there. Something else touched the opening.

"Squeal now. Nice and loud."

Jaye squealed louder as the baton fed into him, dry. He convulsed, grunting, trying to push it out even as Ecker forced it deeper.

"Takin' it like a champ," Thompson laughed.

"Squeal," Ecker demanded, his anger rising.

The throbbing pressure in his aching head and the burn of being skewered on the baton was all he knew. He waited for more brilliant pain to hit — that sharp, tearing horror of his insides ripping open. But luckily Cash had taken him earlier. He was already stretched. Maybe it would be enough.

Ecker squeezed Jaye's sore balls in a hand and began to fuck him with the baton, moving it in and out. Jaye keened, then squealed again.

"That's it, piggy. That's it."

"You think he's gettin' off on that shit?" Thompson asked.

"Course he is! Ain'tcha, you fuckin' farm animal? You subhuman trash?"

Ecker shifted his grip on the baton's handle and began to hammer it into Jaye, fucking him deep and hard. Jaye shouted and tried not to choke. Thompson held him down and hissed, "Yeah, bitch. You little cunt. How you like that now, huh? How you like that?"

"Take the rag out of his mouth," Ecker ordered. "He knows not to scream, don't you, piggy?"

The soaked underwear was plucked out by Thompson, letting them hear Jaye's grunting more clearly as Ecker didn't let up, jamming the stick into Jaye over and over. Thompson leaned down and forced his dirty fingers into Jaye's mouth, pulling his jaw open wider, rubbing over Jaye's tongue. Ecker pulled the baton slowly out and used the end to nudge his swollen hole.

"Say thank you, piggy. Say thank you and I'll make it nice."

Thompson pushed deeper down Jaye's throat, triggering his gag reflex, causing Jaye to retch and cough, his eyes flooding with fresh tears. Then he withdrew the fingers completely and slapped Jaye's cheek.

"Th-thank-thank you," Jaye rasped, his voice breaking. The end of the baton rubbed repeatedly, threateningly across his hole.

Then it fit more deliberately in place and slowly entered him.

Making primal noises, lost in terror, Jaye knew each sound was heard clearly and savored. He quivered, couldn't stop, and the shaking intensified into convulsions. Thompson moved to grip Jaye's thighs and pushed them back, spreading and steadying him as Ecker continued to bury as much as he could of the baton in Jaye's rectum.

"Again, piggy, like you mean it."

Jaye whimpered, feeling dizzy, the bright lights in the room fading at the edges of his vision as things crowded in. "Thank you, sir!"

It was all the way in him then, and he couldn't stop shaking, his teeth clacking together.

"Woo! Just a pig on a spit, ain't he? Pink and porked. And he loves it, don't you, piggy?"

Weaker, he cried, "Yes, sir! Thank you, sir!"

The baton pulled slowly back out until it was completely free. He didn't allow himself to clench back up but stayed open for it. He felt them staring down at his hole. Hands spread his cheeks. One of them hocked up phlegm and spat it thickly into him. "How's that, piggy? Ain't that nice?"

"Yes, sir! Thank you, sir!"

"You want more, don'tcha? You want back on the spit to roast? Does it tickle you in the funny place?"

Jaye hummed to keep from screaming, because the urge was strong, overpowering. "Y-yes, sir!"

The baton pushed back into him, going in fast and deep. Then it kept moving that way, with long, thorough movements that went so far into him, he felt like he was choking on the stick. The stick went farther than any cock had, and there was no hope an orgasm would make it stop.

Fingers dug in by his opening, prying it open wide for the stick to fuck and ride him.

"Squeal."

Jaye complied.

Chapter 20:
Pulling Together

"Jaye! Jaye, come on! You're okay! No one else is here. No one else."

Finally, he came around, blinking. Dixon had Jaye's wrists in a strong hold. Jaye was curled up on his side on the bed, crying brokenly and whimpering as if with pain. There was a red, flushed mark on the side of Dixon's face, about the size of Jaye's hand.

"You see me? You see me now?"

"Y-yes," he hiccupped. His face was wet, his nose dripping. He wanted to hide, but Dixon wouldn't let go, so Jaye just curled up tighter.

"Stop, Jaye. Stop fighting."

He couldn't get past the shame. It was bigger than everything. The only way out of it was on the end of a knife or a loaded gun.

"Please stop fighting," Dixon begged. He did let go then and embraced Jaye, burying his face against Jaye's neck. Jaye reached to touch Dixon's hair. He smelled his skin. Felt how gentle he was.

"I hit you," Jaye said with horror.

"I can take it."

"No one should ever hit you." Jaye felt like he was strangling on the guilt, from all of it. Every part.

Dixon pulled back, searched Jaye's eyes while cupping the side of his face and brushing away his tears. "Where did you go? What was that, huh? You were doing so good."

"I-I'm trying to keep it — k-keep it straight, I — "

"Hey. Breathe. Come on. Deep breath. Good. One more."

"It's all... It's all coming back, trying to get me to run or give up or kill myself or — "

"What is? Sheridan?"

"Yeah. And earlier, with Kris. All of it. You said something that Ecker did, once, and... and it..."

"Ecker's dead. He can't hurt you anymore. I promise."

"Of course he can," Jaye hissed, a pair of fresh, hot tears leaking from his eyes.

"We're leaving, okay? We're flying home," Dixon said decisively, looking panicked and resolute.

"No, Dix," Jaye sighed, breath hitching. "Don't you get it? Tony is still going through this. They're still hurting him the same ways they used to hurt me. Beatings. Torture. Rape. He's even letting Hax fuck him for show! He had a fiancé. A life. He..." Jaye took a sharp, deep inhale, blew it out. He thought of Thompson and all of Ecker's other lackeys that were likely still in Sheridan, doing god knows what to guys like Tony. "He'll do it. He'll fucking kill himself as soon as he gets the chance. I know. Trust me."

"If you're sure of that then why are we here?"

"To try. We have to. We have to show him there's still good in the world too. Decent people. Hope." The welt on Dixon's face looked awful. Seeing it felt like a punch to the gut. "I'm so sorry for hitting you."

"I'm glad you fight back," Dixon told him, with honesty and love shining from his beautiful blue eyes. He kissed Jaye's cheek. "I'm fucking grateful for it every day."

Jaye groaned, covered his face with his hands. The sense memories were slow to fade — the helplessness, the mind-fuck, the hurt.

"Just rest a while, okay?"

"I still want to go out," Jaye protested feebly.

"We will. There's no rush. Breathe a while. We have time."

Dixon found the remote, switched on a local station and sat back on the bed, leaning against the headboard. Jaye shifted to lie next to him, weaving his fingers through Dixon's, brushing with his thumb back and forth over the silky soft skin.

After a while, he asked, "It's not all for nothing, right?"

"Of course it isn't. I know it isn't. We're all the proof you need. What doesn't kill you makes you stronger."

Jaye pulled Dixon's hand close and tried to let the memories go. He listened to the sounds from the hall, from behind the walls, from out on the street below. He anchored to them and the present as best he could.

The saleswoman stared at his tattoos but it didn't keep her from smiling politely or serving them at the check-out counter. Jaye felt more out of place in the upscale clothing store than anywhere else he'd been in three years.

Jaye had carried the clothes to the register after trying them on, but Dixon was the one to pull out his wallet to pay, slipping a Visa card from the letter pocket. Jaye had selected a black button-down shirt and black pants with a dark grey jacket. They were headed to get dress shoes next.

The large glossy photos on the walls reminded him of Rick & Pine in Anchorage. The pristine store with the piped-in music and perfumed air made him deeply uncomfortable. Since he couldn't hold Dixon's hand while he paid, Jaye held onto Dixon's arm instead, resting his cheek briefly on his shoulder as a wave of exhaustion washed briefly over him.

"Would you like your receipt in the bag?" the perky clerk asked. She had an intricate headful of braided dreadlocks, with blue strands woven through. She was shorter than both of them despite her high heels. It was strange to be faced with someone of another ethnicity in such casual settings. In Zus, other than the native population, there wasn't much diversity to speak of, and in Sheridan the gang lines had been clearly drawn to divide men based on visible heritage alone.

"Yeah, that's fine. Thanks," Dixon told her. He put his wallet away and took Jaye's hand again.

"I'm sorry," the clerk said, her tone changing. "But I just have to say, you two make the cutest couple."

Jaye froze. Then he felt his face heating. He stared at the clerk, hit with sudden guilt for... what? Behind the guilt was fear that he was broadcasting his homosexuality to strangers. He tried to let go of Dixon's hand but Dixon wasn't having it. He renewed his grip and smiled at the clerk.

"Thanks. Our one-year anniversary is coming up."

"Aww, that's so sweet! Congratulations," she told them, beaming.

"Thanks."

He took the bag and they headed out of the store. Jaye felt his heart hammering in his chest.

They rounded the corner and headed to the shoe store across the mall's hallway.

"I think we need to get you a drink or three," Dixon commented. "We're fine. Portland is a gay-friendly city. And if anyone thinks otherwise, I'll kick their ass for you, okay? Deal?"

Jaye noticed other people glancing their way, but detected no malice in it, even when he looked through a haze of pessimistic anxiety. He thought again, not for the first time, of how he'd been responsible for killing more than one man, and Dixon had as well. They weren't helpless in any sense of the word. It was just hard to remember sometimes.

"I'm glad Zus isn't this crowded," Jaye realized. "I like how everyone kind of knows everyone else. Feels safer."

"Yeah, I can see that. We'll be back soon. Just try to enjoy the trip, okay? We can make it whatever we want."

Jaye looked up into Dixon's blue eyes, stretched up to give him a quick kiss. "Deal."

Dixon knew the restaurant made Jaye feel as out of place as he'd ever been, so he took charge and brought Jaye along without letting him hang back or slow them down. Though Dixon didn't have as much experience with fine dining as some others, it wasn't as foreign. His parents were foodies who had always flocked to high quality food. It was one of the reasons they'd moved to the lower forty-eight as decisively as they had.

Jaye kept his hand locked inside of Dixon's. The strength of his grip made it hard for Dixon to stop smiling and built up his confidence, knowing Jaye was putting his faith in him to navigate the experience.

The hostess who welcomed them and found them a table at the downtown bistro let her gaze linger on Jaye much longer than it had on Dixon. This caused Jaye to shift slightly behind Dixon to avoid her staring, but Dixon's more plentiful experience with women, having dealt with Brekken his whole life, told him exactly why the woman stared, and it wasn't because of the ink.

The five-minute wait for their table to be ready and the walk to find it confirmed this. Dixon saw several women, some with male counterparts, some with other females, pause their conversation to look, or merely crane their neck or track Jaye with their eyes as they passed.

Of course Jaye noticed too, so when they pulled their chairs out to sit and peruse the menus, he was completely tensed up.

"Maybe this was a bad idea," Jaye murmured. He sat and slouched down in his chair, trying to hide in plain sight. They were located right in the middle of things, with people seated at other tables all around them. The room was cavernous with thick wooden beams above and fascinating decorations that were capturing much less attention than the wildly attractive twenty-two-year-old man Dixon was blessed to call his date.

"Yeah, it sucks being gorgeous and hot as fuck," Dixon commiserated.

Jaye gave him a doubtful glance and raised his menu to hide behind. "I think you're a little biased. I'm a freak, plain and simple. Always have been."

Dixon laughed. There was a whole table to their right, filled with middle-aged women who were frantically whispering to each other and looking at Jaye. He really did look amazing in the new clothes. The dark colors highlighted the stark beauty of his pale skin and dark hair. The ink peeking out of his collar and just beneath his eye gave him an air of danger. His broodiness wasn't hurting him either. But Dixon thought it was really his eyes that made the most impact. After all of that darkness, to see such lightness and delicacy in them made it hard to look away.

"Yeah, you are, just not in the way you mean. Won't be a dry panty in here tonight."

"And since when are you the expert on panties?"

"Okay, maybe not those, but living with a sister for most of your life does give you advantages in understanding the fairer sex."

Jaye pulled himself upright and hunched over his menu. He shot a sideways glance around the room and licked at his lower lip.

"So what are you in the mood for, sexy?" Dixon asked, scanning the offerings. It was a one-sided card with only a few entrées, but what they had seemed maddeningly delicious compared to the caribou meat, frozen and dehydrated, heavily preserved meals they were usually stuck with in Zus. "Steak? Chicken? Eggplant? Hey, there's a bison burger on here. God, everything sounds so good."

"Dix, this stuff is insanely expensive. Twenty-five bucks for a burger?" Jaye gaped. "That's too much. We can't blow our money like that."

"I appreciate your frugal mindset, but we're on vacation — " Jaye snorted. "We can afford to treat ourselves. How often are we in Portland, for Christ's sake?"

"Some vacation. Seeing the sights at the local federal penitentiary and the poor bastards locked up in there all because of the demands of a hardened criminal," Jaye said under his breath.

"Oh, where's the creativity?" Dixon scoffed. "When you were seducing me a year ago, you had plenty of it. Don't tell me Zus sapped it all away. We're here to visit... friends... and spread our goodwill to them, on a glamorous some-expenses-paid trip to a city we never would have seen otherwise. We're out on a formal date for the first time ever and going to forget about everything else for a few hours to appreciate how lucky we are."

Dixon glanced across the table, finding Jaye smiling helplessly at him. He shifted to lean his chin on a hand, his elbow braced on the table. For a full minute, he just smiled at Dixon. Then he said with a sigh, "Okay, I'm convinced."

"Good."

A waiter approached with a pad in hand. "Hi, and welcome to Imperial. I'm Bruno and I'll be your server this evening. Can I get you started with some drinks?"

"Yes," Dixon said with enthusiasm. He grabbed the drink card and scanned it for the weirdest thing he could find. "We'll have two blood orange margaritas, frozen with salt."

"We will?" Jaye chuckled a little, shaking his head.

"Yes. We will."

Dixon noticed the waiter giving Jaye a longer once-over than was necessary and rolled his eyes before he could catch himself, which Jaye noticed because his smile only widened, now spiced with some proud wickedness.

"Very good. I'll have those right up," the waiter told them with one last look at Jaye. Dixon nudged Jaye's foot under the table.

When he left, Jaye leaned forward and asked, "You're not jealous, are you?"

"Course not," Dixon said stiffly.

"Liar."

He sat back, the tension gone. In fact, he was turning on the charm like Dixon knew he could. He spread his legs, smoothed his shirt and gave Dixon a flirty glance.

"You know," Jaye said slowly, his voice a hushed purr. "We might have enough time before he gets back to make a detour to the men's room. I could suck you off. See how you taste with a blood-orange chaser. It's really my only chance to find out."

Dixon felt the blush rising, and with it, Jaye's cockiness soared.

"You're blushing."

"You're killing me."

"Oh, but what a way to go, eh, Dix?" Jaye winked.

Chapter 21:
Filling the Empty Seat

It turned out to be one of the best nights of Jaye's life, but the bittersweet realization came on Cash's dime and at the expense of Tony's health and sanity. They walked through downtown Portland for hours, hand in hand, buzzed on tequila and the jam-packed, human energy of the city. Dipping into a couple of bars, they did some dancing and once they finally headed back to the hotel, Jaye was asleep as soon as his head hit the pillow.

The high lasted all the way through breakfast as well as the hour and a half drive to Sheridan, right through their quest to find the correct visitor parking lot outside the prison, the wait while the car was searched by staff and sniffed by canine units, and until they were walking up to the visitor entrance. The sight of the prison fences and walls didn't strike Jaye as he thought they might, mainly because his chances to view the exterior of the building from a healthy distance had not only been minimal, but during emotionally fraught moments when his attention had been fixed firmly on survival concerns, both in entering and exiting Sheridan.

However, once they began walking through doorways, surrendering themselves to the heart of the beast, an all-encompassing sorrow swallowed his positivity. The heaviness of the security measures, one after the other after the other, began to smother his ability to think or feel much of anything. But Dixon kept his grip on Jaye's shoulder, leading him along, letting him not feel alone. Dixon handled the exchange of identification and the filling out of paperwork for both of them as they checked in. The experience of going through security as a civilian was miles away from the utter humiliation Jaye had felt when he had been admitted three years back, but it still echoed. They walked through metal detectors and went through a pat down. There was no strip search. Each checkpoint they passed through cut them off a little more from the real world where good people were allowed to exist, unmolested and free.

It soon grew too hard to walk. His feet stuck to the tile like they were glued. His eyes wouldn't focus. When Dixon led him into a room with tables and chairs arranged in small clusters, Jaye was almost being pushed along, clinging by the thinnest thread to keep from running from the damned place.

But then he thought of Kris, and Cora, and his old co-worker, Layla, who had never visited, written, or called. He thought of those two eternal, hellish years on his own in FCI Sheridan, knowing no one in the outside world cared if he lived or died. It had torn his heart in pieces to realize no one was coming to check if he was okay when he was in the hospital, after nearly being disemboweled thanks to the blind hatred of a total stranger. How he had been on the verge of the finality of death at only nineteen years of age and no one had cared.

So he sat in the scratched-up, blue plastic chair and folded his shaking hands. He bit down on his tongue and lost the ability to speak when Dixon gripped his leg, whispering in question if he was okay. Instead, Jaye shook his head.

He wouldn't run from this.

He resolved to be there when others weren't. He would man up to fill Tony's empty chair, and look him in the eye when they spoke, and he'd listen with everything in his heart and mind to every single word Tony said.

There was an all-too-familiar bang of a locked door slamming shut, and of many voices carrying through long, cold halls, the rattle of chains and the smell... how had he forgotten the smell? A hint of the animal stink of body odor, mixed with metal and ammonia, poured in thick, stale air.

He shivered and a moan of disgust slipped free before he could catch it. Dixon shifted closer, took Jaye's hand and held it in both of his.

"I'm here. I'm right with you. You're okay. We're here for Tony."

"For Tony," Jaye breathed.

166

For all of his noble intentions, Jaye understood he would never have been able to do it, and sit there in that place of his own free will if Dixon wasn't there at his side. He would have been just like the rest of them — all of the loved people who failed him out of their own stark discomfort.

"Fuck," Jaye groaned, trying to snap out of it, but without a clue how. The urge to vomit was close and the whispering wasn't just coming from around them anymore, but from inside his head as well.

It felt like the air itself shivered, that colors sharpened and the walls closed in. He half-expected to look down at himself and see regulation clothing with his inmate number stamped on it instead of his jeans and shirt.

To focus and shut out the nightmare of it all, he looked right at Dixon, who held his gaze and tried to smile encouragingly like they were only waiting in a dentist's office for a check-up instead of lingering in the jaws of Hell in order to face nightmares. Jaye told himself that if Dixon was really sitting there at his side, it meant Jaye wasn't an inmate. He wasn't locked up again. He wasn't in danger.

"You did this already," Dixon told him softly, his bright blue eyes crystal clear and brilliant with hope. "You conquered it. You're out. Not ever going back, except to visit."

Some prisoners began to file in. The temptation to measure and remember each face was maddeningly tempting, so Jaye didn't let himself start. He just looked at Dixon.

People sat down around them. Conversations started. The extra seat at their table remained empty.

It wasn't going to happen, he realized. Either it was all a trap to lure him there so they could incarcerate him again, or drag him to a storage closet for some bonus torture, or — worse still — they were too late, and Tony had done the unthinkable while they were out having their date night like a pair of selfish assholes.

"Dix..." Jaye began, his anxiety finally winning out and ready to push him to his feet. He turned to check the doorway, looking at it for the first time.

And there was Tony. Jinx. Cash's Puppy.

But oh, how he'd changed.

The shivering air settled. The noise and colors faded. Jaye's body suddenly became three times as heavy as it should have been, anchoring him uselessly to the ugly chair.

The functioning, rational part of his mind warned him not to stare, but he couldn't stop himself.

Tony had always been a fit, slim guy and only a little taller than Jaye. Now he was skeletal, almost all body fat eaten away. His dull, distant eyes were set in dark hollow sockets where they swiveled slightly back and forth, seeming to register nothing. His cracked, dry lips hung open. His cheeks were sunken. His hands, in shackles, stuck out before him in unmoving, trembling claws, the joints looking swollen and misshapen. His prison clothing hung ridiculously from his shoulders and his feet shuffled aimlessly along. Behind Tony, a female guard led him, pointing to their table. Staring blankly, he stopped moving entirely when only barely inside the room.

He had to have been all of twenty-five at most, but he looked ancient.

Then, somehow Tony's gaze found Jaye after passing over Dixon without sticking. Jaye felt the eye contact like a hard gut punch of familiarity. Tony's eyes slipped onward on their journey at first before snapping back to Jaye's face.

"Joh-Johnny. God damn, kid, you cut all your hair off. Boss'll shit bricks," Tony said in a soft, exhausted voice.

"Go have a seat, Jaconelli. Go on," the guard said.

Once he'd registered Jaye, Tony never stopped looking as he shuffled to the seat and sat across the table from them. His clawed hands, connected by a short chain to each other and the longer chain leading down to his feet, rested against the tabletop's edge. He leaned forward, staring harder.

"Would never have guessed, kid. Never," Tony said. The more he spoke, sounding exactly as Jaye remembered, if not wearier than usual, the worse Jaye's horror became. The creature sitting before him wasn't just anyone. It was a friend. Someone who mattered, who had clearly been tortured well past the point of endurance. "Look like a different dude entirely. Older. Bigger. You grow or something?"

Wrenching his voice up past all distracting thought and meaningless emotional reaction, Jaye said as normally as he could manage, "Not physically. It's good to see you, man. How you doing today?"

"Well," Tony said with a slight, crooked hint of a smile. "Better now, I suppose. Just look at you. Feels like old times. Good for me, maybe not so much for you. Damn rare for anyone to come back inside just to say hello. I'm flattered."

But Jaye found he couldn't process the niceties and small talk. Leaping right over it, he felt full-bodied anger take the reins, "Hax is a cold bastard for this, man. Cold as hell."

"Nah," Tony said with a dismissive tone, submissively lowering his gaze and bowing his head. "Hax takes care of me. He watches out. Keeps the others away. You know how it is."

"Doesn't mean I have to like it. It's damn good he's not in here, because I couldn't keep hands off if I tried, not even to stay out of trouble."

"Just a few days left though," Tony pointed out. "I heard — saw — how it was for you at the end. Those last days when Cash was in the hole. At least it hasn't gotten worse."

But that wasn't something Jaye could allow himself to think about, so he didn't. He shut it right out. "You coming to Zus, Tony? You'd love it there. It's real pretty. Quiet. The people are nice. They really care about each other. They'll make sure you've got what you need."

Tony's attention finally broke free of Jaye and drifted to Dixon, his head turning slowly on a pivot along with his eyes like an old man in a medication fog. "You're Dixon Rowe. The Trooper."

"I am. Good to meet you, Tony," Dixon said with a polite smile. Jaye noted it was without a hint of the cop voice, for which he was glad.

Tony's gaze drifted back and forth between them for a moment. "You're good for him. It's not just being out. I can tell just from the way you two are sitting. The way he looks. That's some good watching out, Trooper. Nice to know our boy has found a better life for himself."

"Tony, answer the goddamned question," Jaye demanded.

Tony laughed a little. "Always did have some big balls on you, kid."

"Are you coming to Zus?"

He sighed. Shrugged.

"Where else would I go?"

"You tell me." When Tony glanced away, toward the window, Jaye pressed on. "We're getting everything ready for you. Getting you a place to live. Job prospects. Way out where we are, we need good people to keep the town going. Too many move away to cities. We need you too. A smart guy like you who knows how to talk to people and get along with them can really help folks. You help the town, settle in, and we'll help you back. That's the way it works."

Tony's gaze didn't come back around. "There lots of woods out there?"

"Sure. Plenty. Good for hunting or walking or just to look at."

"I bet the sky's real big," he said, searching the barred window.

"You won't know unless you come."

"Tony, do you need anything? Money or anything?" Dixon asked.

All of Jaye's own fear, his demons and preoccupations, were gone. All he knew, all he felt was desperate fury, because he knew the look on Tony's face. He'd given up. There was nothing left in him that wanted to fight. They were too late.

"I think I'd like a walk in the woods. Get lost for a while. Listen to the birds. You know, I don't remember what birds sound like? Their songs? Mary and I, we lived north of Anchorage so we had plenty of wildlife, but for the life of me I can't remember."

"Hey. Look at me," Jaye said. Tony's dull eyes swung back around. "You don't get to let them win. It's not happening. You're so fucking close, man. Days. Hours. You remember what I went through in here? What I was? What I did? I can tell you as someone who fucking knows, okay? You can get past this. You can find things worth fighting for and living for. It gets so much better once you step out into the fresh air, and you are so close to getting to do that. Just try for me, please? I know some of this is on me, so I'm making it my mission to get you through, whether you like it or not."

"Aww, Jaye. You're my little brother, man. It was on us to watch out for you, not the other way around. The way it went down — it couldn't have happened any different. But I'm not like you. You always knew what it was, that it was your ticket out. You owned it. Changed it in your head somehow so it wasn't what it really was. I'm not that type of guy. What am I good for now?" He held up his ruined hands, looking steadily at Jaye with a haunted, broken gaze. "What good?"

170

"I'll tell you what good. You're a good friend. A good person. When you find a family, you make it your own and do your part. Let us be your family now. Leave all of these assholes behind and come live in the wild for a while. See where it takes you. You don't need hands, just heart, and you've got plenty of that."

"You really mean that, don't you?" Tony asked, like he couldn't believe it.

"I do."

"Yeah, he does," Dixon chimed in. "He hates this place more than anything, but he came here just for you. Think of what it would take to get you to come back here, after you'd gotten out."

Tony blew out a breath, shook his head a little. He pulled himself up a little straighter and for the first time, Jaye could see an echo of the guy he'd once been. His friend was still in there. He just needed a chance to heal.

"Why'd you let him come back here? Knowing about Cash and all?" Tony asked Dixon.

Dixon gave Jaye's hand a squeeze and glanced his way. "Everyone should get a chance at closure. He deserves peace of mind. And he needed a chance to see he's better than this place."

Jaye searched Tony's face for a reaction, a decision, anything.

He got a nod. "Okay, I'll make you a deal. I'll come to Zus if you do me a favor, talking about closure and all."

"What favor?"

"Visit Cash. Just once."

"That's a big ask," Dixon warned.

"Yeah, I know you hate 'im," Tony grinned. "Don't blame you, really. Neither does he. Still, you're out. He's in. Let him say his goodbye, yeah?"

Jaye felt Dixon's stare but refused to meet it. He slowly nodded. "Yeah, all right."

"Jaye."

"No, he's right. It's fair. Good deal to me. You swear you'll make the trip?"

Tony agreed, "Yep. Cross my heart."

"You better, you slippery bastard," Jaye warned.

"Thanks for coming, kid. Means a lot, you know," Tony said in farewell, getting to his feet. Jaye moved to clap him on the back in a half-hug that was eagerly returned.

171

"Hang in there. Count the hours if you need to. Hell, count the minutes."

"Will do, sir. Will do."

Chapter 22:
The Creeps

The process of leaving the prison following the visit with Tony was an eerie echo of the day over a year ago when Jaye had been released. They were signed out. They walked through gates, each layer of security peeling away to leave them that much closer to the freedom waiting on the other side. There was a sense in him to not walk too quickly or seem too eager to go, lest they tag him for suspicious activity and detain him until they got to the bottom of it.

A year ago, he'd waited for them to drag him back inside, to lay new charges on him for Tio or a few other incidents since his initiation into the Disciples. He knew they'd figure out they'd made a mistake, and tear away his chance at escape. Part of him had actually hoped for it, though he would never have admitted as much out loud, even to Dixon. At least if he'd stayed in Sheridan, he'd see Cash again, and he wouldn't have to deal with going out into the world with nothing and no one — no friends, no family, no job, no home, no possessions. In FCI Sheridan, all was familiar. He knew how to work the system. There was a dangerous comfort there.

Now, a year later and in entirely different circumstances, Jaye registered the odd look Dixon gave him. It seemed expectant or confused, spiced with a little wariness. With Dixon's hand on his back, Jaye was led out into the sunlight. He folded his arms and tried not to let it show how his heart was beating so hard. The towers with guards holding long-range rifles were quite close. They could pick him off easily if they wanted, which gave him the destructive impulse to run, screaming, for the complex's exit.

"Come on. Let's get out of here," Dixon said, unlocking the rental car. "Place gives me the creeps."

"No shit."

They got into the car and shut the doors. That little act of sealing out the prison's rank air helped Jaye breathe easier. He leaned back in his seat and took a deep breath, itching to be away.

"I could see it," Dixon said like it pained him as he slipped the key into the ignition and started the engine. "In your face, your posture, and that place... I could see you in there. I don't like it."

Jaye turned to look at him, not knowing what to say.

Because Dixon wasn't wrong.

The phone began to ring.

Grant was first, though Dixon could hear Brekken's commentary in the background. He pictured her pacing in the background, rubbing her arms and worrying.

"How's it going? You go there yet? The prison?"

"Yeah, just got back," Dixon told his brother-in-law. Jaye sat on the edge of the hotel room bed, clicking through television stations, tuning out the world. "Saw Tony."

"As bad as you thought?" Grant guessed.

"Worse. When I first met Jaye, he wasn't exactly doing great either, but this is a whole other level. This guy is actively being tortured on a regular basis. He's got an end in sight, but he doesn't even care much, other than to just have it all over and done. He's not living for anything. We tried to tell him a little about Zus to give him a place to keep in mind and look forward to seeing."

He wanted to talk to Jaye about what he'd agreed to, but he was afraid to ask, knowing he could probably guess the answers.

Dixon walked out of the room and into the hotel's hallway, shutting the door behind him.

"The whole trip is fucking with Jaye's head though, man. He's trying to prove to himself he's past all of this, but how can anyone be? He's still just a kid."

He wanted to get Grant's opinion on the whole Cash thing, but also thought he could guess what the response would be. He'd only make it harder to find a compromise with Jaye, so Dixon kept it all to himself.

"And how are you holding up?" Grant asked.

Looking at the long corridor of rooms, all the same except the numbers on the doors, Dixon pictured prison cells instead. He imagined Jaye being locked inside theirs from the outside, trapped and resigned to it. Locked inside with a monster who only wanted one thing from him. "I've never felt more helpless, to be honest," Dixon admitted. "I can't save him from any of this. Can't save Tony either. I can't make it so that those other men never touched them or forced themselves on them. What can you do after someone's innocence and mental health has been torn away? Being there isn't enough. It just isn't."

"I know, Dix, but still... you've gotta try."

While Dixon hung up with Grant only to get a call from Sesi, Jaye sat on the bed and answered his phone on the third ring.

"Yeah?"

"Talk to me," Brekken blurted. He could hear how tense she was. "Please."

"What can I say here? I mean, really? I hate it. I've never wanted to be anywhere less, but no one did this for me. I need to do it for Tony."

"But you saw him. It's done. You can come home now, right? Isn't your flight tomorrow?"

"Night. Tomorrow night. I, uh." He sighed. "I need to pay one more visit first. I made a deal. Tony would fly to Zus if I saw Cash one more time."

"I thought that was the plan anyway? What kind of shitty deal is that?"

"You didn't hear him, Brekken. I honestly think this is the only way we even have a slim chance he doesn't do something awful before we get a chance to actually help."

"You can't see Cash, Jaye. That's like Dixon agreeing to a one-on-one with Marcus, may he rot in hell."

"He can't touch me," he reminded her. "There are rules."

"But he can make you feel like someone you aren't anymore. I know how these mental games go. I see the way guys like Marcus yank a little string and it collapses everything inside their victim. They set it up that way on purpose."

"I'm no one's victim."

She made a tiny sound of exasperation."Fine. Tell me you actually want to see this douchebag. Convince me."

"Do I want to? No. Do I have to? Absolutely. I know he only sees me as Johnny. As a whore. Would you want to see a guy who only sees you as a whore?"

"Jaye..." Her frustration made her sound eerily more similar to Dixon. "Don't do this. Maybe Dixon can't say this to you, but I can. Don't see this guy. Don't do this to yourself."

"I have to. Not just for Tony. I haven't ever gotten to say goodbye to anyone, Brekken. Ever. Do you know what that's like?"

"You're not bringing him with you, are you?" Brekken said softly, the realization hitting her. "Dixon. You don't want him there."

"I'll see you soon, okay? Thank you for caring so much."

"Love you, kid. You know I do. Please be careful."

"I will. Love you too."

Jaye felt the heat in his face, the pressure in his neck, jaw, and forehead as if his blood was going to pop his head like an overripe tomato.

There was nothing Dixon could say to stop him. They both knew it. So to avoid a huge fight, they said nothing.

Dixon hadn't tried to argue the point. He knew he was outmatched by Jaye's stubbornness, but Dixon was upset. More upset than Jaye had ever seen him. He looked like he was coming apart, like Jaye was actively hurting him in ways it would take a long time to forgive or get over. He kept looking over at Jaye, pleading without words but only energy, raw need, and heartfelt love. To deny all of that, to walk away from it and keep hurting him instead was the hardest thing Jaye had ever had to do. No one had ever given him as much passionate, active, complete unconditional love as Dixon.

Jaye was spitting on that by doing this.

But he still had to do it.

In his mind, he heard distant screaming, banging, fighting.

Johnny!

JOHNNY!

Of all of the countless times him and Cash fucked, one time stood out sharpest.

It was the night after the gang bang porno shoot. Jaye hurt physically, mentally, emotionally, you name it. He wanted to not be touched, to not be expected to give any more than he had. He wanted a chance to heal, rest.

But Cash had climbed down to the lower bunk. Pulled down Jaye's pants. Forced his oversized cock up Jaye's swollen, sore rectum. Listened to him cry into his pillow as he rutted and rode him, holding him down and pulling his hips back into the deep thrusts.

After falling back into that moment, it took a strangely massive amount of effort and force of will to climb back out of it.

"Jaye?"

They were parked in the lot outside the prison visitor's entrance. It was a sunny, warm day.

Jaye was shaking uncontrollably, his clasped hands shoved down between his legs, his body curled forward in his seat, his head bowed.

Softer, "Jaye?"

He grunted. Rubbed his hands over his head.

"You know I love you, right?"

"Please don't," Jaye begged.

"I love you so much," Dixon told him, with his whole heart, wearing it right out there where anyone could smash it and ruin it forever, as if he hadn't learned to hide it away for his own safety. As if he would never learn. "You're not this guy. You're not his. You're more than this. You've always been so much more than this."

He was glad Dixon knew without having to be told why Jaye couldn't take him inside. He would never dream of taking someone whose heart was so horribly exposed around someone like Cash. Not in a million years. Not for any selfish reason that could ever exist.

JOHNNY!

Jaye said the only thing he could. He told the truth. "I'm so tired, Dix. I want it to be over. I want it to stop."

Dixon was breathing hard, charging the air, holding the keys to the car as if they were the keys to everything.

Jaye pulled the handle. He jumped out, shut the door and hurried away.

When Cash came around the doorway, Jaye felt the inner tug, the loyalty, the aches, the sense memories, the old fear and devotion. Before Cash recognized or saw him, Jaye had time to see the new wound circling Cash's right ear, as if someone had tried to slice it right off. It wasn't bandaged, the wound partially healed but still garish. He also looked thinner, his muscles, scars, and tattoos starker with the shriveled nature of his appearance. He wore his age clearly in the lines around his eyes and mouth. Cash was an old thirty-six. Maybe the oldest thirty-six-year-old there had ever been.

Recognition finally hit, and Cash blinked in surprise. He was angry, his upper lip curling, jaw clenching, then he was laughing. Laughing it off as he walked over in his shackles, jingling on the approach like a perverted Santa Claus, his hands tight together in front of him, his feet shuffling along.

Falling into the chair across the table, Cash didn't hide the long look up and down he gave to Jaye's body. It set the tone for the whole visit. Jaye wore jeans and a button-down black shirt with the sleeves rolled up to the elbows due to the warmth of the day. Some of his spider web — his initiation tattoo — showed, crawling down his arm.

"Fuck you for cutting your hair," was Cash's greeting.

"Yeah, well, I'm no one's bitch to ride anymore," Jaye retorted, holding eye contact and not letting Cash push him into submissiveness.

Cash smiled a mean smile.

"Is that so? What about that pretty-boy redhead cop? If you try and tell me you don't beg him real sweet to give your tight ass a hard pounding on the regular, you're a fucking liar. I know how you are. Never seen a bitch wanna spread for dick like you, or get hard and squirt from loving it so much."

"Why are you doing this? Is it just jealousy? What is the point of me coming here?" Jaye snapped. Cash didn't reply, only stared, so Jaye kept going. "What part of this is my fault? Hmm? You getting thrown in the hole? Me getting out when I was due for it? Building a life for myself? Finding someone who doesn't treat me like a ride is all I'm good for? Or how about the shit I dealt with that last week? Do you even know what he did to me? The beatings? The rapes? The mind-fucks? You think that doesn't stay with me every single day? So tell me, Cash. Come on and tell me what exactly I've done to piss you off so bad. I'm here for your guy. For Tony. Because people who get broken down the way he has — the way I have — deserve a hell of a lot better than they get."

Cash stared hard at him, his chest rising and falling. It was hard as hell to maintain eye contact, because he felt the old tickle it created. Those were eyes he'd looked into countless times during some of his worst and most vulnerable moments. It made him feel the old touching. The old poke and wriggle. The fondling. The wide stretch as his slim body fought to take what was being fed into it. He heard echoes of his whimpers and the chuckle they'd draw from Cash as he sank in, balls deep.

"You think, in other circumstances, I couldn'ta given you better?" Cash challenged, his scary, gruff voice lowered.

Jaye had to laugh, but it forced him to drop his gaze. He felt his face heat again. "That what you want, boss?" He added a sarcastic edge to the title. "Do better by me?"

"So what if I do?"

Jaye was struck speechless for a moment. Cash leaned forward, his voice conspiratorial.

"I could do things for you. Take care of your problems. You name it. All you'd have to do is get me your number. Send me some pictures once in a while. Let me write you."

He hated the blush, but it wasn't going away. The ugly desperation in the offer flooded Jaye with shame on Cash's behalf. "Thought you'd have a new bitch by now."

"Oh, I do. Ain't the same. He don't want it like you did."

"Incredible. Really," Jaye said, shaking his head. "And I can guess what kind of pictures you'd want. Those wouldn't get through security, so lemme guess. I send 'em to your guy instead? The one I had to pay in services?"

Cash's eye darted around like he was afraid of them being overheard.

"Not gonna happen," Jaye told him definitively, getting riled, feeling steadier. "I'm in a relationship now. I have someone who takes care of me the way I deserve. I don't need your favors."

"Okay, okay. Look. I'm glad you came to see Tony. Did some good. Hax said he — "

"Yeah, that's another thing," Jaye cut in. "I don't approve of any of that shit. You should have kept hands off of Tony. What the fuck were you thinking? After everything they did to him, you hand him over to Hax? For *that?*"

"He was sharing a cell with one of the blacks," Cash said under his breath, eyes blazing. "Hax treats him a lot nicer than that guy did, and you know how it works in here. You need to give them a reason to keep hands off. No one touches him now."

"No one else, you mean." Jaye shook his head, wanting to hit something. "You've watched, haven't you? Does he cry? Fight? Squirm? Beg? Scream? Or does he just say, 'thank you, sir' because his mind is so far gone?"

"Don't even try to give me that shit, boy," Cash warned. "You know sometimes it's the lesser of two evils that wins out."

"I have nothing to say to you about it, other than you better make damn sure he leaves here in one piece, or I'm holding you accountable."

They just stared at each other for a minute or so. Around them, other visitors hugged in goodbye.

As much as he wanted to hit Cash, Jaye also felt the part of him that used to want to curl up at Cash's feet to bask in how safe he felt around him. It was a false safety, distorted and toxic, just like everything else in that place.

"You look good," Cash told him, a peace offering. "Got a job. A place."

"Yeah."

"If Rowe ever turns on you, you tell me, okay? No one hurts you no more."

"What happened to your ear?"

Cash just smiled.

"Damn, I miss the feel of your mouth, Johnny. Miss other parts even more."

A creeping shiver ghosted up his spine.

"Miss your fire. Your spirit. You were a hell of a kick in the pants. Always kept things interesting."

"You do right by Tony. You swear it?"

"I do."

Jaye stood.

"Goodbye, Cash."

"Hey... don't. Sit a while. We can talk about whatever you want. We — "

"Goodbye, Cash." He held out a hand for Cash to shake.

Sadness, pure and strong, rose up high above everything else then in Cash. Jaye saw it happen.

After a pause, he stood, took the offered hand and squeezed it, chains jingling.

Then he tugged Jaye in close, kissing him on the lips, quickly but deliberately.

Jaye pulled back in surprise just as the guard yelled for Cash to knock that shit off.

Jaye pushed past him, fleeing.

"Johnny! Jaye! Jaye?!"

By the time he was out in the sunlight again, Jaye was panting. Cleared of security, he stood there, dumbstruck, until his heart slowed to a normal pace and the chills faded back.

He tried to let it go. He tried to let all of it go.

He wanted to leave it all there.

It wasn't his to carry any longer.

Knowing that, he kept walking. He saw Dixon standing by the rental car and smiled, feeling all of that weight lift at last.

Chapter 23:
Blood on Sheets

"God, it's good to see you," he'd said, giving Dixon a tight hug. Dixon had wrapped Jaye's smaller, slender form in both arms and lifted him off the ground, his legs kicked up in back and a groan sounded into the crook of Dixon's neck.

"You sound like it's been years."

"It has."

"Are you okay?"

"Better than ever. Let's get the fuck out of here. Forever."

Dixon didn't press it any farther than that. They got in the car. Jaye chugged a Redbull and ate a chocolate bar as they began the drive back to the airport. They'd checked out of the hotel earlier. Now it was just a matter of catching their flight home.

The change in him was fascinating. Before the visit, Jaye had looked physically crunched up into a ball, mentally stomped on, emotionally bound in knots. He'd been living one of his most dreaded moments, knowing there was no way out but through.

Without any way to know what happened in there until Jaye was ready to talk about it, Dixon could only go on what he noticed.

As they spied the airport, Jaye let out a happy cry and leaned over the center console to kiss Dixon's cheek. Smiling a little, Dixon reached over clasp Jaye's leg, but his hand was taken right up, held in both of Jaye's.

They parked and returned the rental. Bags in hand, they strode back into the airport and checked in at the desk. Jaye led the way for most of it, no longer hanging back. He kept fierce hold of Dixon's hand, only letting go of it when Dixon needed it to hand over paperwork or his ID.

They strolled past shops and food stands, splurging on a milkshake for Jaye — another rare find in Zus — and as many exotic types of candy as they could fit in his carry-on bag. Dixon got himself a burger and fries. As he sat down to eat and Jaye popped rainbow-colored candy pieces into his mouth, Dixon focused his phone's camera on him. With the flash of a plain old happy smile, Dixon took the photo, then sent it to Brekken so she'd know they were okay.

"Where should we go on our next vacation?" Jaye wondered with adorable enthusiasm. He sat cross-legged in the chair overlooking nearby gates. "Alcatraz? Guantanamo Bay?"

Dixon laughed and shook his head. "How about someplace nice? We could go see the folks. Head down South."

"Yeah?" Another sugary piece popped through his parted lips. The temptation was too good to resist, so Dixon leaned in for a light, lingering kiss. "You wanna show me off?"

"Always."

"Bet its hot down there. I've never been someplace hot."

"Well, you're hot enough all on your own."

Jaye smiled, then chuckled, his eyes squinted slightly closed in cute joy. "Dork."

"Have you ever been swimming?"

"Nope."

"There we go. Add it to the bucket list."

Jaye nodded toward the concourse. "Gonna go hit the head before we board. Be right back, okay?"

"Yeah. I'll meet you back at the gate," Dixon told him.

Jaye hefted his bag and walked off, sparing one more moment to give Dixon another kiss before he went. A few tables away, a small girl in pigtails giggled, peeking at them from over the back of her chair.

Jaye had the window seat on the flight back. For hours, Dixon watched him gaze raptly through it at the clouds and sky. Thinking of the blue jay tattoo, Dixon realized it was the closest thing to flying Jaye would get. No wonder it mesmerized him.

Dixon's energy, however, was crashing. After days of prolonged, elevated stress levels, Dixon was finally giving in to the need to rest and stop worrying so much. He didn't really want to sleep though, so he reached for Jaye's carry-on bag, hoping to pilfer some candy from it and boost his sugar levels.

Jaye grabbed the bag away before Dixon got a firm grip on it.

"No way. Personal property, Trooper Rowe," Jaye scolded. There was a look on his face Dixon couldn't pinpoint. It was a deliberately featureless wall covering something. But a moment later, an easy smile appeared there instead, like nothing at all was off. Dixon wondered if he'd just imagined it out of exhaustion.

"Okay," Dixon relented, raising his hands in surrender. "Never stand between a man and his stash."

"That's right."

Jaye tucked the bag further under the seat in front of him and returned his gaze to the ether beyond the glass. Maybe Jaye was acting strange, but Dixon was content enough to let him have his quirks and leave it be.

One flight led to another. Dixon did doze on the second, smaller flight, hopping them from Anchorage to Zus, even though it had much more turbulence. He was used to being shuttled around on the puddle hoppers for work, so he knew his iron stomach could take it.

Jaye drove them from the airfield to the cabin while Dixon curled up in the passenger seat for another snooze. He didn't know how Jaye was doing it, staying on and alert so long and with no visible effort. Maybe it was another benefit of having endured FCI Sheridan — staying on guard and energized as long as it took until it was safe to rest. Again, Dixon thought of how Jaye had appeared in the visiting room, like the walls had grown spindling limbs which reached out for him, and the only safety was in slinking down further in his metal and plastic chair, praying the devil didn't come knocking in the place of a friend. That had been every day, every minute, for a hellish span of time.

Dixon knew he would never have made it.

Not in Jaye's place and not in Tony's either.

At least with Marcus there had been consistency. They'd had their routine. Marcus had specific quirks to adapt to. He was gone for long stretches of time. Sure, things got violent now and then, but it wasn't a massive facility filled with countless guys just like Marcus, and it wasn't every day.

Watching the sliver of asphalt tumble away under their tires, the tumbling fields and forests stretching out to the horizon in all directions, Dixon said a little prayer for Tony, that he'd keep his promise and try his best to get to Zus. As someone who knew the oily taste of the barrel of a loaded gun, Dixon hoped there was enough strength left in the guy to make him curious about the possibility of recovery and rebirth.

They rolled up to the cabin. At first Dixon didn't want to move.

Praying had left him pessimistic. That scary, beaten voice in his head whispered that it was too late and too much. Tony would step out onto the highway in front of a speeding truck before he'd bother to come north and follow a dream. What were the use of fantasies when Hell lived inside you and monsters never slept?

"Hey." Jaye nudged Dixon's leg. Jaye bit his lip, his hooded sweatshirt pulled up to hide his short curls. Part of Dixon missed the longer version and lusted after the waist-length tendrils he would never get to twine through his fingers. Those light green eyes were too sharp, too wise for someone who should have been a spoiled, stupid kid with the world at his feet thanks to the luck of being born a white man in America with the face of an angel. How did the world choose who to feed on and who would flourish? Where was the fairness? What was the point of fighting? "You look spooked."

"Yeah, guess I am. The whole world sucks, doesn't it? I mean, when it matters. Good guys get the shaft and the bastards slip right through everyone's fingers."

"Says who?" He smiled like Dixon was worried about nothing, which only left him more baffled. "I know a couple of dicks who had all of their long-overdue bad karma come choke the life out of them. And I know a couple of handsome devils who got their second chances."

"Will Tony make it?" Dixon asked, feeling desperate. When had he gotten so invested in someone he didn't even really know?

"I hope so, Dix. I really do. But no one gets to tell him what he can handle. It's a choice he gets to make. No one can take that one away."

"Did you ever try to end it? Really end it?" Dixon asked in a fearful whisper.

"No. Not once. Never." It sounded convincing. His piercing gaze only sharpened. "When things were as bad as they ever got, all I ever wanted was peace and quiet. That's all. I'd try to bash the ghosts out of my brains, but I didn't want to die. What would have been the point of all of that shit I endured if I was just gonna give up and off myself? I always wanted to live."

"I didn't."

It came out before he could catch it. Then his face heated and he fought to think of how to explain, of what to say to the fury blooming in Jaye's beautiful eyes.

The car's engine was off. It was too quiet, with just the whistling wind around the cocoon sealing them inside.

"You never told me that."

"I know. Sorry. It was back when things were really dire. I don't know. Marcus had just left for the fishing season. My nose was broken. There was blood and semen on the bedsheets again and I just... it felt like it was easier to swallow a bullet than try to wash that shit out again."

It was too quiet for too long. Jaye said nothing for minutes. Then...

"How often did you wash out blood?"

"Too often."

"Yours?"

"Always."

Dixon chanced a glance to his left. Jaye was facing the steering wheel, staring straight ahead at the place where the road met the sky.

"Where was the blood from that time?"

Dixon sighed, rubbed a hand over his face.

"I... tore. The toy was too big. Too dry. He kept using it anyway. I was tied up so I couldn't fight back or stop him." A deep breath. "And my nose. He broke it again when I started to cry."

Jaye let out a sinister laugh. He punched the wheel, causing a short honk. Then he did it again and again, beating on it.

"FUCK!" Jaye bellowed. The word rang in Dixon's ears. "We need to dig that piece of shit up so I can kill him again."

"He's gone, J-bird. I'm just... I'm trying to be honest. I'm trying to say that I know how hard it gets. I know what giving up feels like. And I just really, really want this kid, this fucking kid, to make it through."

"How were you gonna do it?"

"My gun."

"What stopped you?"

"Brekken. She called. I knew she'd have to see my body and..." He shook his head. Cleared his throat. "I'm ashamed of all of it, okay? Every piece. Of what I let him do, of staying so long, of staying quiet, of how far down the spiral I went. None of it is easy. And I know how it must seem from the outside, like it was my fault. I should have been able to handle it. I shouldn't have let myself get in that situation, but for a while it was good, until it was just okay, and then it was not great, and then bad, and then shitty and... The shame was paralyzing. It got away from me. It all did. When it comes to taking care of myself, I'm not strong like you. I'm not. I — "

Jaye grabbed him by the arm, dragged him into a hug and kissed his cheek. His hand cupped the back of Dixon's head and Dixon felt his deep breath. He sensed Jaye inhale his scent.

"I'm sorry," Jaye told him. "I should have been there for you. We should have been there for each other, years ago. But we weren't. Maybe we found each other at just the right moment, when we needed to finally have some good. You fill up all my blank spaces, Dix. You always have. You give me purpose. You take care of me so good. Better than in my dreams. You make me feel like a man who's a hell of a lot more than the sum of his broken parts. I want to be that for you too."

He let go, reached into the back seat for his carry-on bag — the one he'd been keeping out of Dixon's reach since the morning and Portland.

He dug something out of a side pocket.

It was a little box. The lid bore the logo of a jewelry kiosk they'd passed in the airport.

Jaye opened it.

Inside was a ring — a band of plain silver.

Without looking up, he took Dixon's hand and slipped it onto his finger.

"It's not the nicest, but it's better than I could have gotten out here. It's my promise to you, Dixon Andrew Rowe. I'm yours. All yours. I swear I'll take care of you, too, however you need, no matter what comes our way. I'm never leaving you. I'm never letting anyone hurt you like that again. I used to try really hard to take care of people who didn't want to be taken care of, and when I realized that, it almost killed me. To have you, and to have the honor of taking care of you just as much as you take care of me, means the whole damn world."

Dixon cupped a hand under Jaye's jaw, tipping up his chin, and kissed him. His lips were warm, supple, and his sigh filled Dixon with the taste of sugar.

"I love you."

Chapter 24:
Bird in the Wind

Never before had it been so good to work. In the days following their return to Zus, Dixon was quickly swept up in his patrol duties, working twelve-hour days three days in a row. Jaye loved driving himself to and from his job. Because the office was so close to the station, it still allowed him to feel close to Dixon, even if they barely saw one another. He made sure to prepare dinner each day and save some in their fridge for when Dixon arrived home. If he could, he heated up the food so it was ready, and he made sure the fire in the hearth was hot, the cabin cozy.

By the third day, Jaye could see it in Dixon's eyes — apologies for being gone so much and for taking advantage of Jaye's eager hospitality. He was doing their laundry down in town. He was keeping the cabin clean. He packed their travel things away and went shopping to bulk up their food stores.

Jaye never let Dixon actually verbalize those apologies though. Each time Dixon tried, Jaye silenced him with a kiss, distracting him as he knew best and demonstrating the truth of how he felt. Words never seemed to capture the full span of his experience, but Jaye figured if Dixon was going to buy into the fact that Jaye loved being able to do for someone who appreciated it, it was going to be through unmistakable examples of Jaye's confidence and joy.

The question of Tony's fate hung over Dixon much more than it did Jaye. That particular cloud darkened in ways embarrassment for needing nurturing could not.

Jaye knew there was nothing they could do but wait.

And if there was ever someone good at waiting, it was him.

It was only a matter of days, anyway.

The day before Tony was due to arrive, Dixon seemed as far away as ever. Though his schedule was blessedly shorter, giving them a chance to share space for more than the just-before-waking and moments-prior-to-sleeping periods, all he did was sit on the couch, spinning his new ring on his finger. His gaze fixed on a point in mid-air. His brow furrowed.

"You're a good guy, Rowe," Jaye murmured, leaning against the stone edge of the fireplace with his arms folded. "Says a lot about your heart that you care about this kid, but you can't help him. You can't do one damned thing."

"I'm a sucker for hopeless cases," Dixon retorted sullenly.

"Don't I know it," Jaye smiled.

Dixon's eyebrow rose in disbelief. "You've never been hopeless. Sometimes I think you're made of pure faith, like it's etched into your bones."

"When he shows up tomorrow, you'll let it go? Or you'll just worry about other things instead?"

Some of Dixon's tension seemed to ease as he relaxed back into the cushions a little more. That stubborn frown softened.

Jaye knew Dixon well enough to judge how much he could handle. There was plenty Cash had said during their visit that Jaye had no intention of telling Dixon. There was no point in handing a natural worrier more shit to obsess over. Especially when it didn't matter.

Now Jaye knew exactly how desperate Cash was. Cash's need for more of Jaye only allowed Jaye to see his value and self-worth that much clearer. Simply put, it made him feel big, while showing him how very small his former boss had become.

There were some other lessons he'd taken away from Cash, ones that were also not easily spoken of.

"C'mere," Jaye said, luring in his prey. The tight seams between the wooden floorboards pressed beneath his bare feet. The heat baking the air on his right side and the crackle of the burning logs, as well as the subtle nip in the air not yet warmed by the flames, all grounded him in that place — their place on the edge of nowhere. There were no distant voices, no lurking threats. His guard was dropped as low as it had ever been. Dixon had all of his trust, all of his heart.

Holding out a hand to him, Jaye felt Dixon's larger, rougher hand slip into it, fitting so perfectly into place. Blue eyes watched him, asking so many questions and full of more fear than Jaye would ever be able to feel for himself again. Knowing Dixon feared for him was plenty. It made him safe.

Getting to his feet, towering over Jaye, Dixon drew him in just by being, and breathing, and loving.

Jaye pulled off his own shirt, then unsnapped his fly.

He turned his back to Dixon and sighed in pleasure as Dixon pressed up close, one arm coming around to caress Jaye's bare stomach. Dixon's fingertips paused on the scar's ridge, tracing it as he'd done so often.

A kiss came to the skin just below Jaye's ear.

Dixon's hand pushed down inside the front of Jaye's pants, grabbing a handful of his cock. Frowning with how much he wanted, Jaye shivered inside Dixon's grasp — one hand holding him by the cock, the other bringing his chin around as Dixon's teeth scraped gently along Jaye's jaw.

It made Jaye hard. Thinking of that silver ring twisting restlessly around Dixon's finger, of his concern and futile desires to make impossible wrongs right, Jaye let go of everything that had ever held him back. There was no act. He had no agenda. There was no deal he needed to follow through on. All that mattered was the fervent way Dixon tugged on Jaye's cock, the rising heat of his breath, and the simmering need Jaye had to feel consumed and taken. He wanted to be wanted for the love, safety, and devotion he provided.

Dixon let go, crouched to strip the clothes from Jaye's legs, kissing Jaye's upper thigh when he moved to step from the jeans. It took only a moment for Dixon to shed his own clothes and come back naked, his body firm, downy soft with body hair, and deliciously warm.

"On your back," Dixon told him.

Jaye lay down on the edge of the bed, looking up at him, reaching for him and hurrying him down between his spread legs. Dixon pushed Jaye's legs back and fed his opening two wet fingers, kissing away the soft, helpless cries he made at the feel of Dixon's gentle, patient touch.

Jaye skimmed his parted lips over the short ends of Dixon's red-gold hair at his temple, liking the way the velvet texture tickled. The fingers buried themselves in him and he pushed down against the thrust, sighing, praying.

"You're so good to me," he whispered. "Come on. I'm ready."

But Dixon wasn't. Some stubbornness lingered in his eyes as he pressed a third finger in as well, avidly following the ways it drew a frown on Jaye's face, his lower lip caught between his teeth at the ache.

What was he thinking of? Blood on sheets? Begging echoes in dark, cinderblock halls? The dull bang of wood breaking bone? The whir of a camera's lens to focus on hot, flowing tears?

He came in closer, into a hug, his lips against Jaye's neck and his body a human shield. The fingers inside held him as if forbidding the rest of the world entry, and claiming Jaye's intimacy for only himself.

Jaye had never been held so completely. Relaxing into it, his whole body open and calm, Jaye shivered once in ecstasy and felt a drip slide down the shaft of his rigid cock.

More soft kisses peppered over his skin.

The fingers slowly withdrew.

When Dixon began to push to enter him, Jaye growled with the size of his need, but forced himself to be still, be patient.

Dixon's lips hovered over his own, following his ragged breaths, drinking in primal cries while Jaye's body took Dixon in just as impatiently, swallowing him up. He sank in to the hilt and Jaye tightened his hold, wrapping his legs and arms around to capture.

Then he saw the smile, the glimmer of peace and happiness in aqua-hued sparkling waters that were the windows to Dixon's soul.

Jaye didn't want him to move. Not yet. He wanted to savor it. He had Dixon inside, deep and complete. They were one. Dixon had him like no one else had or could.

"This is all I want. Ever," Jaye told him.

Dixon tracked his eyes as if doubting or unable to believe after everything and all of it, Jaye didn't crave more, or that peace had been so easily found.

He knew Dixon would never stop trying to give more, no matter what Jaye did or said.

And that was okay too.

His needs were different sorts.

So Jaye relaxed again.

Dixon began to move.

It started shallow, slow, but the fire in Dixon burned hot. He still carried his anger and fear and questions. They drove him on and he rode Jaye through it all. Panting, rocking against Dixon's increasing, passionate thrusts, Jaye let Dixon take him over and pour all of his cares into the empty places.

"I've got you. I love you," Jaye promised.

Dixon's breath caught, his frown deepened, his lip trembling. He pressed his mouth against Jaye's shoulder and cried out, quaking as he came, twitching against Jaye's body through the aftershocks.

He'd barely calmed down, still breathing heavily as he pulled out and sank down, swallowing Jaye's erection as if starved for it.

Then, Jaye moaned wildly, clasping Dixon's head as it bobbed and he sucked all sense away. Feeling desperate, frantic, Jaye couldn't stop moving, taking the ride, and his thoughts short-circuited as he climaxed in the perfect, wet, close heat of Dixon's mouth.

He crawled up again, curled around Jaye as they both lay on their sides, panting.

There were still so many questions. Jaye saw each one as he brushed back Dixon's sweat-damp hair.

Would the pain ever truly go away? Was there a way to defeat the monsters that would always live in the dark? Most of all, was Jaye's total absence of fight and suspicion just a sign he'd given up, that he was actually slipping away?

The answers weren't Jaye's to give. There was no way to explain in words how the prolonged absence of anything made the presence of something good and real seem like heaven on earth — the greatest blessing.

All he could do was show Dixon his trust and give him all of his love. A quiet, caring voice whispered that it was enough, and that Dixon knew how lucky he was, that it was what really scared him. Only time would prove it wasn't going to be stolen away by demons, ghosts, or fate.

Looking into the sparkling blue of Dixon's eyes, Jaye thought of his promise to Cora, long, long ago, and told her in the quiet of his heart, *I'm flying, Ma. I'm free.*

Chapter 25:
Thick

"You're coming today, right?"

"Duh. Of course," Sesi replied. "I'm driving over now actually."

"Oh," Dixon said with surprise. "Okay. Cool. We'll see you there."

"Yup. Later."

Dixon hung up and shifted the Expedition into gear. Jaye had made them both coffee and was sipping his from a travel mug. It wasn't early, but they'd been up late. The caffeine boost was desperately needed by Dixon, but Jaye looked peppy enough for both of them.

He started down the road. Jaye changed the station on the satellite radio, turning off the nineties alternative in favor of a weird electronica station.

"I honestly don't know how you like listening to this stuff," Dixon said. "It's barely music."

"Yeah, yeah, these damn kids and their music, right, old man?"

Dixon glimpsed his cocky grin.

"I'm not that much older than you."

"Keep telling yourself that." He relaxed back into the seat, shifting his ass lower, and propped his feet on the dashboard. "You know, I did the math. If you'd been a slutty, straight teen, you could have been my father."

Dixon groaned. Jaye laughed.

"Don't tell me shit like that, please. That's just wrong."

"It's true! And hey, I've never met ol' pops. Maybe you're him."

"Gross. And no. Not straight. Not a teen father."

"But you are kind of slutty," Jaye said with a cute expression of apology.

"Excuse me, who's calling me what now?"

"Ooh, burn," Jaye replied with sarcasm. "I own my sluttiness. It's a badge of honor."

"And I love you for it, babe. Besides, no way my kid would get away with bypassing the curse of the Rowe redheads."

"Maybe I've been dying it this whole time," Jaye said with a fake gasp. He turned in his seat, adding more sultriness to his already alluring voice, "Daddy, is it really you?"

"First off, the pubes never lie. Second, gross."

"Oh please, like you'd hate it if I called you Daddy while you were fucking me into the bed."

"I might. You should probably try it and find out."

Jaye laughed again.

Dixon reached for his own mug and took a sip, willing the coffee to hit his system hard. Natural splendor and isolation did come with the downside of having infrequent Starbucks locations. If he wanted a refill, he'd probably have to wait until after the drive home.

Changing moods and conversational tracks, Dixon asked, "You still think the truck stop will be a good fit?"

"Sure, to start. Worked for me. People don't bug you much. Let's you be around others so you don't get too stir crazy. Shouldn't be too physically taxing on him. And if it doesn't work out, we'll find something better."

They'd gotten word through Sesi that a position there was open and waiting for Tony, should he want it. It should have been great news, but Dixon's gut instincts wouldn't let up on the insistently negative feelings he had about Tony. He couldn't figure out why.

Dixon had gotten a call from Tony the day before. It had been welcome reassurance that the kid was still breathing air, but for how long? Tony had sounded awful — even worse than when they'd seen him in person.

But at least he was trying. At least he was still fighting to get out and live.

The drive took about an hour. When they pulled into the lot by the airfield, he saw Sesi's vehicle right away and parked right beside it. A quick check of his watch told him they were right on time, but Sesi was nowhere to be seen.

Leaving the mugs behind, they walked toward the field.

After a short hike, and rounding a low building that housed the small planes and some offices, they spotted a gathering of people near a plane with its door opened.

"Is that him?" Jaye wondered.

"Could be. Maybe they were early."

They walked a little faster.

Dixon spotted Sesi. A slim figure with a raised hood hiding their face approached her. After a moment, she pulled the person into a hug.

Jaye glanced over at Dixon and broke into a jog.

Dixon followed.

"Tony?" Jaye called. "Hey, man. So good to see you. Congrats."

Sesi had let him out of the hug, but Tony was having a hard time tearing his gaze away from her. At first, it didn't make any sense. He was looking at her like she was an old friend, not someone he'd never met and didn't know. And the longer he stole glances her way, even as Jaye approached and drew Tony into another hug, the more it caused a bizarre flare of jealousy or defensiveness to rise in Dixon. He tried to tell himself Sesi was one of the first women Tony had been close to in years who wasn't a guard, but still...

"Thank you," Tony was saying to Jaye, almost too quietly to hear. He tapped Jaye lightly on the back with a clawed hand, mostly making contact with the inside of his wrist. "Thank you so much for this, Jaye. I don't know how I'm ever gonna repay you."

"Don't even think about it," Jaye told him, letting go. "I wanted to. It's good to be needed. And the longer you're here, the more you'll see how much you're needed too."

"Trooper," Tony said, nodding to Dixon. That's when Dixon realized shaking hands was likely an impossibility for Tony now. A glance at his fingers showed them to be slightly twisted and swollen, mostly unmoving with the exception of the thumb on his left hand. A sick feeling rose in Dixon's gut, knowing it was likely the less scarring injury he'd sustained, and that it could have been Jaye instead, had things gone down in different ways. "I appreciate all of your help in getting me here."

Tony looked around, up at the sky, and the wide expanse of the landscape opened up around them.

"I forgot it's like this," Tony murmured. Dixon didn't ask for clarification.

"Mr. Toklo is so excited to meet you, Tony. He's got your room all ready. You're in walking distance of town, so it should make things a little easier, but if you ever need a ride anywhere, I'm sure I speak for all of us in saying we'd be happy to help you out there too. Anyway, come on. Let's get you going, get you settled."

"Thanks, Sesi. You're an angel. You never told me you're beautiful."

Dixon rolled his eyes before he could stop himself.

"Wait, you two have been talking?" Jaye asked.

"Sure," Sesi smiled, her cheeks turning pink. "Tony's been calling me every day for the past two weeks. I had to find out how to help him, right? Plus, he's great to talk to. All of his curiosity about the Inuit culture is another reason I knew he'd be a great fit with Mr. Toklo. His respect for the old ways of doing things will take him far around here."

"You mind if I ride with you?" Tony asked her.

"Mind? I'd love it. Come on."

She took his arm and led him away.

Dixon and Jaye were left standing there, stunned.

"Wow. That didn't take long," Jaye commented.

"I should have known," Dixon sighed. "She's always telling Brekken how few available men there are in town. She's going to have to be pretty damned open-minded and patient though."

Jaye took his hand, leaning on his arm. "I think she can take it. She's a nurturer. Every day, she works with people on the fringes looking to survive, who know how to appreciate what little they have. Tony isn't much different. Seems like a great match to me if they can make it work."

They started to walk back to the vehicle.

"How's he look to you?"

Jaye shrugged. "Tired. The whole process is exhausting though, so I'm not surprised. I just... I don't know. Every time I look at him, I see Hax with that creepy blank look in his eyes."

Dixon pulled to a stop. "What blank look?"

Jaye bit down on his back teeth and stayed quiet.

"What are you talking about? Tell me. Please."

Lynn Kelling

"He took his turn with me, okay?" Jaye said without making eye contact, some of the strength sapped from his voice. "Said he'd break my jaw if he felt any teeth, and I believed him, even though Cash was right there. Had to make it look good, right?"

"Jaye — "

"No. It's not about me." The missing strength surged back, coming in angry. "It's about that fucker taking Tony for a ride for show on the regular. I don't fucking care that it kept the others off. I just hate it! They were friends! Brothers! You don't do that to people who trust you. Because I know how it feels. I know how it goes." The noise of a plane starting up drowned out a lot of his yelling. Dixon was glad, because Tony wasn't really that far away. "I know how he'd make it look rough, that he'd get Tony to act like it hurt and encourage him to fight back. He probably didn't only act the part like I did. I'm sure that shit was genuine. At least Hax doesn't pack what Cash does. He — "

"What?"

"Fuck," Jaye said softly. He started to walk away. Dixon yanked him back.

"What?"

"Dixon, let it go," Jaye said sternly.

"What are you saying here?" Dixon demanded. He flashed back to Marcus, pulling out an oversized dildo and laughing as he forced it into Dixon, and the helpless noises of pain Dixon had made because of it. When his mind tried to overlay those reactions onto Jaye, Dixon felt like he was going to puke.

"He's..." Jaye pulled his hand free, folded his arms. "It doesn't matter."

"He's what?"

"Fine. He's thick, okay? Like a soda can. Like the... the wrong end of a baseball bat. Now you have a real nice mental picture, huh? Fuck. Fuck!"

Jaye started walking quickly away. Dixon was too dumbstruck to follow at first.

He snapped out of it but didn't make it back to the Expedition until Jaye was already inside.

"Dixon!" Sesi yelled from her rolled-down window. "You're following, right? To the house?"

"Yeah, I know where it is. We'll meet you there, okay?"

"Yeah, okay."

With a wave from her and Tony, they were off.

Dixon opened the driver's side door and got in, slamming it closed behind him.

"Why did you never tell me that?"

Jaye laughed somewhat hysterically. "Are you shitting me? Why didn't I tell you the thug crime boss who actually sexually owned me and forced me to have sex every single day had a huge cock? Gee, I don't know, Dix. Must have slipped my mind."

Dixon flooded with shame as his face heated with a blush.

The words stuck in his throat. He forced them out.

"So you — you were u-used to that, I guess. Did you not tell me because now I'm not enough for you, or..."

"Dixon, stop. Stop." Too fast for Dixon to anticipate it, he lunged over, grabbed the lever to slide the driver's seat backward, sent Dixon's seat back as far as it would go, then climbed onto his lap. When Dixon raised his hands, refusing to touch, Jaye took Dixon's wrists and crossed them, pinning them over Dixon's head, holding them to the headrest. "You're fucking out of your mind," Jaye said levelly. "And yes, I acknowledge the irony of me saying that to you, but you are. You've fucking lost it. When Cash first gave me an up-close and personal idea of what he was packing, I asked him to do it. I said he could do it if he kept me alive, but I didn't know what I was asking for. He went in dry. Everyone was watching. I bled for days. In front of many other guys who saw where I was bleeding from and thought it was an open invitation until Ro told them otherwise. It was a horror show. Yes, Cash was more gentle later, in private, but his size only made a bad situation worse. Other guys knew. Dorrance knew. They'd joke about it, how I shouldn't complain when someone else wanted to have a go at my ass because I had to be so loose and sloppy from taking what I did every night. So am I glad you don't make me bleed when we have sex? Yeah, that's a bonus. Size matters. Size is the difference between terror and pleasure. So get the fuck over it already."

Dixon closed his eyes, squeezing them shut. Jaye nuzzled his cheek and Dixon resisted how good it felt, how the hint of wood smoke in Jaye's hair smelled like home, happiness, and heaven.

In his memory, he heard his own startled yelp of bright pain, his voice wavering and choking off as the thick phallus was forced into him without lube. He heard his weak begging.

Please take it out. Please take it out!

No. No!

Marcus, please?

A scream, muffled in bedding that was soaked with tears.

He let his own voice shift into Jaye's in his mind. There was no containing the pain of that, or how awful it was, to know there had been additional layers to Jaye's torture, and there was nothing at all Dixon could do about it.

Dixon's closed eyelids were kissed by a pair of feather-soft lips.

"I keep this stuff from you to keep you from hurting."

"I hurt anyway."

"I know you do."

Jaye kissed his closed eyes again, then kissed his lips. Dixon tugged at Jaye's hold, but it was steely and determined.

"I know it hurts," Dixon confessed, swallowing the words.

Jaye watched him, measuring.

"I know you do."

But he kept thinking about it, how now his nightmare imaginings of Cash raping Jaye over and over again in the dark somehow got even worse, and the ache grew so big, it pulled Dixon down like a hook embedded in his soul. He fought to breathe, his chest heaving. Jaye kissed his parted lips.

"I'm okay, Dix. I swear I am," he promised, sounding so resolute and unassailable.

But Dixon still couldn't breathe. The truth was a weight on his chest, crushing his lungs.

He heard a teenager's cries. A child without parents, without any sort of hope, without even the ability to scream in response to the crimes being actively committed upon his beautiful body.

Jaye was holding him. His chest was against Dixon's chest. The air wouldn't come.

"Feel me breathe, Dix. Breathe with me. Nice and slow. Like that. Good."

"I'll fucking kill him," Dixon rasped.

"You can't. He's damned anyway. He's done. He's gone, Dix. He's not coming back."

For a while, they just sat like that, breathing in tandem.

Then, because he had to, Dixon asked, "How have you survived all of this?"

"I found a way. I had to. Had to get to you, right?"

"Right."

He felt Jaye take his hand and spin the ring around his finger. It felt like a promise, like old wounds healing slowly over.

Chapter 26:
The Worst Secret

They pulled up to a cabin that was at least three times larger than Jaye's. It had a hand-hewn look about it. Jaye didn't remember looking at it so closely before, though it was impossible to totally miss any singular structure in Zus, given the rarity of man-made buildings.

"Mr. Toklo, huh?"

"He's eighty. Netsilik Inuit, which means he comes from a sea-focused culture. Moved here after the kids grew up, for an easier life. More reliable food supply. Never went to school, from what I heard. Just raised to hunt and provide. His wife died two years back. The kids and grandkids moved away. Since he can't read and his memory isn't the best, he needs reminding to take his medications and to have someone there just to keep an eye on things. Plus, he's lonely."

"Everyone in Zus is lonely. He ain't special."

"Yeah, well. He had the room. He's an open-minded son of a bitch. Said his brother did time, way back when, but offed himself ten years later. I think he's trying to balance the scales."

Sesi's vehicle was parked nearby. No one was inside it. Neither Dixon nor Jaye reached for their door handles quite yet though. The wind shrieked as the Expedition rocked on its tires.

There was an outhouse several yards from the main cabin. Funny to think of an old man and a crippled ex-con using it in the dead of winter.

At least it was private.

At least Tony could go do his business without having to guard against an attack, or without wiping Hax's come from his ass.

Fury flared, there and gone, the detonating of a small emotional bomb and the hazy smoke after.

"I can't believe he's really here," he confessed. "The Disciples are infiltrating."

"Guess so. I hope Tony's the last one."

"Me too."

Jaye sat forward, cracked his knuckles.

"I have to talk to him."

"Yeah, I thought so. You want me to wait here?"

"You mind?"

"Nah."

"Can I ask you something?"

Dixon raised an eyebrow at him.

"Why's Sesi want in on this? On Tony? I mean, he's okay looking when he's not so damned skinny, but she didn't even know that before today."

"It's not about what he looks like. She's a hero. She needs to save people. Always has. It's why she became a Trooper even though her whole family was against it because it goes against tradition and because of all that sexist crap; the job keeping her from settling down and having the family they expected from her. She doesn't do things because someone told her she should. She follows instinct. Reads the fucking signs in the wind or whatever, and tries to do the right thing, no matter how crazy it is. You can't fight a calling."

"Yeah. Guess not."

Jaye got out of the car and took one last hard look at Dixon's beaten-down expression before leaving him and trudging up the path to the cabin's door.

There was a large stump pitted with marks from an axe's swing and a small stack of firewood out front. That was familiar enough, but he kept noticing all of the ways the cabin was better than his own — like the larger windows and how there was more detailing on the trim. They felt like personal slights, to the extent that he had to remind himself how his place fit his and Dixon's needs just fine.

But they didn't have an arctic entry like this one, so the frigid drafts didn't blow into the main living space. And they didn't have multiple rooms. Or triple-paned windows. Or multiple fireplaces.

203

But at least they had a toilet inside the building.

"Hey," Sesi said with a small smile when she let him inside. The decorations there spoke to Mr. Toklo's heritage. Many types of furs and skins adorned the walls and floor. Some tools were mounted either for ease of accessibility or purely for admiring, though the axe for splitting logs simply rested by the door in the arctic entry. Jaye also noticed a number of stone carvings sitting on shelves and mantle. They looked handmade, the style of each similar enough that he wondered if the artist was Mr. Toklo or someone in his family. There was also what seemed to be an old lamp in the living area made of stone and oil with a cotton wick, though it wasn't clear whether it worked or not. In an opposite corner was an old television and a DVD player.

Tony sat with Mr. Toklo at a table in the small kitchen. They each had a mug of something hot and were in quiet conversation. Tony held his mug between the heels of his palms as he raised it to his mouth to drink. Mr. Toklo was slim, his face and hands weathered, a welcoming smile on his face. Though he had the look of someone who'd survived a lot, Jaye could tell from first glance that he was not a man who set out to intimidate or show off. Everything about him and his home seemed modest, simple, and tied to the earth. He wasn't stuck in another era, but brought the past along with him to the present with honor and respect.

As someone who had only been terrorized by his past, Jaye found himself to be enraptured of the differences in perspective. Jaye could only dream of someday being able to own his struggles and heritage with as much pride as Mr. Toklo and Sesi's people did. He craved the peace of their outlook, and strove to learn from their example. In them, there was acceptance of the harshness in nature and fate, but plenty of joy and celebration in each small victory.

It felt like the right environment in which to leave Tony. It gave Jaye hope.

It was a different place than FCI Sheridan, but it embraced raw wildness and truth, setting it free rather than locking it away.

"I think it's going good so far," Sesi told them. "Time will tell."

"Yeah. Thanks again for doing this."

She waved him off.

Tony finally looked over to catch Jaye's eye, and Jaye saw he'd sensed their arrival well before he'd gotten out of the SUV. When you were used to guarding yourself as fiercely as FCI Sheridan demanded, it took a damned long time to drop those protective instincts.

"Hey, Mr. Toklo, have you heard anything from the grandkids lately," Sesi asked, moving to take another one of the seats at the small table. "Are they planning a visit soon, with winter on its way out?"

Tony got up and walked over to Jaye.

Weird memories flickered in Jaye's mind, contrasting in sickening ways with the cozy comforts of Mr. Toklo's cabin. They were in the showers, and Tony was laughing at Rat's bleeding nose while Jaye's knuckles throbbed. They were playing cards in the center of Unit 4, with the other gangs divided neatly in clusters all around them. They were in the exercise yard and the bodies of the Disciples made a tight ring around them as Cash took Jaye's ass for a public ride to reward the guys for a job well done — a job of which Jaye knew nothing about. All he knew was the hard tug on his long hair and the wide, aching stretch in his ass thanks to the hard pounding Cash was giving it. The other crew members breathed heavily from all directions, closing in. He heard the squelch of lube with each push, the light, fast, steady slap of flesh on flesh.

Yeah, give it to him, boss.

He can take it, can't you, Johnny. Give it harder.

Do it. Do him, boss.

In the memory, Jaye had caught Tony's eye. There hadn't been hunger there, or lust, but a strange recognition. Why?

"Can we talk?" Tony asked, keeping his voice low. "My room's right there."

He pointed toward a doorway leading off of the main space.

"Sure. You think you'll like it here?"

"Yeah. It's big. Nice. Feels like a home, you know? Not mine, but still."

They walked through the darkened doorway. Jaye closed the door behind them. Tony went to the single window and parted the dark blue curtains, possibly handmade by the late Mrs. Toklo, to let in more light. He lingered at the glass, staring through it at towering evergreen trees that crowded in close. The road cut through them and rock-strewn driveways led to other small homes. Someone in a parka with a fur-trimmed hood followed the road's shoulder, their head down, their steps small, their hands buried in their pockets.

"I was just there, Johnny. Is this even real?"

Jaye let the nameslip go, though it did feel like a bad touch, or bait for the ghosts.

"Sure is, man. Just give yourself time."

"Time. Right."

"You like Sesi, huh?" Jaye leaned against the closed door, his arms folded.

"She's nice, you know? Even Mary wasn't as nice as her. I don't get it, but she acts like she actually cares. She looks at me like I'm a-a person. Like I'm just a guy. A man. Like I'm normal. The guards, they always... well. You know. Why the fuck'm I telling you? You know what I mean."

"Yeah. You're lucky. You've got people. I didn't have anyone when I came here. Almost got arrested again, just trying to feed myself. I was a dumbass."

Tony went to sit on the single bed. There was a divot in the center, like it had been well slept in for years. The only other furniture was a dresser, a nightstand with a lamp, and a small bookshelf, half full of paperback books and other knick-knacks. There was a cross hanging above the door and a stylized painting of a caribou on the wall.

"Look," Tony said heavily, looking down at his ruined hands, cradled in his lap. "I've been thinking on this for weeks, like constantly. So I kind of want to just cut the small talk and get to this, okay?"

"Get to what?"

Tony looked up at him, holding his gaze. It felt just like in the exercise yard, when Jaye was taking cock for show. It created an uncomfortable tickle way down low, behind his balls.

He breathed in the scent of the cabin's wood, using it to anchor him to where he really was. Things had changed. He'd changed.

"I know what you're thinking. I know what you've wanted to ask, but couldn't because they were listening. And no one else gets it, all right? No one. They can't get it because they haven't been there. So I just... I need to..."

"It's okay, Tony. Just say what you need to say."

He sighed, stared out into space, facing the room's shadowy corners rather than the view beyond the window.

"I never liked watching you, okay? I didn't. It always reminded me. But what could I say? To Cash?" He laughed. "I was earning my place. I was no one."

"You weren't a bitch."

"True. Not yet, anyway. But I'm not like that. I need you to know. I don't like that stuff."

"Butt-fucking?"

Tony flinched. Jaye studied the reaction coolly, trying to figure it out.

"When you're locked up that long though, some guys learn to like it."

"I didn't. I never would, okay? Ever."

"Because of Hax? Because of what he did to you?"

"No," Tony frowned. "I keep telling you, Hax was okay. He only did it around the other guys. In the showers or the yard or the common area. But Cash got him stuff to use, so it didn't hurt as much."

"You liar."

Tony gave him a weary look.

"Fine, there was a couple times after lights out, but Thompson was on watch. He'd linger by our door, listening."

"Before or after he started in on you?"

"Both. I couldn't ever... get used to it. Or relax. It was always..."

"Yeah. I know," Jaye said quietly.

"Hax wouldn't talk much, during. I'd start to panic, even when it was just Hax instead of those other shitheads, even this last week. So he'd just do it, you know. He'd just kind of turn himself off, hold me down and go through with it."

"Yeah, I know that too."

"Course you do."

Tony watched him. Jaye allowed it.

Then, Tony told him, "It wasn't the first time, okay? It wasn't that big of a deal."

Jaye stared hard at him, but couldn't get a read. Tony looked old and too young at the same time. His sandy-colored hair wasn't combed. There was more color to his face than there should have been, his lips dark and his eyes big. He was way too thin, his cheeks hollowed. It was too easy for Jaye to imagine Tony willing his way through it, panting, grunting and trying to be cool, to be okay when he was so fucking far from okay.

"What are you talking about, Tony?"

"I'm talking about Hax, and Keyon, and Diego, and everyone else. It wasn't..." he sighed.

"Then who was?"

"My cousin. Older cousin. Drew Lahner."

"Christ. You're serious, aren't you?"

"Yeah. I am."

"He forced it?"

"Yeah. He lives out in Pennsylvania, where I grew up. Or lived, I guess. I heard he got killed. Shot. Just happened a few months back, actually. His murder, not what he did to me. That happened years ago. I heard when he got shot, he was going after some teenager like he used to go after me, and... Anyway."

He rubbed the back of his hand over his upper arm, like his hand had an itch there.

"How old were you?"

"Thirteen. Another teenager. Barely. Guess he had a type."

"How did it happen? Did it happen when other people were nearby, or did he get you alone or what?"

"He was babysitting me, as a favor to my mom while she and my dad took a weekend trip for their anniversary, headed up to New York City. And he..." Tony cleared his throat, restlessly rubbed his arms. His words sped up, coming out faster and faster. "He took my clothes off. Took some pictures. Some video. That was the first day."

Jaye groaned.

"The next, he... he went for it. The real deal. Pushed me over the side of a couch. Held me down and..." A heavy, shuddering exhale. "After, he smacked me across the face a few times when he saw me crying. Said I'd been asking for it, so he had no choice. That it was my fault. That I acted like a whore."

"How the fuck old was he when this happened?"

"Twenty? At least?"

"Jesus."

"I-I think he had a thing for kids, like he was sick. Well, I know he was sick. And after that, I wasn't right in the head. I thought what he did meant I was gay or something, even though I didn't like guys or dick. I started to do drugs. Anything I could get. Pills. Powder. I didn't even ask what it was. Didn't care. I stopped going to school. I couldn't stop thinking about it, wondering what it meant. I'd just leave. Walk out and get high. I kept expecting him to show up at the building to get me. So we moved. They moved me way the hell up to Alaska. But it didn't undo any of it, you know? It was still in my head. I could still feel him inside me. And I was so fucking scared of turning gay. No offense or anything. It just fucked with me completely. So I got worse. Started to steal shit to pay for the drugs. They arrested me for possession and theft. Threw me into Sheridan. And every time I had to watch a kid like you have that happen to them, in front of everybody, I knew somehow. I knew it was only a matter of time before that was me again, doing the taking."

"Tony, that's fucked up."

"I know it. I do."

"Did you tell anyone about Drew?"

"No. No way. They would have called me a faggot and I wasn't. I didn't — Sorry. That's not a nice thing to say."

"You don't think they would have believed you?"

"I just wanted it to go away," Tony told him, pleading for understanding with his eyes. "I wanted it to not have happened. I needed to escape it. That's all I cared about."

"But he could have been going after other boys. He — "

"I know he was. I know, okay? He had other pictures in his bag. He…" Tony blew out a breath. "They'd never treat me the same if I told them. I knew it. And I was right, wasn't I? Because it was never the same after Diego gagged and fucked me in medical while his buddy held me down. Never. I went from being in the crew to being a bitch, just like that. It was out of my hands. That's all I was good for. It would have been the same, only it would have been my family. It — "

"What happened to your parents?"

"House fire. Took out the whole block a few weeks after they arrested me. Some jackass overfed his fireplace and passed out drunk. The carpet caught and *whoosh*."

"I'm sorry," Jaye said, meaning it sincerely.

"I know. At least Drew's dead. At least he's burning for it now. But… sometimes I think about the pictures he showed me of other boys. And the video he took, telling me to spread my cheeks and try to relax. They're still out there somewhere."

Panic twisted Tony's lips and brightened his eyes. He curled forward, hanging his head. Jaye knew the feeling. He had his gang rape porno floating out there too.

"There was no name," he murmured, "in the article about Drew, about the kid he'd been going after. But I know the name of the detective who investigated and... I was thinking of writing a letter or something, but I'd need help. I can't do writing yet. Would you... would you help me, Jaye? Please?"

"Yeah, of course I will. What kind of letter?"

"To the kid. The boy. Just saying I'm sorry. That it's all my fault."

"It's not your fault, Tony."

Tony's voice rose, rasping, breaking, "Of course it is! I'm not a child. I'm not an idiot. I heard what happened to you. How they tried to rip your guts out with you watching it happen. While they fucked with you. What if someone had killed those two assholes first, way before they found you? You would have been spared. You would have been fine. Your whole life would have been better."

"You can't think like that."

"Like hell I can't. All of this." He held up his hands, the bones smashed, then healed in gnarled twists. "This happened because I didn't stop Drew sooner. Because of me, kids got raped. *Kids*."

"You can't take responsibility for the crimes of the monster that hurt you. You were a kid too. You were thirteen!"

"Will you help me or not?"

Jaye didn't like the look on Tony's face. Like it was already settled. Like decisions had been made.

"Only if you promise me you're not going to do anything stupid."

"Cross my heart," Tony said, reciting the words as the shadows behind his eyes told another story entirely.

"You didn't deserve any of this. You were the one hurt here. You're the victim. You deserve a shot at a good, normal, happy life."

All Tony did was smile. But it was cold. Empty.

What words could Jaye use to convince him? What would get through to someone who'd convinced himself his failure to snitch had caused the molestation of countless young boys?

What could he do?

Lock Tony up again to keep him from killing himself? For what? Where?

Send him to a mental institution? Again, where? How? There were no facilities. There was just endless space and plentiful chances to take the easy way out.

Grasping at what little he had, Jaye said, "What about Sesi, huh? You like her. She's trying to fucking help you, man! She's one of the best people I know. She's doing all of this with no motive. None. She just wants to do some good for you. You're really gonna do that to her?"

"She doesn't need the burden," Tony answered. "She's way too good for me anyway."

"Tony, promise me you'll give this a fair shot," Jaye demanded.

Tony let out a deep breath. "Sure thing, boss. Scout's honor."

Boss.

The honorific echoed. Way, way back in the recesses of Jaye's mind, ghosts laughed.

Jaye had to get out of there. It felt like spiders were skittering all over his skin. He stood. Moved.

"Hey," Tony called when Jaye cracked open the door, his back turned. "Cash tattooed your name on his side." He pointed at his abdomen, a few inches above his hipbone, where Jaye's scar from the stab wound was. "Right here."

"Of course he did," Jaye whispered.

You feel that? How I'm still fuckin that hole? That's our deal, right there.

Invisible fingers trailed through the ends of Jaye's long hair, gone for well over a year's time, and he brushed them away.

Jaye met Tony's gaze, felt the strong grip of his hands, holding Jaye down, crying while he was violated from two ends at once by monsters and as a camera watched everything.

He's got bigger balls than you. Trust me, I checked.

Somewhere, Tony laughed, doubled over.

"He's got it bad for you. Real bad," Tony said.

"Yeah, well, I ain't his no more. Neither are you. How about you fucking think on that a little, huh?"

Jaye turned and left.

Sesi watched him walk away from her seat at the table, across the room. Old Mr. Toklo met his gaze steadily, barely smiling, nodding once with an unflinching look like he saw the demons crawling out of the corners, coming for Jaye and Tony, both. Like he knew simple courage was the only weapon that would fight those bastards back, and wished them luck in doing so.

"Jaye? You going?"

"Yeah. Yeah, I am."

She jogged to intercept him at the door. When she did, he said, "Watch him, okay? Real close. He's not right in the head, Sesi. Trust me on that."

"You think he's gonna hurt someone?"

"No, I think he can't do this. I don't think he even wants to try. So watch him. Please." Fingers wrapped in his hair, yanking his head back. More fed down his esophagus, triggering his gag reflex. He swallowed the bile down. "I've gotta go."

"Okay," she said worriedly. "I'll call later."

"Okay. Good luck."

He jogged to the Expedition. Dixon watched silently as Jaye jumped into his seat.

"Let's go home, okay?"

"My pleasure," Dixon replied.

Chapter 27:
Shaken Up but Holding On

The call came on Jaye's cell as they were walking into the cabin.

"Tony?"

"Yeah. Look, I'm sorry about all of that, okay? This day is just fucking with me, man. It's just a lot to deal with. Sesi talked to me a while. So did Mr. Toklo. Told me this amazing story. Can I tell you about it? You got a minute?"

"Yeah, man. Go right ahead."

"Well, he told me about this sea goddess named Sedna. Real freaky chick. Got her hands chopped to pieces by her dad who was basically sacrificing her to save himself. Took an axe right to her fingers, man, over and over. She fell into the sea. Died. Became powerful. Created life there. People make sacrifices to her so they have a good hunt, catch a lot of fish to feed their families, and so they'll be protected. That sort of thing. He really believes it too. Has a statue of her on his mantle. Said his family has made offerings to her before, way back when. Said he believes it gave 'em a run of good luck. They know she was treated like shit, but she's wiser for it, so they try to learn from her.

"Anyway, the moral of the whole thing is supposed to be that anger that gets buried or feeling totally helpless is real powerful. Can't be ignored and needs to be let out. Someone real upset deserves to have someone to listen. I don't know how he figured out I needed to hear that, other than, you know... the hand thing. Maybe it was meant to be. And, hey, if they know how to get some good luck going, I'm all for that. Maybe that's the whole reason why I'm here, right? I mean, yeah, it's rough living with another guy right now, after Hax and all. Fucks with my head, kinda. Especially since I'm in his space and he calls the shots, but he's a good dude. It's not like a woman like Sesi'd want to live with a guy like me anyway."

Jaye tried to get a word in, but Tony plowed ahead.

"Sesi and I are out on a walk right now. I stepped away for a second to call while she checked in with the station about something. I just wanted you to know that it's all coming together for me, okay? Things are making more sense. I'm sorry if I freaked you out before."

"No, I get it," Jaye told him, giving Dixon a look to help communicate the nature of the call. "Things were squirrelly for me for a while there, too. For different reasons, but it's a transition, you know? Being out here gives you more space to think and deal with shit. It'll take time. Sesi and Mr. Toklo won't let you down. Neither will Dix and I."

"Being around you just takes it to another level for me though. It's crazy how I can tell you this stuff. None of the crew knew about my past. All I ever told them was that I tend to have a lot of runs of bad luck, which is where they got Jinx from. I'm glad Drew's worm food. I'm glad I'm out. And I'm glad I've got you all pullin' for me and trying to set me up with this whole new life out here when you've got no real reason to give a shit about a guy like me. I'll show you it's not all a waste, okay? I will."

"All right, man. I hope so. Because all of the bastards that hurt you? Don't give 'em the satisfaction of hurting you more by hurting yourself. You're only letting them win if you do that. Do you really want them to win?"

"Course not."

"Is there anything else you need?"

"Nah. I'm good. It's cool of you to offer, but you've already done too much as it is. We're headed back now. Sesi's gonna cook us dinner — some clam chowder; family recipe, she said — and she's gonna help me rig up a spoon and some rubber bands so I can work a fork better. You know Martinez was spoon-feeding me all of my meals? Fuckin' humiliating."

"You'll get there," Jaye told him. "And he'll never do that shit again, right?"

"Right. Okay, later, Jaye. Take her easy."

"You too."

He hung up. Exhaled heavily with a groan.

"What?" Dixon asked.

The eagerness in Tony's voice coupled with the image of an axe chopping fingers floated through Jaye's mind. He tried to shake it loose, clear his thoughts. He flopped down on the bed on his back, running his hands over his face. "Why did no one ever tell me how much it sucks to be the one doing the head shrinking instead of the one losing his mind?"

"So psychiatry isn't your calling?" Dixon guessed, sitting beside him. He started massaging the tops of Jaye's thighs and it felt so good, Jaye groaned again but for other reasons.

"Psychiatry can suck a bag of dicks."

Jaye dropped his hands away from his face, letting them fall to the bed. The massage helped him relax a little. Dixon leaned over him and pecked a kiss to his lips.

"I thought you liked sucking dick?"

"Well, not a whole bagful. Your jaw would get way sore. And you'd need to rinse that shit out every few dicks or so."

Dixon smiled wider. Then he laughed.

"What?" Jaye asked.

"Marcus had a bag of dicks."

Jaye snorted.

"No, I'm serious. He kept the bag in his closet."

"Of course he did. Fuckin' Marcus, man." Jaye watched Dixon's grin become more introspective. "Did he ever make you suck the whole bagful in one go?"

Dixon's nose scrunched. "No!"

"Well, I wouldn't put it past him."

Dixon draped himself over Jaye's body, trailing his fingers along Jaye's leg.

"I think it'd just get really tedious after the first two, don't you think?"

"Nah, I'd give it three to four. A variety of sizes and flavors, though. The thick ones are way less fun. I'd do long over thick any day."

"Why are we still talking about this?"

Jaye brushed through the gloriously soft, downy hair covering Dixon's arm, pushing his sleeve back to expose more of it.

"You still mad?"

"About Cash? Nah. But I'm sure I'll have some awesome dreams tonight," Dixon told him softly, gazing down at Jaye's legs. "Wasn't mad anyway. Just upset."

He didn't hide anything as he met Jaye's gaze. There was so much honesty in the confession and the whole air about him. Jaye was fascinated. Everyone from Cora to Kris to Cash had always kept secrets. Dixon didn't keep any. Ever.

"I'm so damn lucky to have you," Jaye said. "Can't believe I finally have a family that actually tells me what's really on their minds and doesn't just placate me."

"I'm lucky to have you too. You push me to be a better man than I'd be otherwise."

"Doubt that." He picked up Dixon's hand and pushed his fingers through the gaps to weave their hands together. "Tony told me stuff."

"Figured. Like what?"

He explained about Drew and the downward spiral it set him on. He left out the chopped fingers.

"You think Sesi can handle all of this?" Jaye wondered.

"I do. Yeah." His thumb brushed over the side of Jaye's hand. "In her village, growing up, her best friend was molested by an uncle. He took off once word began to spread, because he knew the community would never let him get away with it. They never found him, but it was the middle of winter and he was on foot, so..." Dixon sighed. "Sesi was about sixteen then, I think. She told me how she tried to be there for her friend, no matter what. The girl's parents were at a loss. Sesi stepped up when no one else did. And her friend is still doing fine. Lives in the village and takes care of several kids within her family. She writes Sesi all the time. But that was another reason why she went into law enforcement. She can't stop trying to help people. And she shouldn't. Tony's in good hands."

"Have you known all of this for a while?"

"Some, not all. She told me the rest on the phone the other day when I was waiting for you to come back from visiting Cash. Kept me busy." Dixon raised their joined hands and kissed Jaye's knuckles. "Is Cash gonna leave you alone now?"

"Yep. I'm done with him," Jaye said with as much confidence as he could. "We're square."

"Mmm," Dixon hummed.

Jaye pulled him down and linked his hands behind Dixon's neck. "Not done with you, though."

"That ring on my finger says as much," Dixon replied, kissing the tip of Jaye's nose.

"Yes, it does," Jaye smiled.

The following week, a fair-sized earthquake disrupted the power grid in Zus, knocking out several lines to those who didn't generate their own electricity or have solar panel arrays. It kept Jaye busy, as he worked with his co-workers to get the lines repaired in several places. He was still learning, and couldn't tackle serious issues on his own just yet. He never worked on live, high voltage lines directly, but only gave support to the trained crew who did. But he did like seeing his work have a major impact on the residents of town. Without the power, food and medicine would spoil, lights wouldn't shine and service in many businesses had ground to a halt.

Dixon was almost as busy as Jaye, putting out different kinds of fires. The property damage was, thankfully, relatively minimal, but the few structures that crumbled required the intervention of the State Troopers to ensure the safety and whereabouts of the residents affected.

Both of them were on the road for days, tackling one emergency after another. They kept in touch via their phones, except when one of them ventured into a blackout zone. When they managed to be at home at the same time for a few hours, their interactions consisted mostly of cozying up close under the covers and snatching what sleep they could.

Jaye tried to keep tabs on Tony as well, especially since Sesi was just as preoccupied with work as Dixon. That left Tony home alone with Mr. Toklo for days at a time. Jaye worried the comparisons between life with Hax would only grow for Tony. Even if he was getting out for work, Tony kept going home to a space he shared with a man he considered to be of a higher social rank than him. It gave Jaye a bad feeling, wondering if they'd made the right call.

A water line had ruptured at the truck stop, flooding a storage area stocked with merchandise. When Jaye spoke to him, Tony sounded tired but energized, talking about his part in an assembly line of employees carrying the goods out to a dry area. The satisfaction in his voice told Jaye everything he needed to know. In FCI Sheridan, it was all too easy to feel like only a burden, contributing nothing worthwhile, feeling unwanted and unneeded. What had they been there, if not undesirables secured away in order to minimize their impact on the running of the world?

Jaye also checked in with his former boss, Tammy Jean Polk, whose spirits rose to see how eager Tony had been to have her load up his arms with towers of boxes, which he had no trouble carrying out across the property. When some of the more elderly contributors tired, Tony carried on with enthusiasm, refusing to take breaks or rest until the job was finished. Tammy made sure there was always a large cup waiting for him with a straw, filled with fresh water.

On the phone with Jaye, Tony talked about that cup with its straw endlessly, saying he planned to bring it back home with him to keep on his nightstand. It reminded Jaye of that first morning when Dixon had brought breakfast along with his offers of help to get Jaye back on track. Jaye never told Dixon as much, but he'd saved one of the sugar packets from that morning, palming it and storing it at the bottom of one of his drawers with other keepsakes he'd accumulated over the past year, like a scrap of a label from one of the cans of soup he'd tried to steal from the Stop and Shop, which he'd found in his coat later that night, as well as a handwritten letter from Brekken saying thank you for being there for Dixon when she couldn't, and for keeping him safe. The drawer also contained a drawing Jaye had done of Grant sitting out on the front porch of his home with the shotgun, watching out for their family, and one of Dixon's business cards with the logo for the Alaska State Troopers and the local station number listed right under Dixon's name.

"Keep the cup in a safe place," Jaye told Tony. "Sometimes it's good to have something to hold and see when things get tough. I've got my own stash."

"Yeah? You do?"

"Yep. Been adding to it since I got here. I don't tell anyone about it, really. It's for me. My peace of mind. I never did have much of anything to keep in my locker before. Not like Cash did. How about you?"

"I have a photo of Mary from our engagement party. She's wearing this yellow dress and smiling so big. Sometimes I leave it face-up, but sometimes I turn it down. Either way, it's good to have. Just knowing it's there. Got a picture of my mom and dad, too, from when I was eight. It was taken on Christmas and we're all standing by the tree, with the twinkle lights shining. You don't have any photos?"

"Nah. But I draw things I want to remember. Just as good, really."

"Man, I wish I could draw. I know what I'd draw, too. I'd draw a big, beautiful picture of Sedna for Mr. Toklo. I think that'd mean something to him. Maybe bring him some good luck in exchange for all his help, and welcoming me into his home and all. Maybe the good luck would bring his kids and grandkids out sooner to see him. They might not make it now for a while, and it's been getting to him."

Jaye got a chill at the mention of Sedna with her chopped fingers and tried to push past it, saying, "You can do anything you set your mind to. Anything in the world. You'll never know unless you give it a try. The good things come from inside. The problems we have — they can't take away the good that's inside us."

"You really think I got any good inside me, Jaye?"

"When you look at that cup Tammy gave you, you're really gonna ask me that? This is just the start for you. I know it."

The next day, he went past the truck stop. Parking his car out front, where he could see in through the glass to the shop inside, Jaye sat a while watching Tony work. He had rigged up what looked like a rubber loop to tie the mop handle to his hand, helping him keep hold of it as he washed the floors. He'd scan the room every few moments, his head down and shoulders a little hunched. If someone caught his eye, he'd look away fast, then glance back again to see if they were still looking. When one of the other employees passed by, clapping him on the shoulder, Tony's face lit with a big smile as he responded with a few words Jaye couldn't hear.

He saw the paradox Dixon often told Jaye he also possessed, in the simultaneous youth and age in Tony. He was only a few years older than Jaye. In another life, he might still be in school, working towards a future instead of just trying to prove to himself he could have one at all. Considering the other employees around Tony, the way they seemed to accept him rather than judge him, as they could have so easily done, gave Jaye a lot of hope. Maybe Jaye's span of time in that same job had helped them open their hearts to another ex-con. Maybe not. Tony had more charisma than Jaye in a lot of ways. He didn't have visible tattoos or an inappropriately pretty face, or seemed younger than he should. He was just a normal guy trying to do the right thing, expecting nothing in return.

Jaye didn't like those hunched shoulders, though, like the weight of others' deeds pressed Tony constantly down, or the way the light in his eyes burned low when he turned his focus back to the mop, the handle slipping through his twisted fingers.

Jaye knew if he went in to say hello, Tony's light would come back. But for how long? How was he supposed to show Tony the future was worth the continued fight, when he'd already been in the ring, swinging away and losing for way too long?

He didn't have answers, but he wasn't ready to give up the fight either.

Chapter 28:
Aftershocks

The call came at three a.m. over Jaye's cell phone. He and Dixon had been sleeping since eleven, both of them exhausted. When they'd gone to bed, the wind had been howling and thunder rumbling. As the ringing yanked Jaye awake, he realized everything was calm and perfectly still, like an indrawn breath before a wild shout.

His dreams had been muddled, with hands grabbing at him, the voice wavering between Cash's growl and Ecker's eerie lilt. He'd been bent over the edge of a couch and kicked out at whoever was behind him as hard as he could. The breath had woofed out of his attacker and he'd managed to get up and twist around, right onto the end of a filleting knife. It hadn't just stuck in him, but had sliced across, his intestines spilling out in a red, wet pile as the knife clattered to the floor. Standing there alone, with only the ghosts as company, he'd heard a voice say, *'Just trying to find the good inside, piggy. It comes from way down deep, just like you said. Just trying to find it...'*

In his mind, part of him was still trying to grab hold of the slick loops and push them back inside, even while he blinked and saw the clear, starry night through the curtains, not a cloud to block their shine, and his ears rang with the shrill shrieking of his phone.

He reached for it, almost knocked it off the nightstand, and finally got hold of it.

A press of a button and he heard, "Get to Tony's, now! I need help!"

"Sesi?"

"Now!"

"Okay!"

The call ended. He stumbled out of bed. Squinting over at him, Dixon frowned. Jaye hopped into the jeans he'd worn the day before, pulled a sweater over his head and lunged for his shoes.

"Gotta go. Gotta get to Tony. It was Sesi. Something's wrong."

"Okay. Okay, I'm up," Dixon said in a sleep-roughened voice, swinging his legs over the side of the bed.

"Dix, I've gotta go!" Jaye yelled, grabbing his keys and heading for the door.

"I know. I know!"

In his pajama pants, Dixon grabbed his heavy coat and a hat and followed.

"I'm driving. You still look half asleep," Jaye decided, jogging to his sedan.

"That's because I am," Dixon admitted, heading for the passenger seat.

Jaye started the car and sped away once Dixon was inside, thankful for the absolute lack of other cars on the road.

Even though there was a Trooper in the seat beside him, he sped all the way to Mr. Toklo's house. Because his phone was blinking to alert him to an awaiting message, he asked Dixon check it for him.

"It's a text from Tony, from about twenty minutes ago," Dixon told him, sounding more awake but also more disturbed.

"What?"

"It just says, 'I'm tired of taking from everybody. I need to make some good luck for once. I'm sorry,'" Dixon told him with an apologetic tone.

"Fuck," Jaye breathed.

Thinking of the dream he'd been having before he'd woken because of Sesi's call, Jaye had too clear of an idea of the types of dreams Tony must have been suffering — a combination of Drew, Hax, Diego, the guys who'd smashed his hands, the other ones who'd raped him after… And that wasn't all. Jaye knew the heavy weight of needing to take from others to get by, and having to swallow pride, submitting oneself to another's generosity. It could be brutally emasculating, even more so than prison where there were no choices. Maybe Tony couldn't see the path to self-sufficiency that the rest of them could. Maybe being taken in by a community only meant Tony felt that much more helpless.

Had there really never been a chance for him?

Terror chilled Jaye to the bone, feeling the implications for himself also. If Tony couldn't do it, maybe Jaye's past would get the best of him eventually too, no matter how hard he fought for himself.

Maybe they were all doomed.

The car flew down empty roads. Small homes whizzed past as little specks of light and civilization amidst miles upon miles of wilderness. Jaye pushed the gas pedal harder, trying to pull Mr. Toklo's home toward them. He did the math in his head, tracking distances. Sesi's apartment was closer to the cabin than they were. She'd get there first, no matter how fast they went.

He stopped thinking. He barely breathed. Going and doing were all that mattered.

The cabin slid slowly into view. A car was parked slantwise out front, half in the road and half on the rocky grass, the driver's side door left swung open wide, some of the interior vehicle lights shining out onto the star-strewn night.

At first, that's all Jaye saw. That vehicle and everything wrong about it — that it was there, that it was left behind in such haste.

At first, he hadn't seen the rest of what was happening.

Afterward, he thought maybe he hadn't wanted to see it. That he'd blocked it out.

"Jaye," Dixon said, as if in warning. He pointed.

Jaye didn't look, but instead sped up to Sesi's Expedition and slammed to a halt, his tires squealing on the pavement.

Dixon got out before they'd even stopped, and he sprinted forward, arms pumping.

With his door open, Jaye stood there, staring, unable to believe what he finally saw.

Tony was kneeling by a tree stump on the side of the house. An empty bottle of booze lay at his feet, knocked over. One of Mr. Toklo's stone statues had been brought out and stood by Tony's side. There were crude words scratched in the dirt, directly beneath the statue. As Jaye moved closer, he saw they spelled out 'For Sedna'. Sesi stood there, hands up and raised, her gaze locked on Tony and his on her as he clumsily held the edge of an ax to his forearm. Dark drips ran in lines down the pale skin.

If he pressed any harder, he could take his hand clean off.

"Tony, you're worth more than this," Sesi told him, her voice barely shaking. "I need you here, with me. Not in pieces. So drop the axe. Listen to me."

Jaye stayed frozen. It finally registered that he couldn't help Tony; not in the ways that mattered. Dixon ran, circling around to come at Tony from behind.

Tony kept looking at Sesi, who never once diverted her attention from him, bless her.

It was just enough. Tony didn't see Dixon until he was right there, kicking the ax out of Tony's feeble grip. It flew on an arc and landed in the dirt with a muffled thump.

Dixon fell to his knees and caught Tony as he slumped sideways. Sesi broke into motion, closing the gap between herself and Tony. Jaye saw the way she shivered uncontrollably and took deep breaths to calm herself before saying anything.

"Thank you," Sesi choked out. "Thank you, Dix."

Jaye found he could move now, too, though slowly, in a fog. Most of all, he wanted to scuff out those words in the dirt with his shoe, or smash the statue to pieces.

He finally noticed, up by the cabin's front door, Mr. Toklo himself, hand over his mouth, gripping the doorframe with wide eyes.

"I... I was just tryin' ta give somethin' back," Tony slurred.

Dixon pressed against the wound on Tony's arm as blood oozed down his hand and onto his chest below where Dixon held it tight. Her face tear-stained, Sesi knelt beside Tony where he was cradled in Dixon's arms. She kissed Tony, her hand held to the side of his face.

"You already give back to me every damn day. But it comes from deep down in here," Sesi told him, hand to his chest. "Look past the surface."

When Jaye got closer, he smelled the alcohol on the ground and soaked into Tony's clothes. Liquor was never in short supply in Zus or any of the Alaskan communities. Jaye knew from Dixon that most of the calls to the department involved alcohol. Anger began to edge past the fear.

Tony was crying. He leaned into her touch and kissed her too.

"I'm sorry. I'm so sorry," he said, over and over.

"We're not letting you do this," she told him, her voice thick with tears and anger, and something softer, too. "We're not letting you give up. You hear me? It's too late for that. I'm here. Jaye's here. Dixon is here. You're not doing this alone anymore. We care about you. You can't give up now without hurting us. Do you want to hurt us?"

"No," he admitted. A grimace of pain crossed his face.

"I don't know if he nicked an artery here, Ses. He needs help," Dixon told her.

"Dr. Canter," she said, pulling out her phone.

She sat back and dialed. Dr. Canter's home was miles away but the closest medical option they had. The nearest clinic was a three-hour drive. Dr. Canter was retired but had a small facility on his property for local emergencies.

Jaye crouched by Tony.

"What the fuck, man? What is this?" he demanded. Tony held eye contact for a mere moment before returning his focus to Sesi.

"Haven't slept much. Keep having nightmares. Can't relax. It's worst when it's dark. When I'm alone. And I know I shouldn't have, but I bought a couple bottles of scotch. But I couldn't... I couldn't fuckin' open them, so I came out here and used the ax to crack the lids off. And then..." He shook, groaning as Dixon continued to press hard against the bleeding gash across Tony's wrist. "Fuckin' *hate* these ruined things. Just wanted 'em gone. Wanted it to stop. Thought if I gave them up for Sedna, at least I could give something back. Good luck instead of only bad. I'm sorry. I know I fucked up. I don't want to die. I don't. Just wanted to take care of other people for once. Sesi, you believe me, right?"

She was talking quietly into her phone. She hung up.

"We need to go. Get you over there. He'll help. Patch you up, okay? Then you're coming home with me. No arguing. If you want to help, I'll show you how to help."

Tony nodded. He cried out as he moved to sit. More blood flowed as Dixon's grip slipped for a moment, dripping onto the dirt where the words were crudely carved. The offering to Sedna had been made after all.

"Go with them," Jaye told Dixon. "I'll follow."

Sesi and Jaye lifted Tony to his feet and steadied him for the walk to her Expedition. Dixon's grip stayed strong. They got into the back seat. Sesi sat behind the wheel. Moments later, they were both driving away and Jaye could only pray it was enough, that they

225

hadn't been too late, and the cut too deep. But the hope was there, all the same, and it was strong.

Dixon suspected it was the first time Jaye had been to Sesi's place. She didn't usually invite people over, just because of how small the apartment was. It was located on the second floor of a larger building downtown in Zus that had been carved up into smaller units. The convenience to the station and the close community living appealed to her in ways it never would to Dixon.

Dixon and Jaye climbed the outdoor stairs to the private entrance and knocked.

When Sesi opened the door, Dixon noticed a flicker of guilt in her expression before a welcoming smile brushed the subtler emotion aside.

"Good to see you," she told them, ushering them through the door and closing it behind them.

Tony sat on a small couch. The neatly stacked pile of linens beside it told Dixon it was either being used as his bed, or was intended to look that way.

The bandage on Tony's arm was visible since his sleeves were rolled up. Hunched forward, his hands dangled between his knees. He met their gazes one at a time. Interestingly, Dixon noticed no guilt in Tony as he had in Sesi.

There was a lot being said in the quiet space, as no one rushed to speak first. A clock ticked the seconds away. A rich scent of spices and meat emanated from the direction of the stove.

The living and kitchen area was combined in a single cozy space. A doorway led to the equally quaint bedroom and a bathroom. There were less signs of Sesi's Inuit heritage around the space, which was much more modern than Mr. Toklo's, though Dixon did notice a few hand-sewn, beaded dolls on a shelf, and plenty of photos of family members in frames on the walls.

There were several reasons why Tony had not been initially invited to stay with Sesi upon his arrival in Zus following his release. Things like Sesi's need for personal safety, and the impracticality of the idea rose to the top of the list. As Dixon fought to hide his disapproval from her, he wondered if they would be given any explanation why those reasons had been thrown out the window.

"Thanks for coming," Tony said to Jaye.

"Doing better?"

"Yeah. Much."

An iPad lay at Tony's side, like he'd just set it down — another sign that he'd been enjoying more modern conveniences since the move.

Jaye grunted, his expression unreadable, which told Dixon a lot.

To Sesi, Dixon said as politely as he could, "Can I, uh, talk to you outside?"

"Just say it, Dix," Sesi replied wearily, waving her arms. "I mean, what's the point? You're gonna tell Jaye and I'm gonna tell Tony. Truth and honesty is important to all of us."

"Fine. Is this really a good idea? You two living together? No offense intended, man."

"Yes," Sesi argued, sitting in a chair at the small table in the corner of the room. She sounded tired of explaining herself before she even began. "It is. We're comfortable with each other. Tony's happier here. I'm happier with him here. It's less isolated and there are always people around for company. I can be here for Tony whenever I need to. So he's not alone."

"He wasn't alone with Mr. Toklo."

"That's different and you know it. Mr. Toklo isn't invested in Tony's wellbeing."

"But you are?"

"Yes!" With a self-deprecating sort of smile, she shook her head. "Sit down. Relax."

"I'm fine," Dixon countered, folding his arms. Jaye moved to sit beside Tony, shifting the tablet to a side table. Sparing one more glance at the neatly stacked sheets beside the couch, Dixon said as forcefully as he could to someone who he considered one of his best friends, "I really need to talk to you outside."

"Fine," Sesi surrendered. To Tony, she said, "I'll be right back."

"That's fine. Hash it out. I get it."

Dixon followed her out through the entrance and down the stairs, where she stopped and turned on him.

"Dixon, I'm fine."

"You don't have family here, Ses. I need to watch out for you! You're like a sister to me, and we don't know this guy. Not really. He was involved in some bad stuff."

"So was Jaye."

"It's not the same. Jaye never stood by while some other guy was getting raped."

"That's not fair. You don't know Tony's history. You haven't heard his side of it. Tony wasn't in any position to fight against his own boss, his boss's second-in-command, and multiple guards in a locked cell in solitary. And it wasn't clean-cut rape. There was some form of consent there."

"You've gotta be shitting me. You're okay with what they did to him? Taking him by surprise, holding him down with multiple armed guards, gang banging him on video while he cried and begged?"

Sesi groaned and covered her face.

"Are you having sex with him?" he demanded.

"That's none of your business." Sesi's hands dropped to her sides and her tone was frosty.

"Wow."

"Don't do that. Don't," she warned. "He treats me with more respect than any guy I've dated in years. He always tells me the truth when it's just the two of us, about anything I ask, any topic. He's been painfully honest with me about a lot of things, even when it doesn't paint him in the best light. He thinks things through. He does whatever he can to take care of me. And it's not just me. He cares about people and consequences and morality and our impact on the world around us, and I like him, okay?"

"He's not a project," Dixon tried. "He's a man with a hell of a lot of problems which you can't solve. No one can."

She rolled her eyes and crossed her arms over her chest. "We can say that about you too. And Jaye. And me. And a lot of other people. Don't judge him for having a moment of weakness and feeling like he had no choice but to give up. We've all been there."

Dixon sighed and paced a little.

"I'm not helpless, Dixon," she said fervently. "I'm a cop. A Trooper. I can handle myself, but I don't need to handle myself with him. He's a gentle guy. He's careful. Thoughtful. More than anything, he's afraid of not being good enough. He's not dangerous. Ask Jaye. Ask him if he's ever seen Tony intentionally hurt anybody, ever."

He could tell she believed that, but he couldn't make the leap.

"Think of how I felt when you hooked up with Jaye. It's the same stuff. He's an ex-convict. A gang member. He stole food. He has a friggin' tear inked on his face. When I met him he was defensive about everything and his behavior was erratic. Jaye was completely unstable. And you were with him all the time. There was nothing I could do to stop you. Would I have ever been able to stop you?"

"No," he admitted, feeling like the firm, metaphorical ground he stood on quickly soften. Like Sesi sensed she was winning, she pulled herself up straighter, raised her chin higher.

"And don't even get me started on Marcus and the bruises. The broken nose. All of the other many signs that things were very much not okay."

He didn't know what to say to that.

"Tony cares about people," she insisted, her dark eyes sparkling. She pushed her long, black hair back over a shoulder. "He lost the woman he loved more than life itself. She left him. He wants to protect me. Watch out for me. Find ways to make me smile when I get home from work. It gives him purpose. You should see the way it's changed him after only a single day, Dix. And I'm not alone here. My walls are not that soundproof. My neighbors are always here at night. If I ever had trouble of any sort, they'd hear. They'd come. Tell me I'm wrong."

"I can't," he said quietly. "But I'm still worried."

"That's because you care about people too," she said with a smile, giving his arm a squeeze.

He tried to find a way to be okay with it, but it still felt like an itch he couldn't scratch. Knowing he was being a hypocrite didn't really help at all.

"Has he ever been rough with you, in any way?"

Sesi sighed and rolled her eyes again. "No, but that's not your business either. Do I ask you things like that?"

There was only one last approach he could try, so he went for it.

"I know Jaye really well. And he knows Tony better than any of us. He is not thrilled about this either. That tells me a lot."

"Well, Jaye is biased, and he's overprotective too. If not more so." Dixon avoided eye contact, but she wouldn't have it, staring at him until he looked back at her. "Hmm? That shit with Marcus? Jaye's impulsive when he's emotional."

229

"He's not emotional right now."

"Dixon," she groaned.

He fell quiet. Not sure what else there was to say.

"I appreciate that you care this much, Dix," she said gently. "I really do. I love you for it, actually. But you have to let me make my own choices. You have to trust me to know my own heart. He..." She fell quiet, her voice dropping off, as if with embarrassment. "He holds me like I'm the most valuable thing in the whole world. More than anything — money, recognition, you name it. I've never experienced anything like that. Not even close."

He bit at his lip, saw all of her determination shining out of her. "Fine. But at the slightest sign of anything wrong, you need to tell me. You have to swear you will."

"I swear."

"No matter what time it is or — "

"Dixon," she laughed. "I swear."

She came over to give him a hug, which he slowly melted into.

"I know what you mean," he admitted after a pause.

"About what?"

She let go and searched his eyes when he didn't answer right away. Blushing, he said, "Jaye holds me like that too."

She smiled again, her eyes shining even more. She wiped at them and hugged him again, whispering, "Good."

Chapter 29:
Vignettes of Hope

"So," Jaye said conversationally, drumming his fingers together. "You and Sesi, huh?"

"Yeah. You could say that," Tony admitted somewhat bashfully. He dropped his head. "We talk all the time. We've gone out a bunch of times, but yeah. I guess now it's the real thing. But I swear I'm not trying to take advantage. I know she's your friend. She's a great lady. Strong as hell, you know? I respect that. And all the ways she's come through for me? I'm gonna pay that back."

"Oh yeah?"

"Yeah. Absolutely. I'll find a way. Take care of something she needs. Or maybe just try to make her happy."

Jaye watched him closely. Beyond the surface embarrassment from the suicide attempt and being caught at bunking with the female Trooper who rescued him, there seemed to be no ulterior motives to detect.

"Just don't try to get away with shit at her expense. You hear me?"

"I'd never, man. Never. Not to her. She's special. She's... I don't know. I can't explain it." He shook his head, looked around the small apartment. "I feel good here. All of those pictures on the walls. The little mementos she collects from the places she's been. The people she's helped. She celebrates living. I'm not used to that. I mean, I think I used to be that way too, before. Before Drew. Maybe I can get back to that. Do you think it's possible?"

Thinking of the naïve kid Jaye had been before Burt and Earl, Jaye knew he'd never go back to that. Not for any reason. But even

231

then, he'd never been a saint. Life had never been easy. Not with Cora.

Still... Being with Dixon had spurred Jaye to grow into a more well-rounded person. Life mattered in ways it never had, even when he was a stupid kid. Jaye understood now why he couldn't be the one to help Tony. Despite their bond, Jaye was a reminder of a place they both desperately wanted to forget. Tony needed someone innocent to draw his hope from, the way Jaye had needed that from Dixon.

"Nah, man," he told Tony. "There ain't no going back. Not to that. But you can move forward to something better. Much better. You appreciate things more. Take nothing for granted. Hold on to the good. You know what I mean?"

"Yeah," Tony grinned. "Yeah, I think I do."

He glanced around again. There was a photo hanging on the far wall, which he kept going back to. It showed Sesi as a younger woman, arm in arm with a few other ladies her age, standing in front of a roaring bonfire. There were many others in traditional garb around them, at some sort of festival. In the background were snow-peaked mountains. Their expressions reflected only joy, love, and acceptance.

"You know what means the most?" Tony asked, his voice a little softer.

"What?"

"She doesn't get freaked out or take off when I get scared. She sticks right there. Right by me. Holds my hand. Looks me right in the eye. Tells me I can do it. Like it matters to her whether I try or not. And she ain't even getting much of anything out of it either."

"She gets you," Jaye pointed out.

Tony scratched at the edge of his bandage, drawing Jaye's attention to it.

"Don't ever pull that shit again," Jaye warned. "You're not a coward. You haven't been through all of that hell in Sheridan and with Drew just to give up now, when everything's finally getting better, are you?"

"I wrote a letter. Like you said," Tony said, avoiding the question by taking the conversation someplace else. "I'm gonna send it to the detective. See if he can pass it along to the kid Drew was going after when he got shot. Sesi got it all down for me this morning. You think it'll help that kid at all? Hearing that he's not alone? That I'm glad he's free of that pedo creep now?"

Thinking of his own lonely nights and days, in recovery after his attack, in prison, in Zus, Jaye answered definitively, "Yeah. Yeah, absolutely I do. It's the worst thing in the world to feel alone, especially when we're not."

"Yeah." Tony chuckled, bowing his head to hide his relief and happiness. "Yeah, you know it."

"Damn right I do."

He nudged Tony's arm, gave him a smile, and drew another chuckle from him.

"Thanks, man."

"Anytime."

The letters didn't come often, or regularly. It was just once in a while. The first one or two he didn't read. He threw them away, unopened. But then he realized it might not be safe to do that.

So he started to open them. He skimmed the contents for threats or danger.

There were never any to be found.

They were pathetic, really.

Prison gossip. News about this guy or that. Who got in a fight and who had beef with whom.

Then the begging would start. Not overt. Subtle. Proud. The undercurrent of desperation was unmistakable.

Cash wanted photos. Calls. He stopped short of asking for video, though he did mention it often. In return, he promised the world. Anything. Everything. Money. Access. Favors. Devotion.

Dixon understood the balls it took for a guy like Cash to write letters like those to a kid who had only been intended to be a prison bitch. But he also knew Cash had the balls, no question.

He ripped them up, undelivered to their intended. Jaye had gotten rid of his old post office box, so the only route Cash had was through Dixon.

Sometimes they were addressed to Jaye. Sometimes to Johnny.

As weeks turned to months, they began to be addressed to Dixon instead.

The begging intensified, became more blatant.

The calls were never accepted, and Jaye didn't have a landline phone number. Cash was wholly unaware of Jaye's job as an electrician. Jaye wasn't listed officially on any websites or directories. So Cash kept trying to call Dixon instead.

Dixon knew Cash was getting it. He could tell as much from the letters.

The pleas for photos stopped. So did the prison gossip.

He only addressed the letters to Dixon at that point, and they contained only conversation, speculation, questions that would never be answered about what it was like up in Alaska, what it was like to be a Trooper, what it was like to get to love someone like Jaye, day in and day out.

Then they stopped entirely.

Dixon was glad.

Tony showed him the paper one day when they came over for dinner at the cabin. He handed the folded page to Jaye, then walked off to check out the drawings hanging on the walls, his arm slung around Sesi's waist. She kept letting her head lean against Tony's shoulder, and seemed more relaxed and smiley than Jaye had ever seen her. She was practically glowing.

Jaye unfolded it, glancing to Dixon who was preparing their dinner by the oven.

Then, he began to read.

Hi Tony,

I don't know what made you write that letter after so long, or what your life has been like, but believe me when I say how very much it means to know I'm not alone. I was thirteen, too. Back then, I never told anyone either, but someone did start to suspect eventually. But Drew had stuck around for months. I thought he was my boyfriend, and I never saw what it really was. In some ways, I'm still trying to, actually.

Because Drew was just the first of many.

He opened to door to so many others and fucked my head up in ways no one gets. But maybe you do. I can still feel what he did. I can sense it. But I can't really explain it, even to myself.

I tried to kill myself less than a year after Drew took his first picture of me. As you can tell, it didn't take, and I'm glad. I'm so damned glad. I never told anyone this, and I'm not sure why I'm telling you, but I think I went somewhere in those couple of minutes when my heart stopped. That place was warm, bright, good, and I felt so much love and understanding there. I guess what I'm saying is, it showed me this life's not all for nothing. Even if you don't tell anyone else what Drew did to you, or talk about how bad it really gets, there's still a place for people like us where we're taken care of and where everything wrong feels right again. So don't give up, okay?

What Drew did isn't your fault any more than it's mine. The only things we're responsible for are our choices and whether we help other people, or hurt them. I've got people who love me now, and who protect me. I try to do the same for them, too. How about you? Do you have someone to fight for? I hope so.

I believe in you, Tony. Hang in there, man.

Evan Savage

Jaye smoothed out the paper's wrinkles. For a long moment, he stared right through the paper, letting it all sink in. When he glanced up, Tony gave him a small smile, then nodded his head slightly in acknowledgement before continuing his conversation with Sesi. He leaned in and kissed her cheek.

Jaye let out a breath. He folded up the paper again, carefully. He thought of fighters, survivors, of boys captured in photos, boys dying, boys living, of the hopeless trying anyway out of sheer faith, of the small steps that make up momentous transformations, and the simple beauty of truth in a liar's world.

He sat down on the couch behind him and stared up at the starry sky glimpsed through the window beside him, holding the letter in his hands, and wondered.

Maybe all of the broken pieces did fit back together after all, making new patterns, creating miracles.

Brekken met them at the door, holding two glasses of wine.

"Hey, welcome." She smiled, though biting at her lip. She was hiding something. "Here. For you."

She handed Dixon and Jaye the glasses, then waved them inside. Grant waited there, standing while wearing an equally suspicious expression. Sesi and Tony sat on the couch in the living room of the small house, and murmured their hellos. Everyone with the exception of Sesi held glasses as well. There was some music playing quietly, but no one spoke.

"Why do I feel like I'm being ambushed," Dixon asked as they all stared at the new arrivals. "What's going on?"

"Just tell them. Like ripping off a bandaid," Brekken encouraged, addressing the room's seated occupants. Sesi held Tony's arm, while turned slightly toward him. Tony's eyes were too wide, his smile strained.

"Tell us what?" Dixon said with confusion.

"No," Jaye gasped.

"No what?"

"Are you kidding me?!" Jaye exclaimed joyfully, laughing.

"What?!"

"I'm pregnant," Sesi said meekly.

Jaye laughed again, let out a whoop and chugged the wine. "Wow, I hate wine. But this is amazing! How excited are you two?"

"What... how... why..."

"You don't seem that surprised," Sesi observed of Jaye. "Did he already tell you?"

"No, but I kind of suspected. He's been paler than anyone who goes on daily hikes has any right to be. And his eyes have been exactly that wide for a long time now. And Sesi, you're the only one not drinking wine."

"How are you pregnant?!" Dixon cried.

Brekken tsked. "Hon, do we need to have the talk? Did Mom and Dad skip that with you because of the gay thing?"

"How pregnant?" Jaye asked.

"I'm due in late December," Sesi answered. "Doc says everything looks great so far."

"Oh my god. This is amazing! You're making a new person!" Jaye set down his empty glass and went to the couch. He leaned down to fold Sesi into a hug, kissing her cheek. "Congratulations."

"Thanks," she smiled, hugging him back with a happy groan.

He let go and turned to Tony. Pulling him up off the couch, Jaye gave him a fierce hug. Tony's grin widened uncontrollably. "You're in shock, aren't you? You're gonna be a dad!"

Tony laughed a little, his face turning pink. "I've always, um, been good with kids, you know. I just never thought. I... Yeah. Yeah, I'm still in shock."

"Well, breathe, man. You can do this," Jaye told him.

"Yeah, I think so. I..." he blew out a breath and looked around at all of them. There was a silent, still moment.

Then he turned to Sesi and got down on one knee.

"No!" Brekken gasped. "Oh my god, where's my camera!"

"What's happening?" Dixon wondered dumbly.

Jaye planted his hands on his hips, looking profoundly entertained at the whole thing.

"Sesi Ahnah," Tony started, his voice hushed and trembling. "You know I love you. The way you see me, your confidence, your heart — it's everything I've ever wanted. I'd do anything for you, and for our child. I want us to be a family. All of us. I want to build a future together. Would you do me the great honor of being my wife?"

He didn't have a ring, but he held her hand in both of his, looking at her with what seemed to be pure, open, honest hope. Seeing it, all of Dixon's initial concerns dropped away.

"Of course I will," Sesi said, her eyes shining. She pulled him close and kissed him hard.

Brekken aimed her camera at them, capturing the moment.

Dixon was dumbfounded.

"Congratulations again, you two," Grant said. "I think we need more wine."

"Much more wine," Dixon agreed.

"None for me, thanks!" Jaye waved. "I'm good."

"Me too," Tony smiled at Sesi, who threw her arms around him, beaming.

The night was wild, the hour late, but their home was their sanctuary.

Seemingly unprompted, Jaye chuckled, his eyes squinted shut with the size of his smile. It appeared to Dixon to come from the innermost core of his heart, shining up through him from sacred places.

When Dixon bottomed out, Jaye's ass pulling him in like it had a mind and will of its own, he let out a moan from way deep down, resting his forehead on Jaye's dark, soft curls, which smelled of coconut, skin, sweat, and him. Jaye's chuckle grew into a bright laugh and he began to move, rolling his hips with proud eagerness.

There were no words to express the beautiful madness it conjured in Dixon, feeling that tug and push, crashing into him like waves. He moaned even harder, and Jaye laughed louder. It sounded free, like flying, like soaring on clouds and dancing on the wind. He intertwined his fingers in Dixon's, kissed Dixon's thumb and sighed breathily.

Dixon's teeth scratched lightly along the side of Jaye's neck, drawing faint pink lines through the bluejay's gray wing. The rolling and crashing grew in strength and force and Dixon panted, trying to survive it, getting lost in it.

Outside the cabin, teeming rain thundered down on the roof, dripping from the eaves, tapping on the windows. Inside, they were warm, secluded, and utterly safe. Jaye had Dixon gripped tightly and wouldn't let go. In turn Dixon had — and took — Jaye. He pushed into the next undulation, his hand wrapping Jaye's slim hip, restless in its quest to take him apart and wring him dry of sense and sanity. He pushed harder, and Jaye's next exhale rushed from him. Goosebumps rose on his skin and his chuckle softened to a contented hum. He nuzzled Dixon's next kiss to Jaye's cheek, drew their entwined hands closer to his chest where Dixon felt Jaye's heartbeat drumming behind his ribs at a steady, wild pace.

Dixon pushed their hands lower, felt the wet tip of Jaye's hardness brush their knuckles. Jaye let him loose, so Dixon grabbed hold of it and tugged. Jaye's sigh bloomed into more laughter and Dixon needed to feel it against his lips, vibrating into his skin, soul, and the air itself, so he pushed in all the way and leaned around to catch Jaye's lips and pumped him harder. The laughter melted into the most fragile whimper and Dixon came, shivering, drinking down Jaye's fevered breaths and small cries. When he came, kissing Dixon back, there was no care in his face, no worry, no weight. Both lost and found, free and safeguarded, Jaye finally flew high and there was no danger, no dread. Just love, life and everything Dixon would use all of his power to give, forever.

If you enjoyed this story, you can sign up for a free membership at ForbiddenFiction and discuss it with other readers and the author at the *Arctic Restitution story page*.

Author's Notes

It wasn't until I wrote *Caged Jaye* that I realized *Arctic Absolution* needed a sequel. In showing the "before" stage of Jaye's life, introducing all of the major players before Dixon came on the scene, I sensed it was necessary to show more of the "after." More than that, I needed to show all of the parts of Jaye's world come together as a greater whole.

In *Caged Jaye*, Jaye loses his family and becomes a warrior. In *Arctic Absolution*, he finds love and hope of something better. In *Arctic Restitution*, I wanted to give him his family back. It's not the one he would have ever expected, but it's more nurturing than the one he'd left behind.

After all Jaye and Dixon have been through before getting to this third book, they've certainly earned a break, as well as a chance to focus on healing themselves. Jaye's mental health issues and Dixon's trauma from Marcus have not gone away. But life doesn't tend to give us perfect spans of respite in which to tend our wounds. For both Jaye and Dixon, Tony is a cosmic push to expand their world view and realize their experiences and strength can enable them to help others. Jaye and Dixon are no longer in imminent physical danger, but Tony is. The urgency of Tony's need can't be ignored. It also shines a spotlight on how far Jaye has progressed since his incarnation as inmate Johnny in *Caged Jaye*.

This novel brings Jaye full circle. After everything, he's able to become once again the carefree, laughing boy he once was, though even more fulfilled than he dreamed possible. Where once he promised his mother to fly far away from their problems, he transforms into a soaring, brave, capable hero. It's the ending I always wanted for him.

I'll admit one of my biggest motivations with this story — if not the biggest — was having Dixon and Cash meet. Cash, who gets some bittersweet moments to hint at deeper layers of his heart, gets to show just how much Jaye means to him. Dixon, with all of his fear and worry, encounters someone who seems to outman him in every single way. But Dixon also learns the power of his love for Jaye gives him weapons he never had to wield before. Being the man Jaye needs does not mean being the man Dixon thinks he should be. In tangling with Cash and Tony, Dixon gets a jarring lesson in understanding his privilege and power. As someone whose inner strength had always been challenged, Dixon is faced with a crime boss who knows no fear. But it's not Dixon's badge or his ability to seem tough that matter in the end, but the yearning in his heart to ease the burdens of those he cares for, as much as he possibly can.

While I'm at it, I'll admit something else too. I never planned on Tony. Though I enjoyed his character as Jinx in *Caged Jaye*, it wasn't until Jaye was sitting frozen in an icy field with a letter in his hands that I felt Tony's layers begin to peel away. He's the kindred spirit I knew Jaye needed — a brother with even more dire prospects and even less hope. And the only person in the whole world who was up to the task of pulling Tony out of hell was none other than Johnny Larson, who knew the way. Jaye is someone who can't give up. He fights, always. Here, I needed him to fight for someone who everyone else had forsaken. But Tony ties Jaye to Sheridan forever. He threatens to keep the ghosts alive, but he's also the proof he has always been right to never, ever give up.

The greatest sentiment I tried to infuse into this story is the idea that survival has a purpose. In navigating the horrifying obstacle courses set before them, Jaye and Dixon have proven themselves. Working towards peace and health might still be their goals, but they have work left to do. There are others who still struggle to endure in darkness and can't see the light at the end of the tunnel unless someone out there takes the time to shout back and show them the way. It's when Jaye understands Tony's desperation and hopelessness that he truly begins to move past his own harrowing experiences. In lifting Tony up, Jaye also lifts himself.

The appearance of Evan Savage from my Twin Ties series was also not planned, but as Tony's story took shape, I felt its echoes in Evan's. If Tony embodied for Jaye memories he initially would rather have left behind, for Tony that person is embodied by Evan. Ironically, it's the understanding they find in each other that becomes their greatest source inspiration. I know for Evan, hearing from Tony has worked wonders, showing him we're never as alone as we think.

There are a lot of layers to this story. Beneath one truth are always many others lying in wait to be revealed. But it's honesty and goodness that pull everyone through. And, as someone stumbles, they are helped back up to their feet by a community they never expected to have.

It was good to bring Jaye home for the first time, and give him a man to care for in ways that only make him feel more alive.

Thank you for reading. This story wouldn't exist without the encouragement of my wonderful readers and the fabulous folks at ForbiddenFiction. I hope it helps inspire you, my friends, to never stop fighting and to see the greatest beauty lies not in our destination, but in the journey.

Lynn Kelling
March 18, 2017

About the Author

Lynn Kelling began writing in order to tell stories that weren't afraid of the dark, didn't hold anything back and always strived to be memorable, forging lasting attachments between character and reader. Her inspiration comes from taking a closer look at behaviors and ideas lurking at the fringes of life – basically anything that people may hesitate to speak of in mixed company, but everyone wonders about anyway. Her work is driven by the taboo in order to expose the humanity within it. Lynn is an artist, designer and lover of any form of creative self-expression that comes from a place of honesty and emotion, whether it's body art or opera. She has had multiple novels published, has written over 50 works of erotic fiction of varying lengths, and always has several novels in progress.

Other Works by Lynn Kelling:
Bare
Between Here and There
Bound by Lies
Cursed Blessings
Deliver Us
Divine Surrender
Double Heat
Dual Affairs
Escape
Expected Lies
Forgive Us
From Temptation
Learning from the Master
Loving the Master
My Brother's Lover
Never Happened
Only the Lonely
Pleasures of Paradise
Song of the Lonesome Cowboy
Trick and Truth
Whatever the Cost

About the Series

Erotic stories set in the world of **Lynn Kelling**'s Arctic Absolution series.

Jaye Larson is an ex-con with a troubled, terrifying past. Dixon Rowe is a good man in a hard world, a cop with a soft spot for saving bad boys. Things change for both of them the night Dixon nearly arrests Jaye for petty theft and decides to help him go... Well, not straight, exactly. As it turns out Jaye is just Dixon's type, and Dixon's interest quickly rises beyond the professional.

As if their growing romance wasn't complicated enough, Jaye's history won't stay behind him, and it turns out that Dixon has a skeleton or two in his own closet. In order to build a future together, the two men have to put the past to rest.

Lynn Kelling draws intense emotion and raw, kinky sex from these characters and their lives, creating a multi-layered romance with deep history and real warmth. She makes Jay and Dixon work hard to earn their happy ending.

About the Publisher

FANTASTIC FICTION *FORBIDDENFICTION*

PUBLISHING *INTELLIGENT EROTICA*

ForbiddenFiction.com is a publisher devoted to writing that breaks the boundaries of original erotic fiction. Our stories combine intense sexuality with quality writing. Stories at Forbidden Fiction.com not only arouse readers through sensations, but also engage them emotionally and mentally through storytelling as well-crafted as the sex is hot.

ForbiddenFiction.com is also designed to be a social reading environment. You'll have fun even if just reading the latest post each day, yet you will have the chance for so much more. Readers and authors can be part of ongoing discussions of specific works and individual authors as well as more general topics.

Sign up for a FREE Membership today at <u>ForbiddenFiction.com</u>